Neighbors and Other Strangers

The Threat of the Criminal Alliance—
Crime, Corruption, Assassination

Gordon Parker
Tales of Crime and Corruption Creator

PUBLICATION
CONSULTANTS
We Believe In The Power Of Authors

PO Box 221974 Anchorage, Alaska 99522-1974
books@publicationconsultants.com www.publicationconsultants.com

ISBN Number: 978-1-59433-833-5
eBook ISBN Number: 978-1-59433-834-2

Library of Congress Number: 2018961909

Manufactured in the United States of America

July

The stench of rotten food wafting from the dumpster filled the darkened alley. Steve Burgess pressed himself against the brick wall of a building. He tried to believe he was invisible. He was in a bad part of the city in the middle of the night. He felt nauseous. He was sweating. It was a warm New Orleans night. That had nothing to do with it. He would have been sweating if it was snowing. He would have been nauseous without the dumpster.

The door was opened by a blonde man so large as to occupy the frame. With close cropped hair and no noticeable neck, he was a mass of muscle. Burgess was a big man, too. But unlike the young giant filling the doorway, he was an overweight, out of shape cop on the down side of middle age. At least he had been a cop. Now he wasn't. Now he was nothing. A frightened man hiding in an alley.

Trent Marshall, a Pulitzer Prize winning investigative reporter, almost got Burgess sent to prison a few years ago. Three of Burgess' colleagues did go to jail. Six others were fired. Burgess didn't get indicted or lose his job, but he was demoted. More recently Marshall humiliated Burgess in front of his boss, Detective Lieutenant Jordan Baron.

After that incident, Burgess went to a bar and got drunk. He was still on duty. He didn't care.

Late that afternoon he found himself stumbling down the sidewalk across the street from Marshall's house in the Vieux Carre'. He had intended to do nothing but shout a curse and raise a middle finger. But just at that moment the pedestrian gate in the brick wall enclosing the old house and its courtyard opened. Marshall and his girlfriend stepped into view. Something came over Burgess. Something he could not control. Without really knowing how it got there, he found a revolver in his hand. He fired two shots across the street, narrowly missing them. As they ducked back through the gate seeking the protection of the bricks, he staggered out of sight as quickly as he could.

He didn't use his service weapon. He used the hideout most officers carried. His was a snub nose .32. Baron made him turn over both weapons for ballistics testing. Knowing what the results would be, Burgess said he was going to the men's room. He didn't go to the men's room. He walked down the hall and out the back door. He didn't go to his apartment. He did his best to disappear. Now he was a former cop on the run. He needed help. He came to the only place he knew.

"He'll see you now," the young man said. His voice was surprisingly soft. Burgess was certain that was the only thing about him that was.

"Thanks," Burgess said as he moved to the door.

The young man turned and walked away. Burgess hurried to follow him, already out of breath. He was led to a private dining room off the kitchen. A well-dressed, older man sat at a table dining alone. A simple meal. Bratwurst on a bun with Creole mustard accompanied by potato salad.

"Thank you, Gart," the man said.

Gart didn't leave. He stood near the door. Behind Burgess.

The older man took the last bite of bratwurst. He wiped a bit of mustard off his lips with a white cloth napkin. Only then did he look at Burgess.

"I hear you're in trouble, Steve," he said. "Big trouble this time."

"Yes, sir," he replied politely. He clearly knew the older man was the alpha male.

"And now you come to me."

"Yes, sir," the former cop replied. "You always treated me good."

"What do you need from me now?"

"I have to get out of town," Burgess said. "I need money and a place to go where there might be a friend."

"Why shouldn't I just have Gart break your neck and toss your body in the river?" the older man asked.

"You could do that," Burgess replied nervously, beginning to sweat again. "But that could bring complications. You never know when a mistake might be made. A mistake that could lead cops in the wrong direction."

"You know better than to threaten me, Steve."

"I would never threaten you, sir," the former cop said. "I'm just pointing out that it's less complicated to help me relocate. A small amount of cash and a suggestion about where I might go. Nothing that would ever connect us."

"Is that all?"

"I would ask one more small favor, sir," Burgess said. "And again this is something that could never lead back to you."

The older man raised his eyebrows. "Yes?"

"I'd like to get in touch with Jimmy Shadow."

The older man was surprised by that request though he didn't let it show on his face. He didn't know if Jimmy Shadow was still working. He was seventy-five himself and Jimmy had to be at least his age. He was one of the best hit men in the business in his day. It was his talent for accomplishing a hit using methods that made it difficult, often impossible, to figure out the cause of death that earned him his pseudonym.

That and the fact that he was never seen. No one knew what he looked like. No one knew what he sounded like. No one knew his real name. No one knew for sure whether Jimmy Shadow was a man or a woman. Communication with Jimmy Shadow was done in the old days with dead drops. The last the man heard Jimmy still used dead drops but in the age of computers had added burst transmissions. Small packets of information sent quickly. Too quickly to be traced by the cops, most of whom didn't have access to the necessary sophisticated computers.

"That could be asking a lot, Steve," the older man said. "It could even be dangerous for you. Jimmy was never patient. If Jimmy doesn't want to be found, you might disappear."

"Believe me, I know that," Burgess said.

"You're not going to give up on this thing are you? You're going to try again, aren't you?"

"Yes, sir, I am going to try again."

The older man considered that. He didn't want to have Burgess killed. It was never smart to kill a cop. Even a crooked cop. He wouldn't be sad to see Trent Marshall done in. The investigative reporter had cost the older man money a few times. He had even come close to exposing the man's power in the city. No, he wouldn't mind seeing Marshall receive what was due him for the trouble he had caused.

If Burgess was going to try again to kill Marshall, the older man would rather it be somewhere other than New Orleans.

"Where would you like to go, Steve?"

"Marshall has a girlfriend who lives in San Francisco. I wouldn't mind tracking him down there."

The man motioned to Gart who moved close to him and leaned over. The man whispered instructions.

"Gart will take care of you, Steve," the older man said. "I don't want to see you or hear that you're in New Orleans ever again."

"Thank you, sir," Burgess said nervously, not sure what was meant by Gart taking care of him.

He followed the young man out of the room. Gart told him to wait in the alley. He was gone for ten minutes. When he returned he gave Burgess an envelope containing $15,000 in cash and a slip of paper with a name and phone number. A San Francisco area code.

In the private dining room, the older man made a phone call. When the call was answered, the man's message was concise.

"A former cop named Steve Burgess will be calling. He has been of some service to me in the past. I would consider it a favor if you will take his call and assist him if, in your judgment, you think it possible without endangering yourself. He can be useful if you're inclined to give him a little work from time to time. If you don't care for what he has to say or what he asks of you, do as you will. I don't need to know."

He gave the mobile phone to Gart with instructions to throw it in the river.

Tuesday, April 26th

Trent Marshall steered the sleek black sedan into the below ground parking garage. The car pulsed like a leashed lion struggling against its restraint. Its engine emitting a low, barely audible roar. Powerful. Eager to be set free.

"Welcome back, Trent," the slim young man in the uniform said.

"Thanks, Bat," Marshall responded. "You keeping everything under control around here?"

The young man laughed. His name wasn't Bat. Marshall had taken to calling him that because he knew about the baton the young man kept out of sight. It looked like nothing more than a cane an old man might use. Trent happened to know it had a lead core that converted it into a potentially lethal weapon.

To Marshall's knowledge Bat had never used the weighted stick. If the time ever came, he was confident the young man would emerge unscathed. They had spent a couple of hours one lazy afternoon practicing maneuvers with the stick as a weapon. Bat had some tricks of his own. Trent taught him a few more. Bat was a security guard. Not a cop. He wasn't allowed to be armed. But he had no intention of going down in a fight if he could help it.

"It's all good here," the young man said. "The thugs steer clear of my building."

"Good job."

"Hey, that's a new car, isn't it?" Bat asked. "What happened to the Caddy?"

"It's in New Orleans," Trent said, referring to his Cadillac CTS-V, the fastest car ever built by General Motors. "This is a Bentley Continental GT Speed. Six liter. V 12. 626 horsepower. Faster than the Caddy."

Bat whistled.

"How fast?" the young security guard asked.

"Top speed…204 miles per hour."

"Did you hit it on this trip?"

"Came close out in west Texas," Trent called over his shoulder as he steered the powerful vehicle into the garage.

He pulled into his assigned parking space. The Bentley cost almost twice as much as the house Trent lived in as a teenager with his father. As an adult he had lived paycheck to paycheck, like his parents before him. His life changed forever when his last living relative, his mother's elderly aunt, died leaving him a thousand acres across the Mississippi River from Baton Rouge. Land that once had been planted in sugar cane. He formed a partnership with a builder. Together they built a world class golf course. They surrounded it with more than a hundred houses. Big houses. Expensive houses. $1 million would barely cover the price of a guest house. The partners each walked away with an immense fortune.

The parking space was assigned to him by Darcey Anderson. Two parking slots came with the condo she purchased as revenues at her firm, DJA Designs, soared. One space sat unused until Trent's first visit the previous August. Darcey's white BMW X-5 was in the other slot. Trent knew she might or might not be home. The condo was only a short walk from her small office building on California Street. Unless she had business outside the office, she usually walked to work.

The Bentley's trunk held only two items. A large black duffel bag. Very heavy. It was one reason that Trent preferred to drive rather than fly. The other item was a standard small, soft-sided roller bag. It contained only what he needed for the drive from his home in New Orleans. Four to five days for most drivers. Fewer for Trent.

Lifting the duffel to his shoulder he pulled the roller bag toward the elevator, reaching it just before the door closed. He forced the door open with his foot, causing the elderly woman inside to scream with fright.

She pressed herself into a rear corner of the elevator.

"Stay away from me, young, man," she demanded, her voice quivering. "Why are you following me?"

Trent spoke calmly. "I'm not following you, Ma'am," he said.

He saw she had already pressed the button for the 15th floor, one of the three top floors requiring a security key for access. He had his own key but since she had already used hers there was no need for him to repeat the process.

"You are following me!" the woman screeched. "You don't live on the 15th floor. You're following me!"

"No, ma'am," Trent said, doing his best to remain calm. "When I'm in San Francisco I live on the 15th floor. I'm not following you."

"I don't believe you. I'm calling 9-1-1 just as soon as I get into my condo."

"Lady, believe me. I'm not following you," Trent said, his patience wearing thin. "If I was following you I would certainly be regretting it by now."

Trent stood still, staring straight ahead. The woman remained pressed into the rear corner. Finally the elevator reached the 15th floor. The doors opened. Most of the condos on the lower floors were smaller. Those on the three top floors were large. There were only four units each on the 15th and 16th floors. The 17th floor held two penthouses. Trent knew how much Darcey's 15th floor unit cost. He figured the price of the penthouses would be more than the Gross Domestic Product of several countries admitted to membership in the United Nations.

Trying to do the gentlemanly thing, Trent held the elevator door open so the lady could exit. She squeezed past him hurriedly and rushed down the hall.

"Don't you dare follow me," she shouted. "I'm calling 9-1-1. You just stay away from me."

The door to one of the condos at the far end of the hall opened. An elderly man stepped into the frame.

"What's all the fuss about out here?"

"This man is following me," the woman said. "I don't know why. He doesn't belong on this floor. He leaped onto the elevator before the doors could close. I'm calling 9-1-1."

"Oh, shut your trap, Jean," the man said. "I hope he is following you. And I hope he does something terrible to you!"

"I see it all now," the woman said as she fumbled to unlock her door. "You put him up to it, James Williams. You're trying to make me pay for my sins. Well, you have to pay for your sins as well. I'm calling 9-1-1 right now. Both of you will be spending the night in jail."

She finally got her door open. After she slammed the door, Trent heard at least four locks slide into place.

He turned to the elderly man. "I'm very sorry about all that, sir. I don't know why she got so upset."

"She does it nearly every day. That's the widow Philby. She's always complaining about something or someone."

"Well, I'm sorry you were disturbed."

"No need to apologize," the old man said, with a nasty laugh. "Watching her running scared is the most fun I have all day." He ducked back inside his own condo and slammed the door.

Trent was left standing in the hall alone. He didn't know which of the two was most unpleasant. The old woman who suffered from abnormal fear of strangers, perhaps fueled by something in her past for which she felt guilt, or the old man who seemed to enjoy her fear.

It wasn't a hard decision. The old woman was irritating. The old man was cold-hearted.

He used his own key to open the door to Darcey's condo. It occurred to him that if the woman did call 9-1-1 there were some things he didn't want to have to explain to the police. He took his bags to the master bedroom and stowed them in his closet. As a precaution he called Bat and told him about the unfortunate incident with Mrs. Philby.

Bat laughed. "Don't worry about it, Trent. She calls 9-1-1 all the time. They have to respond, but they'll talk to me first. They won't bother you."

Twenty minutes later Darcey was home and sitting on the edge of the bed. Trent was in the bed. His upper body was naked. The bedclothes covered him from the waist down. An open bottle of Mumm's Napa Brut Prestige sat in an ice bucket on the bedside table. They each had a flute from which they were sipping.

"What? No gun?" she queried, knowing Trent's tendency to be armed at all times. Even when it was less than convenient.

"I have all the weapon I need," he said, flashing her a devilish grin, as he took the champagne flute from her and set it with his beside the ice bucket.

After dinner they wrapped themselves in robes to sit on the terrace. Darcey had made a quick and delicious meal of scampi with linguini. Trent had opened another bottle of Mumm's.

Darcey laughed. "So you met Mrs. Philby. She's forever claiming people are following her. She believes they're trying to make her pay for her sins."

"That's what she said. And that sadist who lives across from her seemed to enjoy it immensely."

"Mr. Williams," Darcey shuddered. "He's a little scary."

"The Germans have a word for what turns him on," Trent said. "Schadenfreude. Taking pleasure from the discomfort of others."

"That fits him perfectly."

"Interesting that he told her to 'shut her trap' instead of shut up or quiet down," Trent said. "The etymology of the phrase 'shut your trap' also comes from German by way of Old English. It originally was a warning to trappers to keep their traps shut when not in use to avoid injury. Makes you wonder what he did for a living."

"You're being weird, Marshall," Darcey said, refilling his glass with sparkling wine.

"You're right. Enough of this talk of sadists. Do you realize what day this is?" he asked.

"It's Tuesday, April 26th. It was one year ago today that we met."

It had been an eventful year. Trent had built an emotional wall to protect himself after losing his wife, his mother, his father, his best friend. He had sworn he would let no one get close to him ever again.

And then came Darcey. She had come to him asking for help in solving a one hundred fifty year old mystery that was again threatening her family. As they began to unravel the mystery, they suffered betrayal from people they thought were friends. Both Trent and Darcey's mother were kidnapped. Darcey was briefly held hostage by a mad man. A crooked cop fired two shots at Trent and Darcey, missing them by inches. Two good women were murdered as were a psychologist and a security guard at a hospital for the criminally insane.

Trent, Darcey, and her mother survived. One of the villains was killed by Trent to save Darcey's life, a second in self-defense. A third was wounded by Darcey in a shootout with a woman who was preparing to kill Trent. Trent had already put the woman's husband out of action by breaking his nose with a shovel. Those two would likely never be released from prison.

The only one who escaped was the cop who tried to shoot them.

Surviving the attacks and threats, they solved the mystery that had plagued Darcey's family for a century and a half.

In the process, Darcey broke through Trent's protective emotional wall though she had to threaten to shoot him to do it. Given Trent's fondness for guns and respect for those not afraid to use them, she chose the right strategy.

Darcey had difficulty understanding Trent when they first met. Eventually she accepted his love of fast cars and guns. She even came to share it.

She thought it strange that all his cars were black as were most of his clothes. She asked him if that was symbolic. He thought for a few seconds and told her it was. Of what, she wondered? That he likes black, he told her.

She came to understand that Trent was easily bored. He was, she guessed, an adrenaline junkie. He wouldn't go long without finding a challenge. The more dangerous the better. She was frightened in the beginning. But she learned he was fully capable of protecting her as well as himself. More importantly, she discovered that she, too, was capable of defending herself and him. Of using violence if necessary.

He made his first trip to San Francisco in August. Through the year they grew ever closer. Darcey didn't push him. She patiently let him move at his own pace. It was a wise decision. They were starting to feel like a couple.

He invited Darcey and her mother, Betty, to his home in New Orleans for Thanksgiving. They were joined by Ivy and Walter Ford, the elderly, black couple who looked on Trent as a son.

Ivy had worked with Trent's mother at the venerable Coffee Pot, the restaurant in the Vieux Carre' that had served locals and visitors alike for over a hundred years. She was protective of the young white woman struggling to support her son. When a would-be Romeo from the kitchen tried to hit on his mother, it was Ivy who backed him off.

"Don't nobody mess with this girl," Ivy warned. "If you mess with her, you're messing with me."

When his mother passed away suddenly and unexpectedly, Ivy became a surrogate parent to him. After his father took his fourteen year old son to Baton Rouge to live with him, he saw to it that the boy visited Ivy and Walter often.

Darcey hosted them all for Christmas. Her three bedroom condo was spacious enough to accommodate everyone. Trent flew Ivy and Walter to San Francisco first class as part of his Christmas gift to them. They were wide-eyed at the view of the city from Darcey's terrace. Especially the lights of the Golden Gate and Bay bridges at night.

Though there were times she wouldn't have thought so, it was a year that ended well.

Trent took another sip of wine.

"Now there's something I need to talk to you about," Trent said.

Wednesday, April 27th

Trent was frying bacon when Darcey came in and sat at the kitchen counter. He left the bacon to tend itself while he refilled her coffee. He had made biscuits from scratch, which were now in the oven. He would use the bacon grease to make milk gravy. They might be in the beautiful city by the bay, but they were still southerners. Biscuits and gravy. Southern health food.

She called Miles Diaz-Douglas, her executive assistant, to let him know she might be a little late getting to the office. She said she might not be in at all.

"Girl, what is going on?" Miles demanded. "Trent got here yesterday, didn't he? Do you have something to tell me?"

"You never know," Darcey teased. "We want you and Scott to come over for brunch on Sunday. Will y'all be here?"

"I'll make sure of it," Miles said, then added dramatically. "You know I'm psychic, girl. My psychic powers are telling me something is up. I wouldn't miss it for the world."

After breakfast she called Mandy Rillard, her best friend, to invite her to the Sunday brunch as well. Darcey was still struggling to survive in the highly competitive San Francisco design business when she met Mandy.

Now a corporate attorney with one of the Bay area's most prestigious law firms, Mandy came from old money Boston. She had been a key factor in the success of Darcey's design company when she convinced her father to hire her new friend to head up the renovation of an old Nob Hill apartment building. Darcey's success with that building, coupled with Mandy getting her invited to the best parties in San Francisco, was the boost DJA Designs needed.

She also invited Preston Johnson, her neighbor across the hall. They had developed a special relationship when Darcey moved in three years earlier. He was an old man alone who enjoyed the company of a beautiful woman. But only in the most appropriate way. Every other Wednesday they had dinner together. They alternated with Darcey cooking dinner for him one week and her as his guest at one of the city's best restaurants two Wednesdays later.

He was quite old fashioned, insisting that they dress for dinner. He would show up at her door, dashing in a tux, his silver hair and mustache sparkling. She would wear something dressy, just short of sexy, even when they were dining in her condo. And he always brought her flowers.

Trent met him on his first trip to the city. They liked each other immediately. Trent found him to be a fascinating conversationalist with a vast knowledge of many things.

Trent noticed that, though he showed remarkable dexterity for his age, Preston 'wore a stick,' as they would have said in the elderly man's youth. His ever-present cane had a leather covered handle with a gold cross piece. The stick itself was black hardwood. It was a beautiful piece. Trent told him so. Preston nodded slightly, acknowledging the compliment but offering no other details.

Trent discovered he also had a lively sense of humor. When he asked what Preston did for a living before he retired, he was surprised at the reply.

"I was in organized crime."

Later Trent probed again.

"I said I was in organized crime," the old man repeated, a twinkle in his eye.

Refusing to let it go, Trent came back to the subject a third time.

"Well, young man, I was in the insurance business," Preston said, "and if that's not organized crime I don't know what is." The old man rocked with laughter.

Trent heard his phone chirp. A text from Lieutenant Jordan Baron, the New Orleans detective who was Trent's closest friend. He asked if Trent had talked to Christopher Booth. Booth was a detective with the San Francisco Police Department. Jordan had told Trent he and Booth worked together two years earlier on a case involving a man who murdered two coworkers at a San Francisco business and then fled to New Orleans.

Booth had left a message on Trent's phone the day before. Trent responded to Jordan with a message saying he would call Booth immediately.

"It's not a good sign if the cops want to know when you're coming to town, Marshall," Darcey said. "What have you done now?"

"Nothing," Trent said, giving her his best innocent look. "I just got here yesterday. Haven't had time. Well, except for that old woman down the hall. But I didn't hurt her. I swear I didn't."

Detective Sergeant Christopher Booth answered on the second ring. With his phone's speaker on, Trent told Booth he just arrived in the city the evening before. He repeated his claim to Darcey that he hadn't been in the city long enough to get into trouble.

"That's good to know," the sergeant replied. "It fits with what our mutual friend in New Orleans said about you. He said it sometimes takes you as long as a week to stir up trouble. On the other hand, he said it takes Darcey Anderson no more than 48 hours."

Trent laughed. Darcey made a face at him.

"I have a case I'm working on that Jordan tells me you might have some experience with," Booth said. "I'd like to discuss it with you."

"At your convenience, Sergeant."

"Can we meet someplace today?"

"Sure. Want me to come to your office?"

"No," Booth answered quickly. "Definitely not."

Trent was surprised at Booth's quick response. "You're welcome to come over here," Trent offered. "Darcey will be here but no one else."

Booth was a big man. Trent judged him to be 6'4" and close to 300 pounds.

His nose was large and slightly off center. The kind of nose that often marked one who had gone more than a few rounds in a boxing ring. Trent was forty-six years old. He thought Booth ten years younger.

Booth explained that he was working on a money laundering case. He knew that a local mobster named Jonathan Rossi was laundering hundreds of millions of dollars every year. So far he hadn't been able to figure out how he was doing it.

"Have you talked to the folks at FinCEN?" Trent asked.

"The Financial Crimes Enforcement Network. Yes, I've talked to them. They'll be happy to get involved. Just as soon as I assemble all the evidence in a neat little pile and hand it over to them."

"Yeah, they serve a valuable purpose but mainly as a data base and sort of clearing house for law enforcement."

"I'm trying to learn the process. How does someone like Rossi go about moving illegal money into the legal financial system?" Booth said. "I'm a beat cop. This stuff is way over my head."

Trent looked thoughtfully at Booth.

"I don't want to offend you," he said, "but that might be why you were assigned to the case."

"I've already thought about that," the detective replied. "That's why I didn't want to meet in my office. At the very least I'm convinced that Rossi has someone there on his payroll. It might be someone high enough to issue the assignment to me."

"Who assigned you to the case?"

"My captain. Captain Albright. Lieutenant Mitchum wanted it. He thinks it would be a big career move for anyone who can break this case. The lieutenant would have been the obvious choice. But for some reason the captain assigned it to me. I had the feeling it wasn't his idea. He's usually a heads-up guy, but this time he didn't look me in the eye. He didn't seem happy."

"Hmmm. Interesting. Who does he report to?"

"Commander John Witney. Witney reports to Deputy Chief Amanda Justice. And Charles Marvin is the chief."

"Deputy Chief Justice? Really?"

"Really. And she has no sense of humor."

"I'll keep that in mind. Tell me about Rossi. What's his background?"

"Rossi's father, grandfather, and great grandfather were all dons heading up organized crime back in the days when the Italians were in charge," Booth explained. "Rossi is not like the old dons. He understands the world they knew has changed. Once he became head of the Family, it didn't take him long to realize the homogeneity of criminal activity his ancestors once controlled was long gone.

"Rossi's traditional crime family still has plenty of power. But now he has lots of competition. Middle Easterners, Asians, Mexicans, Russians, African Americans, even outlaw bikers. Each gang capable of putting its own army of thugs on the streets at will.

"Rossi is as ruthless as any of the old dons. But he's smart. He negotiated an alliance for the Rossi Family with a Thai gang, Spitting Cobra, outlaw bikers calling themselves the Barons of Lucifer, and a group of middle Easterners known as the Scourge.

"Between the four groups they control the largest share of drugs, guns, human trafficking, most anything illegal you can think of in this city. Given their ethnic mix they're bound to have connections across the country and probably around the world. And they have the combined firepower to keep the Mexican cartels, the Russians, and the African American gangs quiet."

"Impressive. Putting a criminal amalgam like that together couldn't have been easy," Trent said, thoughtfully.

"Money laundering is the key to it all. The biggest problem all the gangs have is how to get their illegal money into the system so they can enjoy it. I said Rossi is smart. He's handling that for them. They're making more money than ever. More of their money is showing up as legal. And I don't know how he's doing it. Jordan told me you worked on a money laundering investigation a few years ago and might be able to give me some help."

"There are lots of ways to launder money," Trent said. "Deposit it in a bank in a country that has no reporting requirements and then move it back to the U.S. Buying businesses that operate on cash. Over valuing invoices for work never performed. Buying a casino if you can get away with it. Real estate manipulation. Buying a bank in a friendly country. Or even in this country, but that's a lot trickier. The intriguing point here is, I think, all Rossi's partners can do those things for themselves. What does he offer that convinced them to join his alliance?"

"That's what I can't figure out."

"Here's the bigger concern for Rossi," Trent said. "He's taking a tremendous risk. If any one of his partners decides he's not making good on his promises, they won't hesitate to slit his throat. Or at least try."

"I worry about that. Rossi's death would unleash a war in this city unlike anything ever seen. Jordan gives you the highest recommendation. He tells me if anyone can figure this out, you can. Will you help me?"

To Booth's surprise the answer was no. "At least not right away," Trent said. "I'm going to be unavailable until mid-July. After that, yes, I'll help. With two conditions."

"Conditions?"

"Yes," Trent said. "Both Darcey and I must be assigned some sort of official status by the San Francisco Police Department."

"I'll see what I can do," Booth said. "But understand I'm convinced Rossi has someone in my office on his payroll."

"That brings us to the second condition," Trent said. "Both Darcey and I must be licensed to carry concealed weapons."

"That's a tough one," Booth said. "I can guarantee your safety. I can have men assigned to protect the two of you around the clock."

"When you have one of Rossi's men in your office?" Trent balked. "No, Sergeant Booth. I appreciate your offer but we have to be able to protect ourselves. If it's any help, we've both been appointed special deputies in Louisiana. Perhaps it could simply be a matter of professional courtesy."

"Let me see what I can do," Booth said. "But you can't do anything for what? Three months?"

"We can get started," Trent offered. "If you bring your files over here, we can start going through them. Who knows? Maybe we'll get lucky and find something significant. We might even come up with a plan."

Friday, April 29th

Trent and Booth spent the remainder of the week going through the files the detective had put together. Booth took a circuitous route to get to Darcey's condo each day. He never went the same way twice.

He drove his own vehicle, an old pickup truck, the first day. On his second visit he took a taxi half the distance to avoid being followed. He walked around the block and hailed a second cab for the remainder of the trip. On Friday he hopped on a cable car, stepping off when he was still a mile from his destination. He went to great lengths to avoid establishing a pattern.

While Booth's files were light on information relative to money laundering, he had details on the Rossi Family, Spitting Cobra, the Barons of Lucifer, and the Scourge. By the end of the week Trent and Christopher knew only one thing for sure about the movement of the alliance's money. It was an international operation. But Trent understood how the gangs operated, both in their own spheres of influence and together. He had the names of the key leaders and charts outlining how each was organized.

The Rossi Family. Spitting Cobra. The Barons of Lucifer. The Scourge.

All from very different cultures. All with similar goals and operations. Taking on one of them was dangerous. Taking on all four, as Booth said in his first meeting with Trent, was a war.

Both men thought they had used the time productively. By the end of the week, Trent told Booth there might be some things he could do before returning to San Francisco in July.

Trent liked the policeman. He found the self-described beat cop to be far more intelligent than Booth considered himself to be. Darcey liked him, too. They considered inviting him to join their upcoming Sunday brunch. But the work Trent and Christopher were doing was far too dangerous. It was best that they avoid being seen together for as long as possible.

It was already too late.

At the precinct, Officer Harry Sherman was looking over Booth's desk. Sherman kept a close eye on the sergeant. He saw him rush out of the office after receiving a phone call on Wednesday. He noticed that Booth downloaded files onto a flash drive, which he pocketed before leaving the office on Thursday and Friday. He was out of the office for most of both days. Sherman was sure something was up. It might be to his benefit to find out what.

"Has anybody seen the file on the Lenore Hale case? I can't find it anywhere. The last time I saw it Booth was looking at it," Sherman said as he rummaged through the papers on Booth's desk.

"I'd wait for Christopher to get back before I searched his desk, Sherman," one of the other officers warned. Sherman was not well liked.

"Yeah, I guess you're right," Sherman said. He walked back to his own desk, palming a small slip of paper. Back at his desk he picked up a stack of papers and pretended to be thumbing through them while he read the note he had lifted from Booth's desk. A New Orleans phone number. A name.

At the end of his shift, Sherman hustled out of the building. He drove to a park halfway between the precinct and the small apartment he rented. Parking in a secluded spot, he took the prepaid mobile phone from his car's console and dialed a number.

"Yes?" was the answer.

"Mr. Rossi, this is Harry. Harry Sherman."

"Yes, Harry. What do you have for me?"

"You told me to keep an eye on Christopher Booth. I found out that he's been meeting with someone this week. The name is Trent Marshall. And there's a New Orleans phone number." He repeated the number.

"Interesting. That could be useful, Harry. I'll see that you're rewarded."

"Thank you, Mr. Rossi," Sherman said. Rossi had already hung up.

Sherman popped the phone open and removed the chip. He would drop the two halves of the phone and the chip in separate dumpsters before he got home. Tomorrow he would pick up another prepaid phone.

Saturday, April 30th

Steve Burgess was never much of a cop when he was on the force. But he was cop enough to keep track of Trent Marshall's movements, albeit with the help of another ex-cop in New Orleans who was also owed his ex-cop status to Marshall.

Burgess knew Trent left the Crescent City en route to San Francisco a few days ago. He knew Marshall had visited San Francisco several times in the last year. He found out that Marshall stayed with the Anderson woman when he was in the city. It took a while but he finally discovered her address.

It was late morning. Burgess was still hung over from the night before. He'd started the day with a shot of gin. That made him feel a little better. It also made him a lot meaner.

He was on the sidewalk in front of Darcey Anderson's condominium building. Her condo was on the 15th floor. A secure floor. This was a reconnaissance mission. Burgess noted the security guard stationed at the entrance to the underground parking garage. He was a scruffy-looking man who looked to be around 40. He had a patch over one eye. Maybe a disabled vet.

He assumed there would be another security guard inside. Both would be unarmed. Both easy to take down if it came to that. Burgess wasn't smart but he knew enough to avoid confrontation with security. That would mean other people would be involved. Police. Burgess didn't do well with other people. Especially police officers. Especially now that he wasn't one.

He nodded to the guard as he passed. The guard nodded in return, watching the shabbily dressed man with his one eye. Burgess revised his opinion. This guy might be a disabled vet, he thought, but he was a vet.

He looked like he might know what he was doing. When he came up with a plan for dealing with Marshall he would try to avoid this guy.

He kept walking. As he passed the glass front of the building he noticed a woman sitting at a desk to the left of the elevators. He took a few more steps, stopped and backed up. The name plate was gold with black lettering. It was large enough that he could read the name. Alexis Brandt. Burgess smiled. The woman ignored him.

He looked back at the security guard. He was watching Burgess. He looked serious. Burgess grinned and made motions with his hands indicating 'a well-built woman.' That brought a small smile from the guard. Not a friendly smile. Just the kind of smile shared between men admiring a well-built woman. Burgess was certain it wasn't the first time a passing man had admired the woman sitting at the desk. The guard probably wouldn't remember him. At least Burgess hoped the guard wouldn't remember him.

The ex-cop was definitely feeling better. The woman might be calling herself Alexis Brandt now. But when he knew her in New Orleans she went by Piper Hodgins. Stripper. Hooker. Druggie. When Burgess came up with his plan for Marshall, Alexis or Piper or whatever name she wanted to use would be helpful.

He was absolutely cheerful now. It was almost noon. He decided to find a bar. He thought he would celebrate the morning's discovery with a martini.

Sunday, May 1st

Sunday morning dawned with bright sunshine. The temperature had already topped 70 before Trent and Darcey's guests arrived. It would reach 78 by the end of the day. Unusually warm for a city that seldom gets above the mid-60s in early May.

Darcey was convinced it was an omen of good things to come.

Trent thought it was a nice day.

Downstairs Alexis Brandt was working at the concierge desk. As the junior member of the staff she was required to work weekends. She didn't mind. At least she didn't have to work the night shift. And compared to her life before she came to San Francisco and lucked into this job, working the desk on the weekends was like a dream. A very nice dream.

Ms. Anderson on the 15th floor was having guests in for brunch today. She had given Alexis the names Mandy Rillard, Scott Douglas, and Miles Diaz-Douglas. Scott owned an investment firm. He and Miles had been among the first gay couples to be married when same sex marriage became legal.

Miles and Scott arrived first. Mandy entered the building just in time to join them in the elevator. Miles led the group into Darcey's condo. In his usual dramatic style, he announced that something was up and, with his psychic powers, he knew what it was.

"And, Trent Marshall, if you think you're going to drag our Darcey away from us, you will have to think again," he said. "We simply will not let her go."

Trent laughed.

"Oh, calm down, Miles" Darcey said. "Trent's back in town and we're having our best friends over for brunch. That doesn't mean there's a conspiracy."

To keep him busy, Darcey set Miles to work making mimosas with fresh-squeezed orange juice. He circled the room offering the scintillating flutes.

Mandy and Scott accepted and promptly moved out onto the terrace. It was well known that sipping wine while watching others cook was the extent of their culinary talent. They were even better at their specialty when they could sit outside on such a beautiful day.

Within minutes Darcey answered the doorbell to admit Preston Johnson, her eighty-three year old neighbor. He entered dressed for the occasion as usual. Tan slacks, navy blue blazer, baby blue shirt, topped off with an old-fashioned ascot. Beige with alternating blue and brown chevron stripes. His silver hair and mustache sparkled in the light of the sunny day.

In one hand he held two chilled bottles of wine; in the other the cane Trent had admired.

"Trent, my boy, please accept this small gift. I know you have become a fan of Mumm's Napa product and rightfully so. But I think you'll find this bubbly to be quite satisfactory."

Taking the bottles from the old gentleman, Trent raised his eyebrows.

"Preston, these bottles are both 2006 Dom Perignon."

"Yes, and you'll note they're both brut, which I know you prefer."

"This is a very generous gift, Preston," Trent said. "Thank you."

"We're serving mimosas, Preston," Miles said, offering the tray. "May I offer you one?"

"By all means," the old man replied. "And my guess would be they're made with Mumm's Napa Brut Prestige. Am I right, Trent?"

"Dead on, Preston," Trent said.

"That's an expensive wine to mix with orange juice, isn't it?" Scott asked, ever the fiscal conservative.

"Right you are, Scott," the old man replied with a wide smile. "And I think Trent will agree with me that the best cocktails, like the best foods, are prepared with the finest ingredients."

"You're absolutely right, Preston," Trent replied as he put the Dom Perignon in the cooler. "My dad always said, 'It only costs a little bit more to go first class.' But then he died broke."

"Perhaps so, my boy," Preston said. "But he no doubt was a man who enjoyed life. And that's the way he should be remembered."

Trent looked thoughtful for a moment. Then he nodded his agreement.

"You look so good, Preston," Mandy said. "So dapper. So handsome."

"You're too kind, Mandy," the old man responded. "I've reached the age when I wake up and if I don't hear anyone saying 'He looks so natural,' I open my eyes."

"Oh Preston, now you're just being dramatic," Darcey said, leaning over to kiss his cheek.

While their guests made themselves comfortable in the sunshine and Miles made sure no one's glass was ever empty, Darcey and Trent were busy in the kitchen. At Darcey's instruction Miles urged everyone to gather around the dining table Trent had arranged for the concierge to place on the terrace.

Darcey and Trent set a plate in front of each guest that was piled with crisp bacon, spicy Louisiana hot links, Potatoes O'Brien in which jalapenos had been substituted for the usual sweet peppers, fluffy scrambled eggs and buttered toast. The banter among the guests became subdued as they enjoyed the mid-day feast.

As their guests finished the last of their meals, Darcey disappeared into the kitchen. Trent and Miles cleared the table. Miles returned to the terrace still chattering on about how his psychic powers told him something big was about to happen.

While Darcey worked with dough she had rolled out, cut into squares and dropped into the deep fryer, Trent made a pot of coffee.

With some pride, she brought to the table a tray of beignets, the wonderfully airy square French doughnuts, dusted with confectioner's sugar, made famous by New Orleans' Café du Monde.

"Ivy taught me to make these the last time I was in New Orleans," she explained, as she placed the platter on the table. "It's her own secret recipe."

Trent followed with a tray containing cups of coffee laced with milk.

"You can't have beignets without café au lait," he said as he set a cup in front of each guest.

"These are delicious, my dear," Preston said.

"And you're so domestic today," Miles said. "The needle on my psychic meter is pegged into the red."

Darcey laughed and held her hand out to Trent. He reached into his pocket for the ring he had been carrying until they were ready to make their announcement.

They were ready. He slipped the ring onto her finger.

"Your psychic powers were right, Miles," Darcey said, happily. "Trent proposed to me on Wednesday and I accepted."

"I knew it!" Miles exploded. "What did I tell you? My psychic powers are never wrong! I am simply amazing!"

Mandy wanted to see the ring. Darcey was anxious to show it off.

"Girlfriend, that's the biggest diamond I've ever seen," Mandy said. She hugged first Darcey, then Trent.

"Congratulations, my boy," Preston said as he shook hands with Trent. Darcey leaned over to hug him so the old man wouldn't have to get up. "And best wishes to you, my dear. Trent is a lucky man."

"Congratulations, Trent," Scott said as he also extended his hand.

"We're planning on late June at the Pines," Darcey said, referring to her family's farm in northwest Louisiana. "We hope you all can make it. I know it's a long trip, but Mom wouldn't have it any other way. Mandy, would you be my maid of honor?"

"Of course," Mandy said. "I couldn't imagine your wedding without me beside you."

Darcey reached down and took Preston's hand in hers. "And, Preston, would you agree to stand in for Dad and walk me down the aisle?"

The old man was silent for a moment. Trent thought his eyes were glistening.

"I would be honored, child," Preston said. "Honored. You have made an old man very happy."

"And what about me?" Miles demanded. "What do I get to do? You're not going to have a wedding without me."

Darcey laughed. "I wouldn't dream of it, Miles. What role would you pick for yourself?"

"Bridesmaid," Miles said. "I want to be a bridesmaid."

"Oh, for goodness sake, Miles," Scott said.

"And what's wrong with that?" Miles said. "You didn't have any problem with me being a bride!"

"He has you there, Scott," Mandy said, with a laugh.

"Besides," Miles said, "I've always dreamed of being a bridesmaid."

"Dreams do come true, Miles," Darcey said. "Bridesmaid it is."

"Trent, I assume some sort of alcohol will be available?" Scott asked. "Preferably quite a lot of it."

"Don't worry, Scott. I'll make you one of my specialties. A peach martini. So smooth you won't know how many you've had until you stand up and try to walk."

"That sounds good," Scott said. "If possible, I'd like one before, one during, and…well, we'll see about after."

"But wait," Miles said, glaring at Trent. "Where do you two plan to live? You don't think you're going to move her to New Orleans, do you?"

"I wouldn't dream of it, Miles," Trent said, a look of mock terror on his face. "I know your revenge would traumatize all of us."

"Don't worry," Darcey said. "We're keeping both homes and will spend time in each. And since it's a morning for announcements, I might as well add this one. I'm going to reorganize the company. I plan to remain as chief executive officer. But in the new organization you, Miles, will be chief operating officer. And I have some ideas on expanding to offer more services. If, that is, it's agreeable to you."

For the first time that morning Miles was speechless.

"I feel faint," he finally managed to say, dropping into a chair.

"Chief Operating Officer, eh? How did that slip by your psychic powers?" Scott asked.

While Trent and Darcey entertained their guests, Jonathan Rossi was enjoying a light lunch in the garden of his large home in the hills of Atherton on the southern end of the San Francisco Peninsula. He chose this house for its privacy, though he enjoyed the theater, the wine cellar, and the pool as well. But the garden was his favorite part of the property. The garden and the privacy.

Rossi lived in the heart of Silicon Valley. He was surrounded by people who had made their fortunes in high tech stocks. Rossi owned no high tech stock. He owned no stock of any kind. Rossi never bought stock. He acquired companies. Companies that he could own wholly. Companies that he could buy for strategic purposes and on extremely favorable terms. More than one major stockholder had found himself unable to resist Rossi's powers of persuasion.

That thought directed his attention to the large guest house at the far end of the garden. No guests were ever invited to use it. It was, instead, where his security detail was headquartered. They were charged with maintaining his privacy. For seeing to the security of Rossi's home and Rossi himself. When necessary they assisted Rossi in exercising his powers of persuasion.

There were six. Three were on duty at all times. All six were armed, on duty or off.

The guest house, with its six bedrooms, was luxurious. The men who provided his security were paid well. They lived comfortably. They were loyal. If Rossi suspected, for any reason, that one was not loyal, the man quickly disappeared and someone new took his place.

Rossi was thinking about the phone call from Sherman, the cop at Sergeant Booth's precinct who was on his payroll. He had heard about Trent Marshall from his contact in New Orleans. He knew Booth had been assigned to investigate Rossi's coalition and their money laundering activities. He had arranged through another cop on his payroll, this one at a level well above the sergeant's boss, to have the job assigned to Booth.

He didn't think Booth was dumb. But money laundering was not something the sergeant knew anything about. He thought Booth would spend a lot of time being frustrated. He thought Booth wouldn't figure out the system Rossi had put together. Trent Marshall could change that.

He thought about the phone call he had received from his New Orleans contact several months ago regarding an ex-cop named Burgess. He had given Burgess a few small jobs, more to keep an eye on him than for any other reason. Burgess had, as Rossi's New Orleans friend predicted, asked for another favor. Rossi told him he would think about it. He hadn't given Burgess an answer.

Reaching for one of the prepaid mobile phones that were a part of doing business these days, he dialed a New Orleans number.

"You called me several months ago about a dirty cop named Burgess. As you said, he requested a favor involving Trent Marshall. How dangerous is Marshall?"

He listened, thanked his friend and ended the call. He handed the phone to one of his security team to be destroyed.

With a sigh, Rossi forced himself to leave his beautiful garden. Business must be addressed. He returned a few minutes later having used a high frequency radio transmitter to send a burst transmission. A message that was both compressed and encrypted. He would receive a reply using the same method when the recipient chose to send it. If the recipient chose to reply at all.

"Why did you decide to have the wedding at your mom's farm?" Mandy asked.

"I don't think we had a choice," Trent said, good-naturedly. He wisely let Darcey tell the rest of the story.

She had called her mother first thing Thursday morning to tell her the news. She had turned on the phone's speaker so Trent could hear the conversation.

"I'm so happy for you, Darcey," her mom gushed. "This is the best news you could ever give me. Well, except maybe when you call to tell me there's a grandchild on the way."

"Mom! Let's not rush things," Darcey said, laughing as she watched Trent's eyes grow wide.

"I'm just so excited," Betty said. "And, Darcey, we have to have the wedding here at the Pines. An outdoor wedding. It'll be beautiful!"

"We haven't even talked about details yet, Mom," Darcey said.

"Darcey Jane," Betty said, "I went to New Orleans for Thanksgiving. I flew to San Francisco for Christmas. It's my turn. It's only fair that I get to host your wedding."

Darcey mouthed to Trent, "She used my middle name!"

Trent smiled. He kissed her ear and whispered, "Tell her we'd love to have the wedding at the Pines." He went back to the kitchen to let the women negotiate the details while he made breakfast.

"Well, OK, Mom, you win," Darcey said. "But we were thinking late June. It'll be awfully hot."

"Don't worry about that. We'll get misters and fans. We'll set up canopies. It'll be wonderful. And you'll be the most beautiful bride ever."

After breakfast both got on the phone to call Ivy with the news.

"Trent, I told you that woman was something special the first time I met her," Ivy said. "I know you'll take good care of that boy, Darcey. And if he don't take good care of you, let me know. He's not too big for me to handle."

She was thrilled to learn that the wedding would be at the Pines.

"I'm gonna call your momma right now, Darcey," she said. "We got plans to make."

"Don't y'all get too carried away, Ivy," Trent said. "Darcey should have some say. This is her wedding."

"Oh, we'll do it up like she wants," Ivy promised. "But y'all got to let us old folks have a little fun."

Jordan Baron congratulated them both and wished them well. He wasn't particularly surprised. He was appreciative when Trent asked him to be his best man. Jack Blake, the sheriff of Sabine Parish where the Pines was located, agreed to stand up with Trent also. Especially since it was an election year. There would be voters at the wedding.

Scott's phone rang. He looked at the number and frowned.

"Sorry," he said. "I have to take this call. It's a client."

"Tell 'em it's Sunday," Miles said.

"Take it in a bedroom, if you want privacy, Scott," Darcey said.

Scott nodded his thanks as he spoke into the phone, entering the condo.

"It seems to me, my dear, that there was never any doubt the wedding would be held at the Pines," Preston said, chuckling. "I knew when I first met your mother that she would be a force with which to reckon when she made her mind up about something. I'm looking forward to it. And I'm also looking forward to another of these delicious beignets and more café au lait. Trent, would you be so kind?" He held his cup out.

"Anyone else for café au lait?" Trent asked.

Miles handed his cup to Trent. "Chief Operations Officers don't wait tables. I'll have another."

"Darcey, you've created a monster," Mandy said, laughing at Miles' theatrics.

"Well, just think of it, Miss Mandy," Miles said. "Who would ever have thought a kid who grew up on the streets would wind up in such an exalted position? Or, for that matter, that this little group would be headed to a farm in Louisiana for a wedding among the horses and cows and chickens and who knows what else?"

"We don't have cows and chickens, Miles," Darcey said. "Only horses. And one donkey."

Preston chuckled. "It's the serendipity of life that makes it interesting, Miles."

As Trent prepared the coffee in the kitchen, the sound of Scott's voice attracted his attention. He looked up to see Scott speaking animatedly into the phone. He couldn't understand what was being said but judging by the look on his face Scott had a visceral fear of whatever was being discussed.

It wasn't Trent's business. He took the café au lait back to the terrace.

Their guests having left, Trent and Darcey cleaned the kitchen. Trent took the trash down the hall and around the corner to the bin located past the elevator. He heard doors opening and closing. He heard Mrs. Philby's anxious cry. James Williams' nasty laugh. Wanting to avoid becoming involved, he stopped just out of sight. The next thing he heard came unexpectedly.

Mrs. Philby's voice became calm. It dropped to a lower register.

"You think you frighten me, James Williams," the old woman said, speaking deliberately. "You think I'm just a doddering old fool. Perhaps I am. But let me ask you something. Did you know I sleep with ear plugs?"

Silence.

"Do you know why?"

More silence.

"Do you know what the letters MRAD mean?"

Still more silence.

"Median Range Acoustics Device," the woman continued. "My condominium is equipped with such a device. If anyone attempts to break into my condominium, they will be met with a sound of such intensity, at such a high decibel level, they will be overcome. The pain will be debilitating. Their ear drums will burst. They will be permanently deaf. I warn you to back off."

She paused.

"Leave me alone," were her final words.

Trent heard two doors close. Williams had said not a word. Trent made a mental note to get ear plugs.

Saturday, June 25th

They had worked quickly to put the wedding together in only two months. Darcey insisted that she didn't want it too big or too fancy. Betty and Ivy grumbled but agreed. Still the old house at the Pines never looked more beautiful. Having been described as the finest example of early 19th century "Dog Trot" architecture in the nation, the ancestral home of Betty Anderson's family, the Belmonts, was in its glory.

The sun was bright. The forecast for temperatures in the mid-80s. Quite comfortable for late June. To be safe, Betty and Ivy, as promised, arranged for a large tent-like canopy to be erected. Fans and misters were set up all around the seating area where the wedding would take place as well as on the edges of the canopy.

Trent stood with the minister in front of the crowd dressed in a white linen suit, sans tie. His groomsmen, Jordan Baron and Jack Blake, wore black suits, also with no ties.

Two of Darcey's cousins were assigned to escort Betty and Ivy down the aisle. As Ivy took the seat reserved for the groom's mother, whispering was heard in the crowd. It wasn't that anyone disapproved of a black couple at the wedding. There were, in fact, several black families, friends of both sides, in attendance. It was a surprise that she was honored by being seated in the chair reserved for the groom's mother.

Not everyone in attendance knew that when his mother passed away unexpectedly Trent became very close to Ivy and Walter. Later, when first his father, then his mother's aunt passed, Ivy and Walter became the only family he had. He insisted that they be publicly acknowledged.

But it was when Miles Diaz-Douglas made his way down the aisle to take his place as one of Darcey's bridesmaids that the rustle of the crowd became truly audible.

Not knowing what to expect, Scott sat muttering quietly to himself, wishing he had another of Trent's peach martinis. Still he had to admit Miles did make a stunning bridesmaid.

Miles happily pranced down the aisle in his black suit and pink linen shirt. He loved the pink shirt. It reminded him of sunsets and strawberry daiquiris. He held a bouquet of white flowers with one pink rose in the center. He took his place on Darcey's side of the minister.

Jack Blake was nervous. "I don't know about this guy, Trent," he whispered. "It's an election year, you know."

"Yes," Trent said quietly, "and do you know how many gay voters there are in this parish?"

"No."

"Neither do I. But you just won all their votes.

"I see what you mean," Jack said, now smiling. He looked over the assembled guests. Wondering.

Mandy Rillard followed Miles. She wore a fashionable black dress and carried the same bouquet of white flowers as had Miles.

The beautiful white flowers of the Spanish dagger, the plant that had come to be known as the Lord's Candelabra in the soon to be combined Marshall-Anderson families, were in full bloom. It was those flowers that Darcey chose for herself and her bridesmaids to hold when they made their way down the aisle.

Trent watched Darcey walking toward him, her hand on the arm of Preston Johnson. The old man was elegant as always in his black suit. The sun glinted off his silver hair and mustache, the gold handle of his ever-present cane. He placed Darcey's hand in Trent's then took his seat beside Betty. He could not have been more proud had he been Darcey's father.

Trent held Darcey's hands. For years he had felt lonely even when surrounded by people who cared about him. He held her hands and felt the loneliness fade into the past. He didn't know what the future held for them. He could hardly wait to find out.

The champagne flowed freely after the brief ceremony. Toasts were made by Jordan and Jack, Mandy and Miles.

Preston rose and tapped his glass, indicating his desire to make a toast. As the guests quieted, he spoke in his cultured tone.

"The phrase locum tenens usually refers to the medical profession. But I beg your indulgence to use it in a more general sense today. It has been my honor to serve locum tenens...temporarily... in the place of your father today, Darcey. I know he would be so proud if he was here. On his behalf, and in spiritual kinship with him, I wish you both a long and happy life together."

As it turned out, Miles was a huge hit with the guests. The sheriff even insisted on having his picture taken with him. But Miles refused... adamantly refused...Darcey's dare to ride one of the horses.

"Absolutely not," he said, defiantly. "That is not the kind of animal I am accustomed..."

"Miles!" Scott interrupted.

Miles caught himself before he said something inappropriate.

"Well, no. I won't do it. That's all."

Everyone laughed. Even the ones who weren't quite sure why they were laughing.

Sunday, June 26th

Alexis was relieved promptly at six o'clock by the guy who had drawn the Sunday night shift. She liked him. He was a funny looking little guy around 30, a bald spot already beginning to show through his short hair. He always seemed nervous around her, but he was polite and he made her laugh.

Monday and Tuesday were her days off. She was looking forward to sleeping late both mornings. It was a short ten minute walk to the Montgomery Street BART station. From there it was just over half an hour and another ten minute walk to the house in Richmond, just north of Berkeley, her home for now. After all she had been through, it was an idyllic place.

She walked briskly, watching the myriad of people crowding the streets of the city. She was amazed, happily so, at how her life had turned around. She had been born Alexis Brandt near Sacramento to a dysfunctional family. In her desperation to escape she made bad choices. Heavily into drugs by 15, she was turning tricks on her own at 16.

Then she met John Neal. He rolled up beside her on his Low Rider. He had an evil smile that turned her on and an endless supply of drugs. He convinced her to go with him to New Orleans. They'd have some fun, he said. There would be easy money, he said. She was stoned. She didn't care. She climbed on the bike behind him and held on.

In the Crescent City, John took her to meet an older man. The man gave John some money and that was the last she saw of him. The next ten years were a maze of strip clubs and motel rooms with strangers who had the price. Every day was a desperate search for another day's supply of whatever drug would let her escape the misery of her reality. They called her Piper. She didn't know who Piper was. It was someone she pretended to be.

Her life took a turn when she was arrested the last time. It happened by accident. The lieutenant wasn't vice. He wasn't looking for hookers. She propositioned him in front of the casino. With a crowd of tourists looking on, he had no choice. He arrested her more out of pity than sense of duty.

As he guided a stumbling Piper into the precinct, Bev Prentiss was coming out.

"Where y'at, Jordan?" she said, greeting him with the uniquely New Orleans phrase.

"Awright, Bev. Awright."

"Who you got there?"

"Don't know her. She calls herself Piper."

"Mind if I talk to her?"

Jordan stepped away to give them privacy, making sure to stay between his prisoner and the door.

Bev ran a rehabilitation program for addicts. She had a special feeling for young women on the street. Girls like Piper. Bev had been one of them. But that was a long time ago. She was over 60 now and had put on several pounds since her time on the street. Today she was dressed in her usual jeans and men's blue work shirt with the sleeves rolled up.

She had helped several women recover from the addictions and move on to happier lives. She had some failures. Some were heartbreaking. But she never gave up on the girls as long as they didn't give up on themselves.

She talked quietly to the young woman for a few minutes. Jordan saw Piper nod her head. He saw Bev speak again. From the look on her face she was speaking sternly. Piper chewed on her lip. She nodded her head again.

Bev seemed satisfied. She left Piper sitting on the bench looking dazed.

"Think you might talk to a judge and get her assigned to me?" she asked. "I think I can help her. At least I'd like to try."

"I'll see what I can do."

The next six months were hell for Piper. By the seventh month, Piper no longer existed. Alexis Brandt had come back to life.

Bev and Alexis decided it was best if she got out of New Orleans. She needed to be in a place where no one knew Piper. Where no one would try to convince Piper to come back to life to walk the streets again. Bev had a friend, a retired nurse who worked with her at the rehab facility, who had inherited a small house in California's Bay area.

When Bev asked, Abby said she would be happy to rent Alexis a room. She was a good choice. She knew exactly what she was getting into. She could help Alexis in her continuing recovery. If problems developed, Abby knew how to handle those, too.

Alexis was almost skipping up the short sidewalk to the small house. Her light brown hair bounced on her shoulders. Her birthday was coming up in August. Abby had promised to take her to Napa Valley to commemorate the occasion. She didn't remember anyone ever acknowledging her birthday. Her first birthday celebration would come when she turned twenty-seven. But the past didn't matter. She was excited for the present. For the future.

Stepping lightly up the two concrete steps to the porch, she unlocked the door and stepped inside. She froze where she stood. All the light seemed to have suddenly been sucked out of the house, leaving her in darkness. Darkness that threatened to close in on her. To crush her.

"Hello, Piper," the overweight slob sitting in Abby's favorite chair greeted her. The small semiautomatic pistol in his hand was pointed directly at her. The Smith & Wesson .40 caliber was popular with people like Steve Burgess. It sported a lightweight plastic frame with stainless steel barrel and slide. It held a fourteen round magazine. As far as semiautomatic handguns go, it was relatively cheap.

Alexis was barely able to speak.

"Burgess," she finally managed to utter. "What are you doing here? How did you find me? How did you get in here?"

"The how isn't important," he said, with a sneer. "I found you and I'm here. That's all that matters. And you're going to help me."

Alexis summoned her courage.

"No, I won't help you," she said. "I'm not going back to being Piper. She's dead and she's going to stay dead. You can shoot me if you want. I won't help you."

Burgess laughed.

"I wouldn't dream of shooting you, Piper," he said. "I'll let you watch me shoot the old woman you live with here. I'll let you stand close to her so you are covered with her brains when I blow them out of her skull."

"No, don't hurt Abby," she pleaded.

"She's safe, Piper," Burgess said, "as long as you do what you're told."

Monday, June 27th

Trent and Darcey arrived at Heathrow airport at 9:05 a.m., London time. Though they had dozed in their adjoining first class cubicles, their body clocks were still set at 3:05 a.m., New Orleans time. They moved in a sleepy daze.

They passed quickly through British customs and found the driver from the Ritz Hotel who had been sent to greet them. As they drove through London's busy streets in the hotel's Rolls Royce, Darcey enjoyed pointing out some of her old haunts from her days as a student at the London School of Design. She didn't ride in a Rolls in those days.

Finally shown to the elegant Trafalgar Suite that would serve as their quarters for the next few days, they showered and fell into bed for a nap.

Darcey was awakened two hours later by voices in the suite's large drawing room. Trent had ordered a room service breakfast for them. A British breakfast as he recalled from his one visit to London several years earlier.

There were eggs baked in stoneware plates with slices of tomato, meaty bacon, a spiral of peppery Cumberland sausage, and grilled mushrooms. There was coffee and a selection of teas. Toast and muffins.

"Welcome back, Darcey,"

The next month went by quickly. They played tourist much of the time.

In London, there was high tea at the Ritz with Champagne, finger sandwiches, scones with strawberry preserves, and clotted Devonshire cream.

Darcey was alone only one day. Trent spent that day at the headquarters of London's Metropolitan Police. Better known as Scotland Yard.

Two weeks in Paris. The Louvre. The Eiffel Tower. Cabarets and bistros in Montmarte. Harry's New York Bar where the French 75, that delightful concoction of gin, lemon juice, simple syrup, and Champagne, was born.

They traveled to Versailles for Bastille Day, France's own celebration of independence. An elaborate celebration featuring light shows erupting from the 50 fountains at the magnificent palace built by Louis XVI. The same palace where Louis signed the agreement that brought France officially into the American Revolution on the side of the American colonists.

In Paris, as in London, Darcey was alone for one day. Trent spent that day at the Ile de la Cite', headquarters of the Paris Police Prefecture. The director of Interpol drove in from his headquarters in Lyon for the meeting.

From Paris they flew to Italy for a week in a Tuscan villa that once housed an olive press on a still working vineyard and olive grove. They drove into Florence one day to visit the Galleria Academia Firenze, the home of Michelangelo's Statue of David. Trent had seen the statue and thought it the finest art ever created with stone and chisel. He still marveled at the artist's ability to carve veins in the stone hands.

He thought Darcey's gaze lingered a bit long on David's famous exposed genitals. He pointed out the political symbolism of the statue was in the eyes, casting their stern warning glare in the direction of Rome. Symbolic, he said, of the determination of 16th century Florence to remain independent. Darcey didn't seem interested in politics. Or David's eyes.

As in London and Paris, Darcey spent one day alone while Trent drove back to Florence to meet with the Anti-Mafia Investigation Department, the Finance Police, and the Carabinieri, all of which had an interest in the Mafia and money laundering.

Sunday, July 3rd

Alexis met Burgess at the BART station as he had directed. Only a few days ago she had awakened each morning anxious to see what the day would bring. The rebirth of Alexis made her feel she was exonerated for the sins committed by the girl Piper who had occupied Alexis' bodily shell for so long.

She shuddered as she caught site of Burgess moving toward where she sat on the bench, his body moving in a haphazard fashion not usually associated with humans. He dropped onto the bench beside her.

"I know Trent Marshall is here," he said. "I know he's staying with the Anderson woman. I want to know their schedule."

Alexis felt her new life slipping away. Ms. Anderson had been very nice to her. She didn't want to betray her. She remained silent.

Burgess turned his face to look at her, the folds of skin on his neck flapping with the movement. He opened his jacket slightly so she could see the butt of the semiautomatic handgun.

"In case you're thinking of not cooperating, Piper, keep in your mind the picture of yourself covered with your friend Abby's brains."

Alexis hung her head. She would try to protect Abby and avoid betraying others as best she could.

"They're out of town."

"Where are they, Piper? Don't play games with me," Burgess snarled.

"They got married," Alexis said, her voice barely audible. "They're in Europe on their honeymoon."

Burgess laughed.

"Married?" he said. "Now that presents some possibilities. I'll have to give that some thought. This could get to be fun."

Alexis stared at the floor beneath her feet.

"When will they be back?"

41

"They get back on July 24th," she said.

"Good to know," Burgess said. "OK. You can go."

Alexis stood quickly. She started to walk away.

"Oh, and Piper…"

She stopped.

"Happy Fourth of July," Burgess laughed. His revolting laughter followed her as she hurried away.

Saturday, July 16th

Burgess had immediately reported the information regarding Trent and Darcey's schedule to his San Francisco contact. Rossi called on Saturday morning.

"You'll receive instructions on where and when to pick up a package on July 22nd. Specific instructions on how to use the contents of the package will be included. Arrange entry into the Anderson woman's condo on that day. It must be that day."

"I'll be ready."

"You'd better be," Rossi said. "Don't mess this up, Burgess. You'll regret it if you do."

Rossi ended the call. He tossed the prepaid mobile phone to the closest security guard. It would be destroyed.

Wednesday, July 20th

Alexis trudged up the short sidewalk to Abby's house. She wasn't skipping up the walk. She didn't feel like skipping since Steve Burgess reappeared in her life. July had been miserable. When she opened the door, she realized her misery was just beginning. It would also soon be over.

Abby was on her knees in front of Burgess who sat in the old woman's favorite chair. The barrel of Burgess' semiautomatic was in her mouth.

"I need your keys, Piper," Burgess said, not bothering to greet her.

She held out her hand, which still held her house key.

"Not that key, stupid," Burgess said. "You have key cards that will let me take the elevator to the 15th floor and into the Anderson woman's condo. I want those keys."

"No," Alexis cried. "No, I won't give you those."

"Your choice, Piper. Say goodbye to your friend."

"Wait. Don't kill her. She never hurt anybody

"The keys."

Her shoulders slumped. She reached into her handbag for the two key cards linked with a small chain. She handed them to Burgess.

"Which is which?"

"The gray one lets you access the secure floors," she mumbled. "The white one opens any of the unit doors."

"Good girl, Piper," he flashed his evil smile as he pulled the trigger. As he had threatened, the .40 caliber bullet took off the back of Abby's head. Her brains flew across the room, some of which landed on Alexis.

Alexis' shriek of horror was short-lived. The second bullet Burgess fired struck her squarely in the forehead.

Piper died months earlier. Alexis joined her today. Her friend Abby was waiting for her. They would not be going to Napa.

Friday, July 22nd

Burgess' phone rang at seven o'clock in the morning. He was more hungover than usual. But he was at least alert enough to remember that this was an important day. A day with serious consequences if he failed.

He fumbled for the phone, managing to locate it before the call was directed to voice mail. He didn't recognize the voice. The caller gave no name. He gave Burgess an address where he was to pick up the package. He told Burgess to take no longer than an hour to get there.

The address turned out to be a Thai restaurant on Larkin Street in the Tenderloin. The neighborhood now known as Little Saigon. It was only a few blocks from the cheap residential hotel near Market Street where Burgess lived.

Burgess stopped across the street from the restaurant. He watched for a few minutes. It was an old habit. A matter of survival. He had no intention of walking into a trap. He didn't trust anyone. And he was unarmed.

He knew the cops would find Piper and her friend soon. He wasn't concerned about finger prints as he had worn surgical gloves. But he didn't want to hold on to any evidence linking him to the murders.

He had dropped the magazine in his pocket along with the expended shell and the bullet already chambered. He had wiped the gun down and dropped it on the floor. No prints. Serial number filed off. He would get rid of the magazine, individual bullets, empty cartridge casing, and gloves in multiple trash receptacles on his journey back to the city.

There was no way to connect him to the murder of the two women. But now he wished he had the gun back.

It was early. There were few people in the restaurant. He wasn't sure it was open. There was an alley running along one side of the restaurant. It was dark. He could see no movement.

After five minutes he was satisfied. He crossed the street. As he approached the front door there was movement to his left. Someone was in the alley. Burgess reached under his coat. There was no weapon there but whoever was in the alley wouldn't know that.

A young Asian man stepped from the alley. He wore a hoody, which prevented Burgess from seeing his face.

"You Burgess?" he questioned.

"What if I am?"

The young man held out a small box. A box about the size a watch would come in.

Burgess took the box with his left hand. He kept his right hand on the imaginary gun.

As soon as Burgess took the box, the young man disappeared into the dark.

Burgess took the box back to his room to open it. Whatever was in the box had cost Burgess most of what remained of the money the man in New Orleans had given him. He had been living on the small jobs Rossi had assigned him

Inside the box was a vial. Droplets of condensation clung to the glass. It looked something like the vials that nurses use to take blood. It didn't contain blood. It contained something far worse. So horrible Burgess almost dropped the vial. He laid it carefully on the bed. He didn't trust the table. He feared it would roll off and break. He didn't want the contents of the vial to escape.

The creature was larger than a tick. Smaller than a spider. It looked like something that might result from a mating of the two. Or something created by a mad scientist.

It was black with small, angry streaks of red. It had several short legs. Burgess couldn't remember how many legs a spider had. Was it eight? Six? He thought the small monster in the vial might have eight legs.

It had two pincer-like protrusions where its mouth should be. Burgess couldn't tell if it had eyes. Its head, at least what Burgess assumed was its head because of the pincers, moved from side to side. The pincers seemed to be searching for something. Maybe they were sensors. Burgess didn't want to find out.

The box contained a piece of paper with specific printed instructions, which he read carefully. Then read again. He was sweating. He had not expected this. He reached for a half empty bottle of cheap red wine. Filling the glass he had used the night before, he drained it. His eyes never left the small, ugly little creature constantly moving inside the vial.

Burgess worked out a plan. He shaved. He even washed his hair. He put on his one suit, white shirt and tie. He hoped the wrinkled condition of his clothes wouldn't be noticed.

He spent most of the day at a bar next door to his hotel. He ate a sandwich and fries for lunch. In the afternoon he nursed his drinks carefully. He only ordered another when the bartender began to scowl at him. The thought of the caged nightmare in his pocket was reason enough to stay sober.

Sobriety, temporary though it may be, was also required when the time came to put his plan into action. He didn't want to appear drunk on the streets of San Francisco.

Not that he cared about San Francisco one way or another. It was a puzzle to him. The street on which he lived was one of the most dangerous in the city. Yet only seven blocks away was the Art Moderne Rincon Center, a famous building that started as a post office built by Franklin Roosevelt's Works Projects Administration in 1940. He read that in a brochure a former tenant left in the apartment he was renting.

At five o'clock he paid his tab and started the walk through the Tenderloin and Chinatown up to Nob Hill. He had waited until the offices closed for the day. The sidewalks would be crowded. Workers would be anxious to get home or to their favorite after work hangouts to start the weekend. Hopefully there would be people entering the Anderson woman's building. Burgess wanted to blend with those people. He thought that was his best chance to get by the security guards and the concierge. Just another working man tired after a long day.

By the time he reached the building, the hoped-for crowds of workers had been released from their cubicles. The sidewalks were jammed with mobs of rushing people. A block down from his target building, Burgess pushed his way into the middle of the moving human raft. He was winded from keeping pace with the younger people around him. He managed to keep up.

As they came abreast of the target building, Burgess was relieved to see a small group turn into the lobby. Two of them stopped to talk to the concierge. He saw no sign of a security guard.

Burgess used the temporary distraction of the concierge to move quickly to the elevator. Four others were already in the car when he entered. They all punched in the numbers of their floors. Only Burgess had a key allowing him to access one of the secure floors. No one noticed when he used it.

Alone in the elevator as it moved upward the last few feet to the 15th floor, Burgess pulled on a pair of leather gloves. Not only did he wish to leave no fingerprints, he didn't want to be bitten when he released the monster in his pocket.

Piper's pass key gave him easy access into the condo. He took a minute to look around. It was far different from the dump in which he lived. That made him angry. The anger made him even more determined to press ahead with his plan. He went down the hall to the bedrooms.

His instructions were to find folded clothing that Trent wore next to his body. Tee shirts. Shorts. Pajamas. He was careful as he went through the drawers and closets. He didn't want to leave signs that someone had been there. When he opened the drawer containing the Anderson woman's underwear, his resistance slipped. He couldn't help rubbing a thong over his face. His eyes closed and he let out a low moan as he did so. He tried to carefully put them back as he found them.

The next drawer was the one he sought. It held the soft black pajama pants and black, long-sleeved tee shirts in which Trent slept. He had been told the creature could live for up to four days with only a little water. Eventually it would have to feed on blood or die. There was time.

In the bathroom he ran water onto a dirty handkerchief he had brought with him. He used the wet cloth to slightly dampen a small area inside one of the folded shirts Trent slept in. Very carefully he removed the glass vial from his pocket. Aiming the opening directly into the dampened fold of the shirt, he removed the stopper and gave the vial a light tap. The creature moved slowly out of the vial. It sensed moisture and quickly lost itself within the folded cloth.

Dropping the now empty vial in his pocket Burgess closed the drawer, relieved to be rid of the potential torment. His lips twisted into a repugnant smile as he thought about Trent pulling that shirt over his head.

Monday, July 25th

It was an eighteen-hour flight from Rome to San Francisco, including a layover in Philadelphia. The taxi stopped in front of their building after ten o'clock Sunday night. In Rome it was already eight o'clock Monday morning. Neither of the weary travelers wanted to even think about Monday morning.

The concierge, a new man Trent didn't recall seeing before, helped them with their luggage. Darcey and Trent were both exhausted. Neither bothered to shower. Darcey found her favorite gown; Trent grabbed the first long-sleeved tee shirt and black pants in his drawer. He was too tired to notice the slightly damp spot on his shirt.

He fell into bed with Darcey. Both fell asleep immediately.

Trent awakened before Darcey. He went first to the kitchen to start a pot of coffee. Then to shower. To wash away eighteen hours of travel from the day before.

He had shaved and was standing naked in front of the mirror in the bedroom brushing his hair when Darcey woke up.

"Mmmmmmm…now there's a view that makes waking up worthwhile," she said.

"After seeing this sight every day for a month, I figured you would be getting tired of it," he replied, mugging for her in the mirror.

Darcey laughed.

"You're not getting away that easy, Mr. Marshall. I'm not one of those take'em-to-London-Paris-and-Tuscany-for-a-month-and-then-dump'em kind of girls."

"I have to call Christopher Booth or I'd make you pay for that remark," Trent said, pulling on his boxer shorts.

"Yeah, yeah. You're all talk."

Darcey suddenly looked serious. Puzzled.

"I never noticed that mole under your arm," she said.

"I don't have a mole under my arm."

Darcey jumped out of bed and quickly crossed the room.

"Oh, no!" she exclaimed.

"What?"

"Oh, no!" Darcey repeated.

"It isn't a great comfort to have you standing behind me saying 'Oh no' over and over," Trent said. "What is it?"

She ran to the kitchen where she found a small, plastic container with a snap on lid. Reaching into her purse, she found a pair of tweezers.

"Be very still," she directed. She gently clutched what she now realized was an appalling insect with the tweezers. Moving slowly so as to extract the two small ungulas, the talon-like protrusions the creature had sunk into the warm flesh under Trent's arm. The pincers moved round as though in anger once Darcey pulled them free and dropped the ugly little thing into the plastic container. She quickly snapped the lid in place, trapping the small monstrosity.

"What is that?" Trent said. He raised his arm. In the mirror he saw the tiny pin-pricks where the insect had attached itself to him. The skin around the small dots was slightly reddened.

"Is that a bed bug?" Darcey asked. She set the container on the dressing table, not wanting it in her hands.

"No, I've seen bed bugs," Trent said. "That's not a bed bug. That's not anything I've ever seen before."

"Do you think you picked it up in our travels?" she asked, still horrified.

"That doesn't seem logical. You never noticed it before this morning," he said, with a leer. "And you saw me naked from every possible angle over the past month."

"I don't think this is funny, Trent."

"It's no big deal, Darcey. Just a tick or something. I'm fine."

"We're going to make sure of that," she said as she picked up her phone and dialed a number.

"Who are you calling?"

"My doctor. We're taking this...this thing to him to send to a lab and let him look at that bite. I've only been married a month and I'm not taking any chances on losing you."

Wednesday, July 27th

Darcey was surprised when Trent told her he was taking her to the Tadich Grill for lunch. The restaurant is a legend among San Franciscans. Tadich Grill is the third oldest restaurant in the nation. Only the Union Oyster House in Boston and Antoine's in New Orleans came before the Tadich.

It is a no reservations place. You stand in line to wait for a table. Even Tony Bennett stands in line when he's in town.

Trent insisted they get there by eleven o'clock so they would only have to wait for forty-five minutes or an hour. As it happened, it was a slow day. They were seated within forty minutes. Trent kept a close look out. He didn't see Tony Bennett.

Darcey ordered a small Caesar salad and seafood curry. Trent convinced the chef to make a Bay Shrimp Louis for him and followed that with lamb chops. Rare.

The Caesar salad was excellent, Darcey pronounced. Romaine lettuce crisp and fresh, selected at five o'clock that morning by the chef.

Trent's Bay Shrimp Louie, he said, brought back memories. As a teenager, he had spent weeks in the summers roaming Alaska with his father who worked for an oil company. In Alaska the small crustaceans were called Petersburg shrimp. For most of the 20th century the small Southeast Alaska town of Petersburg processed millions of pounds annually. But the always precarious economics of the seafood industry shifted resulting in the closure of the Petersburg cannery. In recent years local entrepreneurs started a new company to once again process Petersburg shrimp for a promising market.

"We should go to Alaska," Trent said. "I've always thought it's the most beautiful place on Earth. And this Petersburg shrimp processing plant might be worth investing in."

"Count me in," Darcey said. "I'd love to see Alaska."

Her seafood curry included bay shrimp, Dungeness crab and large prawns, served over rice with a mango chutney.

"It's sweet and spicy," she said.

"Ah, just like you," was Trent's rejoinder.

Darcey laughed.

"Don't get your hopes up, big boy. I have to go back to the office after lunch."

"Well, there's always tonight," Trent said, with confidence

They lingered over lunch. It was mid-afternoon by the time Trent left Darcey at her office and walked the four blocks on to the condo. In the lobby he noticed that Alexis wasn't at the concierge desk. The friendly, though nervous, man who usually worked weekend nights was on duty. Clarence, Trent recalled.

"Hey, Clarence," Trent greeted him.

"Good afternoon, Mr. Marshall," Clarence replied, with a tentative smile.

"Where's Alexis? Doesn't she usually work Wednesdays?"

"Well, uh yes, she does, Mr. Marshall. Usually. But Alexis hasn't shown up for work since last Wednesday."

Trent was surprised.

"Has anyone talked to her?"

"The manager tried calling her several times but she didn't answer. We don't know what's going on with her. Maybe she decided to go back where she came from."

"I hope she's OK," Trent said. "She seems like a very nice person."

"Oh yes, she's very nice," Clarence said, in a tone that made Trent think he had more than a casual interest in Alexis.

"See you later, Clarence," he said as he stepped into the elevator. Just as the doors were beginning to close Clarence said something that got Trent's attention.

"You and Alexis have something in common, Mr. Marshall. I mean both of you coming from New Orleans and all."

Trent stuck his arm between the closing doors, causing them to open again. He stepped out of the car.

"Alexis came from New Orleans? Are you sure?"

"Well, uh, she mentioned it one time when we were talking. I don't know if that's where she was born. It was where she lived before she came to the Bay area. A coincidence that you're from New Orleans."

"Yes," Trent said. "A coincidence."

Trent didn't believe in coincidence.

Upstairs in the condo he called Detective Sergeant Christopher Booth. The detective was skeptical.

"What does that have to do with our investigation? Maybe she got a better offer. She used to live in New Orleans. Lots of people live in New Orleans. Could be only a coincidence."

"There's no such thing as coincidence in crime, corruption, and politics, Christopher. I think we should look into her disappearance and do it quickly. In the worst possible case, I will apologize for wasting your time. The best case could be we would save our lives."

Booth said he was on his way.

The building manager was cooperative. He liked Alexis. He told Booth she was a good worker. Never late. Never caused any problems. The residents of the building all spoke highly of her.

They tried calling her one more time. Still no answer. Booth told the manager that he had no warrant and couldn't require it but he would appreciate knowing where she lived. He said she could be in trouble. If so, maybe Booth and Trent could help her. The manager pulled her file and gave them a home address in Richmond.

The drive through Oakland and Berkeley took most of an hour. Booth parked next to the curb rather than pulling into the driveway. As they got out of the car an elderly man walked by, a small dog tugging on a leash. Trent wasn't sure who was walking who.

"Are you the police?" he asked.

Christopher said he was.

"Well, it's about time," the man said. "You're finally here. I've called three times this week. You probably have heard of me. Siemanszko is my name. Casey Siemanszko. Casey from my baseball days," he added proudly.

"Yes, of course," Booth said, playing along with the old man. "Tell me again why you called."

"Don't you know?" Casey said. "Lord knows I talked to enough of your people. You should know."

"I do know, Casey. Do you mind if I call you Casey? We have to be careful in cases like this. Have to be sure of all the facts."

"Sure, you can call me Casey," the old man said, beaming. "I was pretty good with a bat in my day."

"That's what I've heard," Booth said, humoring him. "Tell me again about your complaint."

"Well, the smell," Casey said. "That awful smell. And it's coming from around here. From this house, I think. Something has to be done about it."

"Thanks so much for contacting us, Casey," Booth said. "That's why we're here."

"Just being a good citizen," the old man said as he resumed his walk, his dog tugging at the leash.

Christopher and Trent had already caught the smell coming from the house. Both knew what it meant.

They rang the doorbell. There was no response. They expected none.

Booth tried the door. It was unlocked. He pushed but the door didn't budge. Something was blocking it. They suspected they knew what the something was. Christopher could have forced his way in but they feared disturbing a crime scene.

Booth went around to the back door. It was locked. He didn't think they had to worry about disturbing anything at this door. He kicked it hard. The cheap wood was no match for the big cop's foot. Trent followed him in.

The smell was overwhelming inside. Booth covered his face with a handkerchief. Trent didn't carry a handkerchief. He regretted it. He was wearing his usual black pullover shirt. He pulled the tail up to cover his nose.

The two women had been dead for a week. Both bodies were in an advanced stage of decomposition. It was not a sight for a weak stomach. For any stomach.

They had been through the stages of hypostasis and rigor mortis. They were bloated. Swollen as to be unrecognizable. Their color was blotchy. Some parts turning black. The skin was beginning to blister and split.

Trent thought the woman whose body was wedged against the door was probably Alexis. She at least had a head. The other woman, Trent suspected, had the barrel of the gun in her mouth when the killer pulled the trigger. Most of the back of her skull was missing.

Both men had seen all they needed to see for now. They pushed their way through the broken door and out of the house. Both moved to the far end of the back yard, gasping for air. Clean air. Booth called the Richmond police homicide department.

Detective Sergeant Nancy Patrick was first on the scene, followed quickly by two black and whites. She directed the uniformed officers to mark the crime scene, then joined Christopher and Trent. Christopher introduced Trent to Sergeant Patrick. She had short dark hair, dark eyes, and sharp cheek bones. Trent thought she was an attractive woman. Even sexy in more feminine attire. Today she wore a no nonsense charcoal gray pants suit. When she spoke, her voice matched the no nonsense pants suit.

She and Christopher were friendly toward each other. Friendly enough to make Trent wonder. But now was not the time.

Christopher told her he had kicked in the back door. He told her it was pretty bad inside.

"I guess I have to see it anyway," she said. He offered her his handkerchief to cover her nose and mouth. She accepted it and squeezed through the shattered door.

As Trent and Christopher had done, she came out gasping for air. She placed a call to the forensics crew to let them know they would need masks and oxygen. There was no way they could do their jobs until the bodies were removed and fresh air could be let into the house.

"It's going to take a lot to make that house livable again," she said, still breathing deeply.

Another unmarked car rolled up. A bald man whose belly matched the shape of his head bounced out.

"What are you doing here, Booth? You're a little out of your jurisdiction, aren't you?"

"Hello, Captain," Booth said, not in the least put off by the man's attitude. "Captain Terry Wooster, meet Trent Marshall."

"A civilian? You're bringing civilians with you? I want to know what's going on and I want to know now!"

"No problem, Captain," Booth said, cheerfully. "I'm not here on police business. We were just worried about a friend of ours who hasn't been showing up for work lately. Turns out she had a good reason. Her body is in there along with another woman. They've been dead, I'd say, about a week."

"You got a warrant?"

"Why would I need a warrant?" Booth said, continuing his friendly misdirection of the bumbling captain. "I told you we were just worried about a friend. No intent to search. No intent to arrest. Not investigating any crime."

"No warrant and you entered the premises anyway?" the captain accused.

"Yes, like we would if we smelled smoke or natural gas or heard someone calling for help," Booth said. "In this case it was the smell of decaying bodies."

"Why didn't you call my office?"

"I did. That's why Sergeant Patrick is here overseeing these officers as they secure the crime scene."

Captain Wooster's face turned red with fury.

"I'll be talking to your boss about this, Booth. You have no business poking around in my town."

He hustled over to where the uniformed officers were working and began shouting orders that made little sense. Trent noticed the officers didn't pay much attention to him.

The New Orleans connection is bothering you, isn't it?" Christopher said as he drove them back into the city. "It could be coincidence, Trent."

Trent looked at him.

"Yeah, I know. There's no such thing as coincidence in crime, corruption, and politics."

"You're a fast learner," Trent said. "You seem to know Sergeant Patrick pretty well."

"Yeah, pretty well," Christopher said, suppressing a self-satisfied smile.

"Well enough to ask her for a favor?"

"Yeah, I know her that well."

Given their filling lunch at Tadich Grill followed by the less than savory events of the afternoon, Trent declined dinner. Darcey said she would just have a light snack. Trent waited until after she had eaten before telling her what they had found in the small house in Richmond. He didn't go into great detail. Darcey was grateful.

He told her he had learned that Alexis moved to San Francisco from New Orleans. That was a red flag for him, he said, reminding her that he didn't believe in coincidence.

"I should have known she was from New Orleans," Darcey said.

"Why would you know that?"

"Jordan called me several months ago and asked me if I knew of any jobs that might be available for a young woman who had escaped the streets and was doing a good job of turning her life around. The building had an opening on the concierge staff and I told him about it."

"Why didn't you tell me about that?"

"I don't know. Didn't think it was important. I forgot all about it until now. He never gave me a name. When Alexis came to work here I didn't even know she was the one he had called me about."

He made them each a French 75. They sat on the terrace watching the fog roll in.

Trent reached for his cocktail and almost dropped the glass. He clinched and unclenched his hands. Stood and walked around the terrace.

"All you all right?" she asked.

"I think so. My hands and feet feel numb. There's no feeling at all. Strange. I'm sure it's nothing."

Darcey wasn't so sure. She was glad they had an appointment with the doctor tomorrow.

The pizza arrived only a few minutes before Detective Sergeant Nancy Patrick got home. Detective Sergeant Christopher Booth had been home for a couple of hours. He had showered, changed into shorts and a tee shirt. The double murder in Patrick's jurisdiction made it a longer day for her.

Booth handed her a glass of chilled Chardonnay when she walked through the door of the apartment they shared in Walnut Creek. He kissed her. She let him hold her for a few minutes. It was their evening ritual. A metamorphosis from the tough cops they had to be on the job and an ordinary, likable couple in love when off duty.

"To the shower with you," he said, as he swatted her bottom playfully. "Go wash off the cop smell. Don't let the pizza get cold."

After they finished the pizza, Christopher poured her another glass of wine and opened a second beer for himself. They sat outside on their small terrace.

"Trent asked if I know you well enough to ask a favor."

"What did you tell him?" she asked.

"I said I thought so but you were pretty tough to work with."

She laughed and gave him a punch to his well-muscled shoulder.

"So, what's the favor?"

"He wants to know if you could get some of the DNA from the body blocking the door down to Jordan Baron in New Orleans."

"Whoa. The Rooster would go nuts if he found out I did that," she said. The Rooster was what Richmond cops called Captain Wooster. Christopher thought "an old hen" would be a more appropriate appellation. He was always clucking and flapping his wings.

"Lieutenant Baron can go through official channels and get it that way."

"Nah," Nancy said. "It's too much fun to mess with the Rooster."

That brought a chuckle from Christopher.

"Why does he want a New Orleans cop to check her DNA?"

"It's what sent us to Richmond. The woman was a concierge at the building Trent and Darcey live in. When he didn't see her on duty today he asked her stand-in what was up. The guy said she hadn't shown up for work for a week. Then he said it was funny that she and Trent both came from New Orleans," Christopher explained. "That got Trent's attention."

"Could be coincidence," Nancy said.

"To quote Trent, 'There is no such thing as coincidence in crime, corruption, and politics.'"

"Hmmmm. I never thought about that. He might be right. I'll see what I can do."

Thursday, July 28th

Dr. Smith was six feet four inches tall and weighed less than 200 pounds. That explained why all his colleagues, the nurses, and most of his patients called him Dr. Slim. He was easy going and a good doctor. He wore a traditional white lab coat. The woman in his office wore one, too. He introduced her as Dr. Angie Raymond. Trent and Darcey thought her presence didn't mean the news was good.

"You have contracted a zoonotic disease, Trent," Dr. Slim explained. "That simply means a disease that can be transmitted to a human from another species. It's not uncommon. More than half of the viruses and bacteria that make us sick are spread that way. This one, however, is a little more challenging. That's why I asked Dr. Raymond to join us. She is a specialist in treating similar diseases."

"I'm always up for a challenge," Trent said, trying to sound cheerful for Darcey's sake.

"Well, you have yourself a stick of dynamite this time," Dr. Slim said.

Trent reached over to take Darcey's hand.

"I guess the important thing is the length of the fuse," Trent laughed.

"We don't know that."

The acerbic answer came from Dr. Raymond.

Darcey was silent. Pale.

"What do we know?" Trent asked.

"The bug that bit you is unlike anything we've ever seen," she responded. "It has traits of the ticks that cause Lyme Disease. In fact, when we examined the spirochetes, the bacteria that cause Lyme Disease, that was our first conclusion. On closer examination we found an aberration in the microorganisms."

"And in English that means…" Trent questioned.

"We've never seen anything like these spirochetes before," Dr. Raymond said. "We haven't seen anything exactly like what you have. It bears resemblance to Late Stage Lyme Disease but it isn't. It's something more than that."

"How do you treat this…this whatever it is?" Darcey asked.

The doctors exchanged glances. Dr. Slim spoke.

"We don't have a definitive answer to that, Darcey," he said. "Dr. Raymond and her colleagues will continue to study the spirochetes. We are hopeful they will find the answers. Meanwhile, we will treat it as we would Late Stage Lyme Disease. Heavy doses of antibiotics."

"There's one more thing," Dr. Raymond said. "In Late Stage Lyme Disease, the symptoms don't show up for several months. Sometimes even years. In this case they could show up much sooner. Within days. We don't know that for sure. It's possible."

"What are the symptoms?" Darcey pursued.

"There could be any of several. Confusion. Disorientation. A numbness in the hands and feet. A stiff neck. Joint pain. Headaches. In severe cases we've seen hallucinations. Hearing voices. Insomnia is common as is exacting fatigue. In rare cases the pupils will dilate allowing the patient to see clearly in total darkness but requiring glasses with heavily darkened lenses in light. Also, there have been rare cases in which the patient's hearing becomes hypersensitive. Mood swings are common as are heavy sweating and tremors."

Trent sat quietly. He let Darcey do the questioning. He was thinking.

"If any of these symptoms develop will they be permanent or temporary?" she asked, thinking of the numbness Trent had mentioned.

"Hopefully, with treatment, they will be temporary," Dr. Raymond said. "But we really don't know. And I want to emphasize that Trent does not have Late Stage Lyme Disease. We think it's something similar but more potent. Until we know more, our only option is to treat it as we would Late Stage Lyme Disease, as Dr. Slim said, with heavy antibiotics."

"Trent's hands and feet were numb last night."

Dr. Raymond was surprised. "It's highly unusual for a symptom to show up so quickly. May I examine your hands, Mr. Marshall?"

"Examine away, Doctor," Trent said, trying to sound cheerful as he held out his hands.

"Close your eyes, please," she said. With his eyes closed, she gently touched the palm of his right hand with her forefinger. "Do you feel that?"

"Yes."

With her thumb and forefinger, she gave a moderate squeeze to the web of skin between the thumb and forefinger of his left hand. "And that?"

"Yes, I felt it."

She had him remove his shoes and socks. She repeated the process with his toes and the sole of his right foot, paying close attention to the plantar, the ligament connecting the heel to the toes. Trent showed no sign of numbness.

"So, the numbness was temporary. I'd say that's a good sign," Dr. Raymond concluded.

"Now I have a question," Trent said. "Where did this bug come from? We recently traveled to London, Paris, and Tuscany, where we stayed in a rural villa just outside Florence. Could we have picked this thing up in any of those places?"

"Perhaps," was the doctor's inconclusive answer. "There are ticks in Europe and in this country that carry the Lyme Disease spirochete. But, as I said, we've never seen anything like this before. It's likely that it developed in a tropical region. Africa or South America. Perhaps Southeast Asia. With globalization and the accompanying movement of millions of people from those areas into Europe and North America we're seeing many diseases we've not seen before. I suppose by some coincidence the insect could have been in a hotel room, brought there unknowingly by an immigrant worker."

Trent was doubtful. He didn't believe in coincidence.

Darcey asked the question the others were thinking.

"And if the antibiotics don't work? If you can't find a cure?"

It was quiet in the room. The two doctors looked at each other. Dr. Raymond looked away. Dr. Slim answered the question.

"Enjoy the time you have together, Darcey."

Jonathan Rossi took the call in his office. It was one of his associates in Rome. Rossi wasn't happy with the news. Trent Marshall had met with the Direzione Investigativa Antimafia, the Guardia di Finanza, and the Arma dei Carabinieri while he was in Italy. All three branches of the Italian police establishment dealt to one degree or another with money laundering. He was not pleased.

"Molte grazie," Rossi said before hanging up.

He stared thoughtfully out the window for a few minutes. Then he placed a call of his own.

"How long is it supposed to take for this bug to work," he asked when Burgess answered the phone.

"The directions that came with it said to expect about three months," Burgess replied, nervously. Talking to Rossi always made him nervous. "But he will be very ill for most of that time."

Rossi didn't thank Burgess. He ended the call. He had kept Marshall under surveillance since he returned to San Francisco from Europe. He knew about the appointment with the doctor today. He didn't know how much the doctor knew or what he told Marshall and his wife.

He wasn't sure he had three months. And he had to consider his partners.

Rossi had successfully wooed his three partners into a fiduciaria, a trust of sorts, by convincing them they all would see greater profits, which would be more quickly moved into legitimate businesses. He allowed them to convince him to be the amministrazione, the administrator, of the trust because of his contacts with key European contacts, which they believed to be more efficient, not to mention less risky, than were theirs.

Rossi's partners, however, were not aware that the fiduciaria was in reality a tontine. A 17th century financial structure in which the assets and profits were divided among the survivors if one partner was eliminated. The last surviving partner received all the assets and profits. Rossi had created a tontine of criminal organizations. He intended to be the last survivor. But the timing of the elimination of the other three partners was Rossi's decision and his alone. Marshall could interfere with that. He was dangerous. Sick or healthy. He could cause a lot of trouble for them. Rossi thought he would have to move quickly against Marshall. He thought Burgess had outlived his usefulness. He placed another call.

Burgess was alarmed. He didn't like getting calls from Jonathan Rossi. He especially didn't like getting calls when Rossi sounded displeased. He knew that when Rossi was displeased people disappeared.

He was in the bar next to the cheap apartment hotel where he lived. He had been feeling good about the way things were going. He was celebrating with a bottle of cheap Champagne and two Chicago-style hot dogs. He didn't know what fine wine was supposed to taste like so the cheap bottle seemed good do him. He was enjoying the piquant taste of the hot dog. Now Rossi had ruined his fun. He thought he should find another place to live. Another gun.

He had found a baseball bat shoved into the back of the small closet when he first moved into the cheap apartment. It was the only weapon he had. It would have to do.

Darcey was late getting home. She carried two books. She found Trent on the terrace, a gin and tonic in his hand. He was staring at nothing.

"Ivy warned me you get like this," she said.

He didn't turn his head.

"It's not every day a doctor tells you to enjoy your time together," he replied. "That's medical talk for 'You're not going to make it, pal.'"

"Maybe. Maybe not. I stopped by a book store on the way home and picked up a couple of books I thought you might like to thumb through."

"Something like 'How to Die with Dignity'," he said, sarcastically.

"No. That would be encouraging you to feel sorry for yourself," Darcey said, "and I'm not going to do that."

She tossed one of the books to him.

"This is a biography of Frederik Faust. He wrote hundreds of short stories and novels. Most under the pen name of Max Brand. He was an alcoholic and had a heart attack at the age of 29. Doctors told him he had to stay in bed or he would die. He continued to work and drink for 23 years. He was a war correspondent during World War II. Killed in battle in 1944 at the age of 51. He lived 23 years, Trent, in a time when the only treatment for heart disease was bed rest."

Trent held the book. He didn't know what to think. She tossed him another book.

"This is a biography of John Holliday," she said. "Better known as Doc. He was diagnosed with tuberculosis in 1873 at age 22. There was no treatment. He traveled the Wild West as a gambler, a gunfighter, a killer. He feared dying in bed. He tried as hard as he could to get killed but nobody came along who could outshoot him. He died in a sanitarium in Colorado in 1887. According to Hollywood, his last words, as he looked at his bare feet at the end of the bed, were 'Now that's funny.' He lived for fourteen years with tuberculosis at a time when there was no medicine for that disease. None. So, like Faust, he drank a lot."

"What's the point, Darcey?" Trent asked.

"The point is, Trent Marshall,' she said, "is I love you. We've been married a month. You've contracted an illness, just like Faust and Holliday. The difference is they had no medicines. No treatment. No cure. Yet they lived for years. You are going to be pumped full of antibiotics. There are doctors studying whatever it is you have. They're likely to figure it out and come up with a cure."

Trent pulled her onto his lap and took her into her arms. He held her close.

"You're quite a woman, Darcey," he said.

"You're right. I am," she replied, kissing him again. "And there's no way I'm going to let you sit around feeling sorry for yourself. We're going to beat this thing. Meanwhile we will enjoy the time we have together."

Trent laughed.

"Now you sound like Ivy," he said.

"And there's one more thing."

"What's that?"

"I want to get pregnant," she said, softly.

"What? Are you crazy?" he exploded. "What if I don't make it? Then you'd have to raise a child all by yourself. No, Darcey. No way."

"You can be so selfish, Marshall," she said. She leaped off his lap. "Can't you understand this isn't all about you?"

"How do you figure that? I'm the one who's dying. It seems pretty clear it is all about me."

"You're the one who might be dying, Trent, with the emphasis on 'might be'," she replied, heatedly. "So yeah, what if you don't make it? A few weeks ago, I promised to live the rest of my life with you. How do I do that if you're not here? What do you think that would be like for me?"

She paused, wiping the tears away with her fingers.

"At least if we had a child, a part of you would still be here. Can't you see how wonderful that would be for me?"

Trent couldn't think of anything to say. He held her in his arms. She clung to him. Tears flowed.

When there had been enough tears, Darcey kissed him again.

"Now I'm going inside to finish up some twice baked potatoes. You're going to make each of us a gin and tonic. Then you're going to grill us a ribeye. After dinner, you're going to make us more gin and tonics, and we're going to watch a rom-com."

"What's a rom-com?" he asked, following her into the kitchen. He reached for the Hendrick's gin.

"A romantic comedy," she said. "A chick flick."

"They told me marriage was give and take. I guess this is what they meant."

"If it makes you feel better," she said, "you don't have to pay attention to the movie. You can sit here with me and read about Doc Holliday. He ought to be testosterone provoking enough for you."

Friday, July 29th

Darcey was surprised to find Trent sitting at the kitchen island drinking coffee and wiping a huge semiautomatic handgun down with a soft cloth. A very nasty-looking rifle lay on the island.

"Are we going to war?" she asked as she poured herself a cup of coffee, adding a little cream.

"We are at war, sweetheart," he said. "Alexis' murder was the declaration. I have no doubt it's connected in some way to the case I'm working on with Christopher. That means someone knows who we are. They'll probably come after us at some point. When they do, they'll find out we don't go down easily."

"OK, I won't argue with you. That thing you're so lovingly caressing looks like the biggest hand gun I've ever seen."

"It's as big as you can get," Trent said. "It has a ten inch barrel and fires a .50 caliber round. Because of the size, the magazine only holds seven rounds but it's so powerful you shouldn't need that many. It's a Desert Eagle. Developed by the Israelis. Now produced in this country under license. It has a range of over two hundred yards. There are rifles that aren't effective at that range."

"Is that for me?"

"No, this one will be going with me. This is for you," he slid the rifle toward her.

"You're joking, right?" she said. "I can't walk around San Francisco with this thing. What is it anyway?"

"It's the latest model of the M16," Trent explained. "It was first used in Vietnam but had some defects back then. There have been some improvements and it's now an effective weapon. Thirty rounds in magazine. It's fully automatic but if you have to use it that way remember it works best if you fire three round bursts. It has a range of five hundred yards. At closer range it's more accurate if you aim a little high. As to carrying it around town, here's your gym bag." He tossed the pink and black bag onto the island.

"Trent, I'm not going to lug this thing around with me, gym bag or no gym bag."

"Darcey, we're dealing with some seriously bad guys here. We need serious firepower to protect ourselves."

"No, Trent. We'll do it like we've done it before. If I sense trouble you're on my speed dial. You can come running with that small cannon. But the big one stays here."

"Well, keep it under the bed on your side then. The gym bag, too. At least you can protect yourself if they come at us here and I'm not around."

"Life with you is never dull, Marshall," she said as she picked up the rifle to get familiar with it. Trent showed her where the safety was, how to chamber a cartridge, and change out the magazine.

"Yeah, boredom is what we fear most," he said, kissing her. "I'll talk to Christopher today about getting us into a shooting range to practice with these things."

"Good idea," Darcey said. "I grew up with a rifle in my hands but never one that was fully automatic. Meanwhile, I feel sorry for anyone who comes at us. We have a fair chance of taking them out."

"Better than fair. Hey, we need to take a selfie to send to Jack Blake. He'll be envious."

Trent spotted the tail as soon as they pulled onto the street from the parking lot. Two swarthy men in a BMW Z4 hard top two-seater. He smiled. They thought they were driving a hot car. Fast enough to keep up with their quarry. Had it been anyone else in any other vehicle they would have been right. They didn't know Trent Marshall. They didn't know he was driving the fastest passenger car on the road.

"If you can give me directions and get us out of a speeding ticket I can lose the guys tailing us," he told Christopher. Booth was an experienced cop. He didn't turn his head to look.

"Go for it," he said.

"Hang on. I've always wanted to be Steve McQueen," Trent said.

They teased the tail for a while, twisting and turning through the city. Christopher's expert knowledge of which streets connected to which interstate and where served them well. As they approached the entrance to one interstate Trent pushed the accelerator to the floor and crossed two lanes of traffic, ignoring the blowing horns and obscene shouts coming from the cars he shot past. The tail didn't have time to respond.

To be on the safe side, Christopher had directed Trent onto an interstate that went north when they wanted to go south. Less than two miles and just over a minute later he directed Trent onto a second interstate that would curve to the south. The tail was nowhere in sight. Trent slowed down. But not much.

He brought the Bentley to a halt in front of a modest home in Palo Alto. Modest for a billionaire. For normal working people it would be a palace. It was the home of a man whose name most people had never heard. He was a technology genius. It was his mind behind many of the technological developments that changed the world in the late 20th and early 21st centuries.

Unlike many of his fellow high-tech luminaries Ross Brown wasn't greedy. Money bored him. His wife had to force him to attend monthly meetings with the people who handled their investments.

He wasn't interested in power. He had turned down offers to be CEO or at least a director of several companies.

He liked tinkering. Sometimes his tinkering made him, and others, billions. He seemed oblivious to his net worth. He bought the huge house for his wife and two children. His parents lived in the guest house. He spent most of his time, as he always had, in his basement workshop.

The man who opened the door was past fifty. His dark hair was shoulder-length and streaked with gray. He wore a full mustache beneath a hooked nose. His smile was friendly. He seemed slightly off center. In the manner, Trent thought, of an absent-minded professor. He wore jeans and a very old and worn tan work shirt with a patch over the pocket monogramed with his name.

As he led them into the house, a woman about the same age but very stylishly attired appeared from somewhere.

"Ross, I can't believe you're greeting guests wearing that old shirt," she said, sounding exasperated.

"Sherry, it's my favorite shirt," he said. "It's comfortable."

"It's the shirt he was issued in his first job, delivering refrigerators or something," the woman said, shaking her head but giving him a kiss on the cheek even as she reprimanded him. "Hi, I'm Sherry Brown."

Trent and Christopher introduced themselves. No one mentioned that Christopher was a cop.

"I'm off to pick up our grandsons," she told Brown. "Don't forget your mother is making dinner this evening. And you have to change your shirt before we go."

"Yes, dear," Brown replied as his wife swirled out the door. He grinned at his guests. "That's how you stay married for thirty years."

The newlywed in the room made a mental note.

Brown led them downstairs to his basement workshop. The place he liked to spend most of his time. Trent was awed to be there. He knew the work Brown had done years ago in his basement laid the groundwork for the technology explosion that was to come.

"How can I help you guys?" Brown questioned.

Brown held the highest security clearance offered by the United States government. Trent and Christopher held nothing back.

Christopher briefed him on the alliance among the four criminal organizations. He told the tech wizard how the alliance had increased the profits to the four partners and allowed them legal access to more of those profits. At the same time the other major crime organizations not included in the alliance were being weakened. They were in a serious situation. A war among these organizations could break out at most any time. If that happened, Christopher told Brown, he was not sure the police resources in the Bay area could handle it.

Trent said he was beginning to have a rudimentary understanding of how the alliance was formed and how it operated. He reported on his recent meetings with British, French, and Italian police agencies, and with Interpol.

What he heard in Europe fit with what Christopher had learned. He told Brown he was now focused on figuring out how the group was moving money quickly, in large amounts, with apparently small risk. He said he had some ideas but there was more work to be done.

"This is all very interesting," Brown said. "Very interesting. But where do I come in? This isn't exactly the kind of thing I have much experience with."

Trent smiled. Brown just gave him the perfect opening for the fillip he was holding in reserve.

"When we get this thing figured out, we need someone to help us play a little trick on the bad guys. We need someone who can create the ultimate computer game."

Brown's mustache quivered as he grinned.

"That I can do."

Christopher noticed Trent rubbing his knees as they talked to Brown. He noticed Trent moving slowly, leaning heavily on the bannister, as they walked up the stairs leading from the basement.

Outside Trent stopped for a moment before walking toward the car.

"Are you all right?" Christopher asked.

"My knees," Trent replied, breathlessly. "Hurting badly."

"Lean on me. Let me help you walk to the car."

"No!" Trent exclaimed with alarm. "Don't let anyone see me weakening. Let me catch my breath. Pretend we're talking."

"We don't have to pretend. We are talking."

Trent laughed as though Christopher had told him a very funny joke. The cop managed a smile, which dimmed as he watched Trent start toward the car. He was walking slowly, but with no noticeable limp. Christopher knew he was making a great effort.

"Have you ever driven one of these, Christopher?" Trent asked as he tossed the remote key to his companion. "Why don't you give it a try?'

Trent climbed in on the passenger side, grimacing as he swung his legs painfully into the car.

"I'd love to. Thanks." Christopher managed a strained smile as he caught the key.

Once they were back on the highway, Trent told Christopher the whole story. The mysterious bug. The symptoms that were beginning to show up. Everything.

"The doctors don't know exactly what this thing is. They don't have a cure. They pump me full of antibiotics and tell me they're trying to find a cure."

"Is there anything I can do?" Christopher asked.

"Not a thing. Look out for yourself. I know you have my back. I'll do my best to have yours. It's only fair that you know there might be a time when I can't hold up my end of the deal."

"You'll beat this thing, Trent. You're a tough guy. You'll beat it."

"Yeah, I'm tough, all right. But I don't know, Christopher," he said. "I might not be tough enough this time."

"Well, get tougher then. You have people counting on you."

"You're right. I'll make it. I come from good stock. Did you know I had an ancestor with the Texans at the Alamo?"

"Impressive."

"It would be," Trent said, "if he hadn't been among the small group from Goliad who fought their way into the Alamo."

Christopher grinned. "I can see you doing that, too."

Trent laughed.

Bat was envious when he saw Christopher driving the Bentley into the underground garage.

"Hey, Trent, when can I have a turn behind the wheel of that thing?"

"Soon, Bat. We'll take it out together soon."

"I'll hold you to that, Trent."

Trent waved agreement and directed Christopher to his parking space. As they had at the Brown house, Trent walked without apparent impediment to the elevator. Once inside the car, he slumped heavily against the wall.

He had called Darcey from the car. She met them at the door. His painful knees had gone about as far as they could go. Christopher and Darcey helped him to the couch. She braced his back with pillows while the big cop gently lifted Trent's legs onto the cushions.

"I figured you were armed, Trent, but that black ops holster I just brushed my hand across feels pretty big."

Trent reached under his shirt to pull the Desert Eagle from its holster. He handed it to Christopher.

"A Desert Eagle. Quite a gun. The .44 is legal in California. The .50 caliber isn't. I assume this must be the .44."

Neither Trent nor Darcey said a word.

Christopher handed the big weapon back to Trent before reaching beneath his jacket to the smaller semiautomatic holstered on his hip. "Beats my Smith & Wesson M&P Shield."

"I don't know about that," Trent said. "Extended magazine."

"Yep. Nine rounds."

"I'd go into a fight with that weapon."

"How about you, Darcey? Are you armed, too?" Christopher asked.

"I have a weapon. Not on me but here at home."

"What kind of weapon?"

"You might be better off not asking, Christopher," Trent said.

"You want me to get the two of you into a shooting range but you don't want me to know what you'll be shooting," the cop shook his head. Then he laughed. "You'd better hang on to this guy, Darcey. You'll never find another one like him."

After Christopher left, Darcey lightly massaged Trent's legs, being especially gentle with his knees. She wished she could take some of his pain into her own body by osmosis. Perhaps to an extent she did. He told her the pain was beginning to ease.

That evening she marinated some tilapia in soy sauce, white wine, olive oil, ginger and green onions. She steamed the pieces of fish and green onion, warmed the marinade and served it all over rice.

After they ate, Trent walked slowly out to the terrace. Darcey poured them each a glass of Merlot and joined him. They enjoyed being together.

It was late. Fully dark inside Burgess' cheap apartment. He sat in a chair placed midway between the door and the one dirty window. A rickety fire escape led from the window to the alley below.

He didn't know who was coming. He didn't know when. He was certain someone would come for him. The baseball bat lay across his legs. A duffel bag holding his few possessions was by his feet.

He heard the noise at 1:15 in the morning. A good hour from their perspective, he thought. They assumed he would be drunk. Passed out at that hour.

The noise was loud. A motorcycle. Maybe two. If there were two bikes, maybe Burgess should change his plan. He waited a few minutes longer. He heard the sound he was waiting for. Leather boots on metal steps. The assigned killer was coming up the fire escape.

Moving as quietly and quickly as he could, Burgess picked up the duffel bag, the bat concealed within its folds, grabbing two thin towels on his way out.

In the lobby the night desk clerk, as usual, was sound asleep. Burgess eased out the front door. On the street he went into an act. He became the drunk they expected. He staggered the few feet to the alley, stopping when he saw the man with the two bikes. The lookout.

Horatio saw Burgess at the same time. He was bearded, sleeves tattooed up his arms, a big belly hanging over his belt. He was wearing a black tee shirt and sleeveless denim jacket with his gang colors. Barons of Lucifer.

Horatio was not his real name. It was what his brothers in the gang called him. He knew they were making fun of him by giving him a name that sounded smart. He knew he was not smart. Bonehead was what his father had called him. He didn't mind that his brothers made fun of him now. He knew they were his friends. He had never had friends before.

Burgess was scared. These guys were bad news. Nobody to mess with. But the ex-cop had nothing to lose. He staggered into the alley, mumbling under his breath.

Horatio watched.

"Get out of here," he said.

Burgess giggled, pretending to misunderstand. He stepped closer to the lookout. He almost dropped the duffel and looked confused before getting his feet tangled up and tripping himself. He fell directly in front of Horatio. The bearded man tried to draw the pistol in his belt but didn't have time. Burgess raised himself to a kneeling position, swinging the bat as hard as he could at the lookout's knees.

With a howl Horatio dropped to the ground, rolling over to clasp his damaged knee caps. Breathing heavily Burgess rose to his feet and brought the bat down again, this time onto the left side of Horatio's head. Twice. Three times. Horatio collapsed soundlessly. His hands and face turned pale as blood rushed to his injured brain in a hyperemic reaction. The increased blood supply wouldn't revive the dying brain.

Burgess took the revolver and looked it over. It looked old but well cared for. It wasn't American made. It looked like the revolvers the French police carried in those Inspector Clouseau movies he used to laugh at.

The revolver's cylinder swung out to the right for loading. Burgess found six rounds in the cylinder. Small caliber but the weapon was ready.

Quickly searching the man's pockets he found a dozen more cartridges and a wad of money. He stuffed it all in his own pockets. One of the bikes was fitted with saddle bags. He pulled them off to search later. He tossed the duffel and the saddle bags between two nearby dumpsters.

Opening the gas tanks of both bikes, Burgess dropped the end of a towel into each. He watched as each towel soaked itself with gasoline.

He struck a match from the bar that had been his hangout for the past few months. The gasoline-soaked towel lodged in the fuel tank of the first bike leaped into the flames. Burgess moved as quickly as he could to wedge himself between two dumpsters deeper in the alley.

It took only seconds for the flames to travel down the towel to the main tank. The explosion reverberated off the walls of the enclosed alley, lighting it up like the Fourth of July.

Above his head Burgess heard movement on the fire escape again. This time a voice.

"What's going on down there, Horatio?" came the voice from the fire escape.

Burgess almost laughed out loud. Horatio! The big ox he had just killed was named Horatio.

The next sound Burgess heard was that of boots rattling down the metal fire escape.

Burgess stepped out from his hiding place long enough to light the second towel ablaze. He ducked out of sight again and cocked the revolver.

The second man came into sight. He was also a big man but unlike Horatio he looked more muscle than fat. His arms were tattooed with sleeves also. His head was bald and tattooed. He looked big and strong and colorful. He carried a rifle in his hands.

Burgess didn't need the pistol. The second gas tank blew just as the big man landed on the ground. The explosion knocked the man back. He landed against the wall. Hard. A flying shard of metal from the bike pierced his midsection like a lance. He tried to pull the metal out of his body. For a few seconds Burgess feared he would succeed. But he didn't. His arms fell to his side. His eyes stared straight ahead. They saw nothing.

Burgess tossed the bat into the flames. He picked up the rifle and secured it in the duffel. He knew the alley came out on the next street over and the overweight ex-cop huffed his way in that direction. He could hear sirens but with luck he would be blocks away and unnoticed by the time they arrived.

Saturday, July 30th

The pain in Trent's knees was gone when he awoke on Saturday morning. Symptoms he had felt so far seemed to be temporary. Short-lived.

Christopher called to tell them he had arranged for the use of a private shooting range on the south side of the city. It was owned and operated by a friend of the detective who owed him a favor. He agreed to close the range to the public for two hours.

They arrived at the address Christopher gave him promptly at eleven o'clock. They knew their tail was following them. Trent figured there would be nothing new for the pair to learn today. They knew he and Darcey were married. They knew he was working with Christopher. The only thing they would learn today was they were armed. They would have to be thickheaded to not have assumed that already.

They met Christopher in the parking lot. Trent was not completely surprised to find Richmond Detective Sergeant Nancy Patrick with him.

Christopher, with a wide, proud grin, confirmed that his relationship with Nancy was good enough to ask for a favor. Nancy said she had already taken care of the matter.

Christopher took them through the retail gun shop to the owner's office in the rear of the building. There they met Jess Hickok, sitting at his desk beneath a large reproduction photograph of the infamous gunfighter James Butler "Wild Bill" Hickok.

"No relation at all," the affable shop owner said. "But the customers get a kick out of it."

Inside the range, Trent was the first to lay his weapon on the shelf in front of his firing position.

Hickok whistled as he saw the Desert Eagle. "That's a beauty. Mind if I take a look at it?"

"Not at all," Trent said.

"Say, this is a .50 caliber. Not legal in California."

Trent didn't say anything.

"That can't be right," Christopher said, casting a steady glare at the gunsmith. "Looks like a .44 to me."

Hickok caught on quick. "Oh yeah, I see my mistake now. Still it's a beauty."

If the Desert Eagle impressed Hickok, his eyes about popped out of his head when Darcey drew the M16 from her gym bag.

Hickok was no fool. "And I know that's an AR-15 because M16s aren't legal here. Another beauty."

Christopher felt a little outclassed when he laid his Smith & Wesson on the shelf at his position. Even Nancy's Ruger, with its 15 round magazine, out classed him.

"Say, that Ruger is aluminum. As I recall that means it's one of the earlier of the P series. Maybe a P-85. They had some safety issues in the beginning but fixed them. Stopped making'em by the end of the century but they're a good handgun."

Donning ear protection, the five of them spent the next two hours blasting away at Hickok's targets. The gunsmith himself even got a chance to try the Desert Eagle and M16.

By the end of their time, Trent was satisfied Darcey could handle the fully automatic weapon if she had to. Christopher was glad she was on their side.

Rossi stared out over his peaceful garden as he lunched on a variety of cheeses. There was Caciocavello, a sharp version of provolone. Gorgonzola Dolce, a sweet version of the strongly flavored cheese. The last was a La Tur, a unique mixture of cow's milk, giving it a creamy texture; sheep's milk, providing a buttery element; and goat cheese, adding a tangy quality at the end.

The cheeses he was eating on slices of Italian bread were the only thing satisfying about his day.

First the two men he had assigned to tail Marshall and Booth on Friday reported their failure. They couldn't keep up with whatever car it was Marshall was driving. If it was helpful, they told Don Rossi, Marshall and Booth dodged them getting onto an interstate that would head them north toward Concord. Or maybe even Modesto.

Then the pair of would-be assassins supplied by his partners, the Barons of Lucifer, had let themselves become the victims. He couldn't believe they had let that drunken slob of an ex-cop Steve Burgess outsmart them.

He didn't like to use his own men for such jobs if he could avoid it. But he might have to do that.

Meanwhile, he had other business to attend. He picked up yet another prepaid cell phone and dialed a number

Burgess slept until well past noon. He had checked into another cheap, rundown apartment hotel located on a garbage-strewn block of Eddy Street at the edge of Little Saigon. He registered as John Hudson. He tried to keep his face down so the desk clerk wouldn't get a good look at him. But the man was half asleep and more than half drunk. He wouldn't remember what "John Hudson" looked like.

He awoke in a hebetudinous state. Even more lethargic than usual.

He needed a drink. But there was nothing in the apartment to drink. Nothing to eat. He would have to go out for groceries and booze. He thought it best if John Hudson stayed out of sight for a few days.

But first he wanted to see what he had taken from the bumbling hit men. Opening his duffel bag he found a lever action rifle. Working the action he popped out a shell. A Winchester .44-40 caliber. Like something he would expect to see in a western movie.

A revolver that looked like a 50 year old French police handgun and a 19th century-style rifle. Their choice of weapons was puzzling. But at least he was armed. He would hide the rifle in the apartment. The hotel offered no maid service so it wouldn't be found. The revolver he would carry concealed. He remembered he had taken 12 extra bullets for the revolver from Horatio's pockets.

Opening the saddle bags he was pleasantly surprised to find a thick stack of bills. He counted $2,000. That was probably what they were paid to take him out. It was what his life was worth.

There was also a box of cartridges for the rifle. Nothing else.

He had enough money to live for a few weeks at the hotel he was in with some left over for food and booze if he was careful. At least the two bikers had bought him some time with their lives.

Jordan Baron called from New Orleans in the afternoon. He had the results of the tests on the DNA samples Nancy had sent him.

"She went by the name of Piper Hodgins down here, Trent. She was arrested more than a dozen times for prostitution, drugs. Nothing big. I was the last one to arrest her. She solicited me in front of the casino with witnesses. I don't work vice but given the situation I didn't have a choice. I helped her get into a rehab program run by a friend of mine. The last I heard she had cleaned up and left the city."

"She was working here in our building and doing well, Jordan," Trent said. "Everyone liked her. And she was staying clean. I have no doubt about that. Folks out here think it was a coincidence that she and I both came from New Orleans, and that she wound up working in this building. That was no coincidence. Darcey told me she mentioned the opening on the concierge staff to you."

"Yeah, and here's something else some might try to explain away as coincidence. Nine of her arrests were made by an old friend of yours. Steve Burgess. Charges were dismissed each time because the arresting officer failed to follow up."

"Where's Burgess now?"

"Not sure. He disappeared not long after his ill-fated attempt to shoot you."

"Something tells me he's in San Francisco. If I'm right he found Alexis. That means he was staking out our building. Can you get Burgess' fingerprints up to Sergeant Patrick?"

"I'll get 'em to her right away. In fact, I'll get her a full report on him."

"Thanks, Jordan."

"So how's married life?" the New Orleans detective asked.

"Great most of the time," Trent said. "But she makes me watch rom-coms with her."

"What's a rom-com?"

"You don't want to know." He laughed as Darcey slugged him on the shoulder.

Scott Douglas felt the dread flow through him when the phone rang. It was a blocked number. He knew who blocked it.

He never should have become involved with Rossi and his allies. It started with a few favors that weren't exactly illegal but Scott knew were marginal. It didn't take long before he was deeply involved in Rossi's elaborate money laundering scheme. It became easier to look the other way as he facilitated many off the books transactions. He became a criminal.

Scott answered the call on the third ring. It wasn't smart to keep Rossi waiting. He wasn't a patient man.

"Yes, Mr. Rossi. How can I help you?"

Rossi said it was necessary to make a large transfer of cash. He wanted Scott to take care of it immediately. The funds were to be delivered to an organization called Al Dawla al-Islamyia fil Iraq wa'al Sham, which was headquartered in Iraq. Scott didn't recall ever being ordered to transfer funds to this organization. Anything to do with the Middle Eastern group in the alliance went directly to offices of the Scourge.

Something about this transaction didn't seem right. As he listened to Rossi's instructions, he opened his laptop and googled the organization. He felt a chill go through him when he read that the acronym for this organization was Daish. This was ISIS. The Islamic State of Iraq and Sham. Sham being the Arabic name for Syria.

Scott knew what he had become. He had not refused his own share of the profits for what he had done. He could live with stepping over the line in financial transactions. He would not become a traitor to his country. He told Rossi he wouldn't do it.

There was silence. Long seconds passed. Finally, Rossi spoke.

"You are refusing to do as I ask? Do I understand you correctly?"

"Yes, Mr. Rossi."

"Do you understand what this means?"

"Do what you have to do, Mr. Rossi. I am many things. I'm not proud of what I have become. But I will not betray my country and that's what you're asking me to do."

"I see. The consequences will be serious."

That was the last thing Scott heard before the line went dead. He could only assume he would also soon be dead.

Rossi was thinking differently. He needed Douglas. It wouldn't do to lose him now. He had become integral to Rossi's organization. He had to think of a way to keep Douglas alive, even healthy, yet convince him to follow orders.

Trent and Christopher decided it was no longer necessary to avoid letting their adversaries see them together. They were savvy enough to know they weren't hiding anything from the bad guys. Having decided that, they determined to enjoy a pleasant evening together.

The four of them were sitting on the terrace of the Nob Hill condo enjoying an excellent Prosecco, the Italian equivalent of Champagne. Trent had briefed them on what Jordan reported and the likelihood that Steve Burgess was the man Nancy was looking for. He told her Jordan was sending her Burgess' prints and anything else he thought might be helpful.

They had dined on ribeyes that Trent and Christopher grilled accompanied by a delicious sweet and spicy dish of sautéed beets, fennel and radishes that Darcey had prepared. Nancy was a novice cook but anxious to learn. Darcey thought they would become friends.

They sipped the Prosecco and looked out over the city. So beautiful. From where they sat it seemed so peaceful.

All four of them knew the peace was deceiving.

Sunday, July 31st

Darcey awoke to find Trent lying very still beside her. His body was motionless. His eyes darted around the room.

"Are you all right?"

He motioned for her to be silent. He spoke to her in a whisper. "There's something you need to know, Darcey."

"What?" she questioned.

"Not until I'm sure we're alone." He got out of bed, reaching for the Desert Eagle lying on the nightstand. Noiselessly he left the bedroom, methodically searching each room.

"There's no one here but us, Trent," she assured him.

"There were people here earlier. I had to be sure they're gone."

"What is it you have to tell me, Trent? It must be serious."

"It's very serious, Darcey," he said, looking around. "We're in the Witness Protection Program."

Darcey was tempted to believe him. He seemed so sincere. But she remembered hallucinations were among the symptoms they might expect to see. The doctors said they were rare with this sort of thing but it could happen.

She took his hand and guided him back into bed with her. He let her take the Desert Eagle, which she placed on her nightstand for the moment.

"Why, Trent?"

"Why what?"

"Why are we in the Witness Protection Program? What did we do?" she asked, speaking very softly, gently. Reaching slowly to take his hand.

He looked confused. She waited.

"I...I uh...." he stammered.

Darcey held his hand in hers. She leaned in and gently kissed his forehead.

"I can't remember," he finally managed to say.

"It's OK, sweetheart," she said. "Lie down now. Rest."

He let his head relax into his pillow. His eyes closed.

Darcey held his hand until his breathing became steady. She let him sleep as she carefully got out of bed. She would call Doctor Slim Monday morning to let him know about the pain in his knees and now this hallucination.

She smiled as she walked down the hall. Knowing Trent there was always the possibility that it wasn't a hallucination. Meanwhile, she carried the Desert Eagle with her to the kitchen.

After starting a pot of coffee, she began to prep for one of Trent's favorite breakfasts. Migas. The Tex-Mex scrambled eggs that had been the first meal he prepared for her when they were thrown together in New Orleans. She chopped an onion, a poblano pepper, a tomato, some garlic. She had tortillas for heating and eggs ready for scrambling.

She was optimistic he would be back to normal when he awoke. She wanted to have his breakfast ready.

Rossi awoke on Sunday morning with the solution to his Douglas problem. He actually felt admiration for the man who had the courage to stand up to the don. Douglas knew Rossi wouldn't hesitate to kill him. He knew Rossi could make his death slow and painful. Yet he stood up to him.

Rossi admired that. It didn't change what he intended to do.

In his office he picked up another burner, the prepaid cell phones of which he had a plentiful supply, and dialed Scott Douglas' number. When Douglas answered, Rossi's message was short. Directly to the point.

"I am taking Mrs. Rossi and our children to the theater on Tuesday evening. Not my favorite way to spend an evening but one does things to please one's spouse and to instill culture in one's children. You should think about Miles."

He paused and listened to the silence.

"Think about Miles tonight. Think about him again tomorrow. And get the job done by the close of business."

Rossi ended the call. Scott had not said a word

For long minutes Scott sat staring out the window. He, and the room, were unaccompanied by sound. Only his thoughts.

He and Miles lived in a top floor condo in a small building on Capra Way in the Marina district. They had an enviable view of San Francisco Bay, the Golden Gate Bridge, and, Scott shuddered to consider the symbolism, Alcatraz Island.

He heard Rossi's message. There was no mistaking it. He was glad Miles was upstairs in their bedroom. He liked to sleep in on Sundays. Scott needed to be alone. He knew what he had to do. He didn't know if he would be able to do it with Miles watching him.

With a sigh Scott turned away from the view he and Miles enjoyed so often. He crossed the room to the small desk on which sat his laptop.

Trent seemed himself when he awoke and joined Darcey in the kitchen. He had only one question.

"Where's the Desert Eagle?"

"Right here," Darcey said, taking it from the drawer in which she had put it earlier and laying it on the kitchen island. "But first, tell me something. Are we in any trouble?"

"Of course," Trent said. "We're always in trouble."

Darcey laughed. "But are we involved in anything like…oh say…the Witness Protection Program?"

"The Witness Protection Program? Where would you get that idea?"

"Welcome back, my happy little amnesiac," she said as she slid the Desert Eagle over to him.

The remainder of the morning was pleasant. Trent was delighted with the migas Darcey prepared. He thought the hallucination he experienced earlier was worrisome but not unexpected.

Darcey told him she had to go into the office in the afternoon. She was meeting Miles. They had a presentation scheduled for Monday and needed to rehearse. It had to be professional to give their potential new client complete confidence in their team. There was too much money involved in this project for anything less than a perfect presentation.

Meanwhile, she wanted him to take it easy while she was gone. It was going to be a nice day. Maybe he might want to think about surprising her with a nice dinner when she got home.

Fortunately, Miles waited until Scott had finished what he had to do before tumbling downstairs in his usual striking manner. He had to meet Darcey at the office, he told Scott. They had to finish up a very important presentation scheduled for Monday.

Blessing his mate with a quick kiss, he rushed out the door. Scott watched him go. There was sadness in his eyes.

He waited fifteen minutes. Then he, too, left the condo. He saw the two men in the dark sedan parked across the street from his building. They didn't try to be discreet as they pulled out to follow slowly behind him. They didn't care that he saw them.

Scott walked the few blocks to the Walgreen's on Chestnut Street. He bought a pack of Marlboro Lights. Scott had quit smoking years ago. But like many former smokers he sometimes still had the craving.

He thought his future looked sufficiently dim today that it didn't really matter if he had a cigarette. He might as well enjoy the once beloved vice a last time.

He opened the pack, tossing the torn bits of cellophane and foil into the trash can stationed just outside the door. Doing his best to make it appear the same motion, he dropped a small, padded envelope into the large mail box anchored permanently in the concrete near the trash can.

Having accomplished his task, he allowed himself to enjoy the cigarette. Scott always loved to smoke. When he was younger he would smoke anything. Cigarettes. Cigars. Marijuana. He even remembered as a boy smoking muscadine grapevine with some kids he met when he was visiting his grandparents in Florida.

He enjoyed the cigarette he was smoking now. But he had no intention of taking up the habit again. It was a diversion for what he had to do. He tossed the remainder of the pack into another trash can he passed on his walk home.

"Does the name Jonathan Rossi mean anything to you," Scott asked when Trent answered his call.

Trent was immediately on full alert.

"Yes, it's very important. How would you know that name?"

"Because I was foolish enough to become involved with his business. I have broken the law and I'm not proud of it. But I'm being asked to do things now that I will not do. I will not betray my country, Trent."

"We need to talk, Scott. Do you want to come over here? Want me to come to you? Meet somewhere?"

"I'm sure I'm being watched. I'll be followed if I leave home."

"Then I'll come to you. I'll think of a way to get into your building without attracting attention. Hopefully whoever is watching you doesn't know me."

"I'll leave it up to you to get in."

"There's someone else who should be in on this conversation, Scott. I'm sorry to tell you that I'm working with the San Francisco Police Department on matters involving Rossi. If you're ready to give him up I have to get my police contact involved," Trent warned.

"Bring him with you, Trent. At this point whatever happens is whatever happens."

It wasn't hard to find Christopher. He and Nancy were having a leisurely late Sunday breakfast at one of their favorite restaurants on the waterfront. Trent called down to the concierge to send them directly to the 15th floor.

It didn't take long to brief Nancy on the work Christopher and Trent were doing. Christopher immediately understood that the phone call from Scott could be the thread they were seeking to begin the unraveling of Rossi's alliance.

They decided Christopher and Trent would go to the Marina district and just walk into Scott's building. If they were lucky the men Rossi had watching Scott wouldn't recognize them.

Nancy, and her Ruger, would go to Darcey's office. She would tell Miles the truth. She would tell him what could be the truth. With Christopher and Trent busy, Nancy was bored. She wanted to hang out. She would let Darcey know something big was happening. They would tell her the rest of the story when she got home. They would let Scott decide how best to tell Miles and when.

But first it was necessary to rid themselves of the two men still watching their building. Christopher made a phone call and got a black and white on the way. He asked for another uniform car to be posted a block away. He didn't think the two men out front would cause any real trouble but if they did he wanted the officers to have back up standing by.

Trent called down to Bat at the parking lot security booth. Bat normally worked during the week but was filling in for the weekend guy to make a few extra bucks. He was enthusiastic when Trent told him what he had in mind.

Trent, Christopher, and Nancy went down to the lobby but stayed by the elevators. It would be difficult to see them from outside but they had a clear view of the street. They would be Bat's back up if he needed help before the black and whites showed up. Trent didn't think the young man would need help.

Bat walked across the street, his baton in hand. The two men inside were also watching the young man as he approached them. He stopped by the driver's side. The men tried to ignore him.

He rapped lightly on the driver's window, asking him politely to roll it down. The driver didn't like it but he complied.

"Good afternoon," Bat said. "I've noticed you guys have been parked here for several days now. More importantly the building management has noticed it. I've been directed to ask why you're here."

"None of your business, junior," was the reply.

Bat remained calm. He even smiled.

"Yeah, you're right. It's none of my business. But my boss wants to know. And we all gotta follow the boss' orders, right?"

"Tell your boss to mind his own business," was the reply.

"No, I'm not going to do that," Bat said. "You see I need this job."

The driver made a mistake. He reached out to grab Bat by the shirt, trying to pull him forward. The young guard brought his weighted stick around and down, striking the man's wrist. There was a cracking sound. The driver screamed, his broken wrist going limp.

The man in the passenger seat leaped out, his hand going under his jacket. Bat was considering how to defend himself against a man with a gun on the other side of the car. He needn't have been concerned.

The arrival of the two officers in the first black and white was timed perfectly. Tires squealing as the car slid to a stop, both officers leaped out with weapons drawn. The man on the other side of the BMW had drawn a weapon, which he now promptly laid on the ground as ordered by the officers. He leaned forward to put his hands on the car. This was not the first time he had been in the position.

The three watching from inside the building took the elevator down to the garage while the men assigned to watch them were distracted by being cuffed and helped into the two black and whites now on the scene.

Christopher laughed all the way down.

"That kid is good, Trent," he said. "We could use him on the force. If he's interested I'd consider recommending him to the Academy."

"He'd be interested," Trent said.

After dropping Nancy at Darcey's office, they parked the Bentley around the corner and two blocks up from Scott's small building.

Unfolding his big body from the Bentley's passenger side, Christopher dropped his sunglasses down onto his nose.

"I believe you are docent on this tour of the Marina," he said to Trent, obviously enjoying his role as a Marina resident enjoying a sunny day. "Lead on."

Both were dressed casually. Trent was also wearing sunglasses. They talked animatedly as they strolled leisurely down the street. Trent gestured wildly as he told what must have been a hilarious story to Christopher judging by the big man's laughter.

When they reached Scott's building they didn't hesitate. Trent continued talking, to Christopher's apparent amusement, as they entered the building. It wasn't a secure building. The elevator took them directly to the top floor.

"Thanks for coming, Trent. I'm not sure I deserve much consideration."

"It took a lot of guts to make that phone call, Scott."

"Well, I was motivated by hemophobia," Scott said. "I fear the sight of blood. Especially my own. Or, worse, Miles'."

"We'll do our best to make sure you're not bothered by your phobia, Mr. Douglas," Christopher assured him, "assuming you're ready to help us."

"I don't have any choice, Sergeant," Scott replied bluntly. "I'm not going to do as he has directed. I won't betray my country by providing funds to terrorists. Rossi has made it clear that if I don't do what he wants me to do he will punish me. His idea of punishment isn't particularly humane. If I can help you take him down, I'll be protecting myself as much as anything else."

Christopher nodded. "All right. What can you tell us? What's Rossi's game and what role do you play in it?"

"Rossi formed what he calls a fiduciaria, a trust, if you will," Scott began to explain, "I'm essentially running his financial transfer operation. His money laundering."

"How is it done?" the policeman wanted to know.

"Through a system known as hawala," Trent responded. "Am I right, Scott?"

Surprised, Scott nodded in the affirmative.

"Hawala is an ancient system of conducting business requiring minimal records that allows the participants to avoid regulation and taxes," Trent continued. "It's a system that first appeared in the ancient Middle East and eventually spread as far as Italy, South Asia, and Africa. It's called hundi in India. Rossi and his partners use independent business people, investment firms, and a few banks in several countries around the world as their hawala partners."

"I still don't get it," Christopher said. "How is the money moved without being found out?"

"Say you want to get $10,000 to someone in Thailand. You contact your hawala partner there and request that payment be made," Scott took up the explanation. "Your partner takes a small commission for his trouble and makes the payment."

"So how does that guy get his money back?" Christopher asked.

"Any number of ways," Scott continued. "It might be as simple as returning the favor at a future date. But Rossi's system has worked so well much more of the gangs' illegal money has been freed up for investment in legitimate businesses."

Trent took up the tutorial. "So, for instance, the gang who owes you the money owns a company that sells telecom gear, much of which will be stolen goods, by the way. They ship you $20,000 worth of high tech gear but only invoice you for $10,000."

"That's right, Trent," Scott confirmed. "There are many ways to do it. Inflated or deflated real estate transactions are popular. The list is really endless. The key is there is not much in the way of a paper trail and no reporting of transactions to any government."

"And when there is a need for a quick transfer of large amounts they simply do a rapid transfer between hawala partner banks or investment firms. Very difficult to catch and the transaction simply isn't reported. Which all means," Trent said, honestly, "that at every point along the way someone has to turn his head."

Scott had a hard time looking Trent in the eyes. "That's right."

"And you've been that guy in San Francisco?" Christopher asked. "You've been turning your head as you participated in these transactions?"

"Yes, Sergeant," Scott confirmed. "That's correct. I'm guilty. Am I under arrest?"

"Let's just say you shouldn't make any plans to leave town in the next few days," Christopher said. "After that, we'll see."

"Scott can help us bust this thing wide open, Christopher," Trent said. "And I don't think you have to worry about him trying to run at this point. His best chance to survive is to stay put, work with us, and hope we can protect him. If he runs, Rossi will see that he doesn't get far."

Christopher nodded. "So how do we use this information to shut Rossi's operation down?"

Trent looked pensive.

"When I was a very young boy, my dad took me fishing one day. He had a lightweight .410 shotgun with him. We were walking along a small creek not far out of Baton Rouge. All of a sudden, he stopped and pointed to the other side of the creek. There was a hole over there. He handed me the shotgun and told me to try to fire into that hole."

Christopher and Scott listened, wondering where this was going.

"I aimed and pulled the trigger. Even then I was a good shot," Trent smiled as he remembered. "Fired a handful of small shot directly into that hole."

"And?" Christopher encouraged.

"And out came rolling a ball of snakes. Must have been thirty or forty of them, all tangled up and striking at each other."

Scott shivered at the image.

Christopher grimaced. "What's the point, Trent?"

"The point is as long as there was nothing to stir them up until we came along, those snakes were content to coil up together. As soon as an unknown element was introduced they struck out. They didn't know who fired the shot into their cave so they started attacking each other."

Christopher smiled broadly. He was beginning to get the picture.

"The key to hawala is trust. Everyone involved has to trust that their money is safe. If we figure a way to break their trust, we can sit back and watch Spitting Cobra, the Barons of Lucifer and the Scourge go first after Rossi, and then for each other. We provide the incentive, then watch them strike at each other like that bed of snakes."

"We know who the snakes are," Christopher said. "How do we get 'em hitting at each other?"

"We have to think of some diversions, some sleight of hand," Trent said. "And it's time to let our friend with the computers get to work. If, that is, Scott can supply us with some names and locations."

"I didn't know what was going to happen today after Rossi called, Trent," Scott said. "I thought it possible I might not live much longer. To be safe I dropped an envelope containing a flash drive in the mail to you. It lays out every link in Rossi's chain. You should receive it by Tuesday."

"That's great for a backup, Scott, but we need to move now. Can you send that same information directly to another computer?"

"Easily."

"Hang on a minute." Trent dialed a number but was careful to mention no names when Ross Brown answered. He spoke quietly to Ross for a couple of minutes. He wrote down an internet address.

"Scott, can you do a data dump and send it all to this address? It's an unidentifiable URL. Sort of the computer age version of the dead drop. You won't know who you're sending to and it's untraceable."

"I don't need to know," Scott said. "I don't even want to know," he added as he sat down at his computer and started striking keys.

"Christopher, can you round up a few of your guys, ones you know you can trust to help us? We need someone to keep an eye on this condo but we can't let Rossi's men see them. We also need a couple of guys to watch Darcey's office. And they have to be very discreet."

"I can find some volunteers."

"Get on that, if you don't mind. Then we need to take a look at what investigations might be lurking around on Spitting Cobra, the Barons of Lucifer, and the Scourge. Maybe we can start to disturb our nest of snakes. We don't have to make any arrests that will stick. All we need to do is bring some bad guys in for questioning. Maybe hold 'em for 48 hours, or for as long as we can. If Rossi's mole in your office sees it going on, so much the better."

They left separately. Christopher went first. He would wait in a bar near the Bentley until Trent joined him.

"Do you want a gun, Scott?"

"No, Trent, but thanks."

"Are you sure? I can provide you with a pretty effective semiautomatic handgun."

"I'm not a brave man, Trent," Scott said, self-effacingly. "I don't know anything about guns. I'd do more harm than good."

Trent nodded.

"Besides, if your spouse was as excitable as Miles would you want a loaded gun lying around?"

Trent had to laugh. And he had to admire Scott's sense of humor in the face of menacing forces.

They saw no lookouts on duty when they turned onto Trent and Darcey's street. Trent stopped at the security booth. Christopher leaned over to tell Bat he was impressed with the way the young man had handled himself. He handed his card to Bat, telling the guard to call if he was interested in an appointment to the Police Academy. They left Bat with a grin that threatened to split his lips.

Upstairs Darcey and Nancy waited for them. Trent mixed rum and cokes for each of the four. They sat on the terrace as the two men briefed their mates on the day's activities and on their plans for destroying Rossi's fiduciaria.

Both men thought it only fair that the women know what was going on as, like it or not, they were as involved as anyone. Also, since Burgess had murdered two people in Nancy's jurisdiction, she was professionally involved. That wasn't lost on her.

"Maybe I should talk to my chief to get permission to work on this with you, Christopher, as a joint operation."

"You can't talk to the Rooster about this. He'd probably call a press conference," Christopher said, truthfully. "The last thing we need is for our plan to become public knowledge."

"No, I'll go over his head. We do it all the time."

"I can talk to my captain," Christopher said. "I'll do that tomorrow. We can use all the guns we can get."

Earlier that day, before all the excitement started, Trent had split two mirlitons and softened them with a few minutes in boiling water. There was lump crabmeat in the refrigerator.

Since Nancy was anxious to begin her apprenticeship in the kitchen, the men stayed on the terrace with their second cocktails. In the kitchen Darcey showed Nancy how to make the "Trinity," the sautéed onion, celery, and sweet pepper that is the basis of so many Louisiana dishes.

They added the crab, some garlic, and other spices to the pan, mixing it all well and allowing it to heat through. Scooping the seeds from the mirlitons, which Darcey told Nancy were also called chayotes, they filled the hollow squashes with the crab stuffing, sprinkled them with bread crumbs, and put them in the oven to bake.

Feeling quite proud of herself, Nancy accepted another rum and coke. She and Darcey joined the men on the terrace.

In the hills of Atherton, Don Rossi was furious. He tossed the burner he was using across the garden. One of his security team rushed to retrieve it. And to stay out of the don's way.

First, that dunce of an ex-cop Burgess, dumb as he was, outsmarted the two Barons of Lucifer sent to take him out. Today Rossi was told he murdered two women in Richmond. And now the drunken slob had disappeared, leaving Rossi with two police forces nosing around in his business

Then the two halfwits he assigned to watch Marshall managed to get themselves arrested. One of them had assaulted a security guard. A kid, no less. The kid had broken the big, brave Mafioso's wrist with a stick.

Rossi was tempted to let them sit in jail. He knew he couldn't do that. No telling what they might say to the cops. He had already dispatched a lawyer to get them out. When they got here, he would see to it that they would both beg to have only their wrists broken.

He was at the end of his patience. Douglas had better get money moving Monday or there would be more than broken bones. There would be bodies.

Monday, August 1st

Captain Fess Albright was already at his desk when Sergeant Booth tapped on his door at seven o'clock Monday morning. He had got into the habit of arriving early when he first began to rise in rank on the force. He felt obligated to be on the job when the first of the day shift began to arrive.

Christopher briefed the captain on the status of his investigation. Albright was surprised at how much Booth had accomplished. Surprised and impressed.

Then Booth told the captain what he had in mind. He asked permission to put together a multi-force team, including the San Francisco and Richmond police departments, as well as some federal agencies. They would also, he said, be working with police in Great Britain, France, and Italy, as well as with Interpol.

"You're asking for a lot, Christopher," the captain said. "You're describing a big operation and you want to do it in a week."

"No sir," Christopher replied. "I want to do it today."

Albright didn't blink. He turned his chair to stare out the window. He admired Booth. This was the kind of operation that would have excited him when he joined the force more than thirty-five years previously. Now he was near retirement.

He had been ordered to assign the investigation into Rossi's activities to Booth. He knew that was deliberately done with the expectation that Booth's inexperience in rooting out money laundering schemes would result in the investigation going nowhere. Now Booth was asking permission to begin an operation with the potential to destroy Rossi's alliance and cripple four of the leading criminal organizations in the city.

He had compromised in the past and wasn't proud of it. He was inclined to approve Christopher's plan and go out of office feeling good about being a cop. But he wasn't dense either. If he made a misstep, he could wind up with no retirement at all.

"Let me think about it," he said, as he turned back to face Christopher. "I have to go downtown for a meeting. I'll be back in an hour or two. We'll talk again then."

As he left the captain's office, Christopher hoped he hadn't made a mistake speaking to Albright. If he had, people could die. He respected Albright. He knew the captain sometimes had to play a political game, but he thought at heart the man was a good cop. He didn't think he had made a mistake.

Darcey watched Trent closely as they had coffee before they each began their busy days.

"Are we in trouble today?" she asked.

"No more than usual," he said.

"And we're not in the Witness Protection Program?"

"Not yet," he said, "but the day is just begun."

She thought it would be a day without symptoms.

Albright knew he was walking a fine line as he strolled into the Third Street headquarters of the San Francisco Police Department. The cop in him wanted to tell Christopher to go for it. The old man in him wanted to protect his retirement. He honestly didn't know which of them would win.

He raised his hand to tap on Deputy Chief Amanda Justice's office door, but it wasn't closed. It was standing open by only an inch. Just enough for him to hear the conversation going on inside the room.

Justice had her back to him as she spoke on the phone. Though she was trying to keep her voice down he could clearly hear her side of the conversation. He felt himself grow cold as he heard what she was saying.

"Please, Mr. Rossi, I'll take care of this. I set it up as you wished. I regret that mistakes have been made. But I assure you I will get things under control. You have nothing to worry about."

That was enough. Albright was still cop enough to make his decision. He walked down the hall to the Chief's office. He and Charles Marvin had started on the force together almost four decades ago. He trusted him without reservation. Albright thought that if his trust in Marvin was misplaced then his entire life was a waste. He had nothing to lose.

"Good morning, Diana," he said as he entered the chief's office. Diana had guarded the chief's outer office ever since Marvin was appointed to the job more than a decade earlier.

"Well, look who decided to go slumming today," Diana teased. "How are you, Fess? Haven't seen you in a while."

"A cop's life is never his own, Diana. So many doughnuts to eat. You know that," letting his wit show in the conversation, something he would never do back in his office. "Is Charlie around? I need a few minutes with him."

Diana announced Albright's presence. The chief told her to send him right in. The few minutes turned into an hour.

At the end of the hour, the chief told Diana he wanted the conference room next to his office set up as a headquarters for a special team being put together. He wanted the room ready for occupancy by noon and without notification to anyone else. He wanted it accomplished in complete secrecy.

Captain Albright's men, he told her, would provide a list of names. Only the people on that list were to be allowed into the room. No one else was even to know that the team existed. No one.

While Diana hustled to carry out her instructions, Chief Marvin was making phone calls. The first call was to the chief of police in Richmond. Other names were on his call list for the morning, including the FBI's Special Agent in Charge for San Francisco.

Returning to his own office, Albright called Booth and Lieutenant Billy Mitchum into his office. He told Booth that the chief had approved creation of the special task force. The chief, he said, was making the appropriate calls and had established a conference room next to his office as headquarters for the team. No one else on the chief's staff would be involved. Nor would anyone else know of the team's existence.

Albright said he wanted Mitchum involved but made it clear that this was Booth's operation. He wanted them to work together.

As the two younger officers left, Albright's smile was wide enough to show his teeth. He hadn't felt so good about being a cop in a long time.

Albright wasn't surprised when Deputy Chief Amanda Justice showed up in his office just before noon. She didn't bother knocking.

"Good morning, Amanda," he greeted her. "It's not often we see you down here."

She wasn't particularly friendly. "I have other things to do, Fess. But now I want to know what's going on with Sergeant Booth's investigation."

"He's making progress, Amanda. I'd say he's making significant progress."

"Give me details."

"I'm afraid I can't do that, Amanda."

"It's Deputy Chief Justice, Captain Albright," his superior reminded him, in no good humor. "Did you forget that? And I'm giving you a direct order. I want to know what's going on."

"I'll send you a report by next week."

"I said I want to know what's going on, Albright. I want to know now."

"I'm sorry, Amanda. I can't accommodate you."

"You're going to regret this," she said, as irate as she could remember being in her life.

She was trembling as she left the building. She was a deputy chief of police and she was scared. She tried to think of her options. She was too frightened to think clearly. She suddenly had a vision of the humiliation she would suffer if this ended in her incarceration. Given other possibilities that might come to mind if she gave in to panic, humiliation and incarceration would be the preferable alternatives.

By midafternoon, Booth and Mitchum had assembled their multi-force team in the conference room that was established as their headquarters. Since Rossi had been forced to pull his lookouts from the Nob Hill building, Trent had no one following him to police headquarters. They included Scott via a secure Internet video link.

SFPD Chief Charles Marvin, with Richmond Police Chief Bradford Dundee and FBI Special Agent in Charge for San Francisco Joel Harris on either side of him, spoke very briefly. He told the assembled team that they were assigned to a joint project called Operation Den of Snakes. He said he wanted them to set aside any professional differences and work together, quickly and efficiently. He assured them that he, Chief Dundee, and SAiC Harris would have their backs.

"Just get the job done," he urged, before the three agency chiefs left the room.

Trent and Scott provided a briefing on the structure of Rossi's fiduciaria and the hawala system used to move significant amounts of money without detection or risk. Booth and Trent outlined the plan they had developed to disassemble it.

The first order of business was to get trusted officers to cover Scott's condo, Darcey's condo, and the office in which she and Miles worked. They were instructed to be careful to avoid notice.

Assignments were made to members of the group. Team members got busy making calls and opening files on various devices.

Scott was available to answer questions. Trent spent time talking to Scotland Yard, the Paris Prefecture of Police, the three Italian police agencies with which he had met, and Interpol. He and Booth also spoke with Ross Brown, though they were careful not to mention his name.

At five o'clock Scott's phone rang. It was a blocked call. He didn't answer. It was the first time he ever failed to answer that call.

On the other end of the line, Rossi's anger was becoming uncontrollable. Today was threatening to be even worse than the day before.

Amanda Justice suddenly couldn't force a cop two levels down from her to give her a report. Why was he paying her? He had thought it a good joke having Justice on his payroll. Now it would seem the joke was on him.

By the end of the day, Douglas had done nothing. No money had been moved.

Then Harry Sherman, Rossi's mole in Booth's office, reported that Booth and Mitchum had been called into Albright's office. They left a short while later, taking half a dozen officers with them. Sherman couldn't find out where they were going or what they were doing.

More money wasted on useless cops, Rossi thought. When he got this mess straightened out, there would be some changes made.

Motioning for two of his security team, he began issuing orders. He went back into his office and, using his high frequency radio transmitter, sent a burst transmission. He needed competent help. He needed someone who had never failed.

It was dark when Trent finally made it home. He rode up the elevator again with Jean Philby. She did not become hysterical. Neither did she speak to him. When they reached the 15th floor, Trent stood aside to let her exit first.

Mrs. Philby walked slowly toward her condo at the far end of the hallway. She saw James Williams standing in his doorway as she came abreast of him. She paused for a few seconds. Still she didn't go into her hysterical routine. Nor did she lower her voice to threaten him. She walked on by.

She didn't see the semiautomatic handgun he was holding out of sight. From the angle from which he was looking at Williams, Trent did see the weapon. But the old man made no move to use it. He watched Mrs. Philby until she was inside her condo. He closed his door as the sound of the four locks on her door sliding into position, one by one, reverberated down the hall.

Trent made another mental note. He had to talk to Christopher about these two old people.

Darcey's day had gone long as well. She had picked up a large order of chicken wings on her way home. Trent made peach martinis. They each had two martinis and several wings.

Martinis and chicken wings and a few precious moments alone together. Trent thought they were following the doctor's orders.

Jimmy Shadow once again read the message received in the burst transmission from Jonathan Rossi. Jimmy was considering a response. Or whether there would be any response at all. This was the second time within the past few weeks that Rossi had signaled for help. Perhaps Rossi's troubles were approaching the overwhelming. Jimmy was beginning to think further involvement could be dangerous. Maybe disastrous.

Jimmy Shadow hadn't survived so long by flirting with disaster.

Tuesday, August 2ⁿᵈ

It was four o'clock in the morning when Darcey was awakened.

Trent was standing in the middle of their bedroom, looking around as though he didn't know where he was.

"Trent?" she asked, cautiously.

"Yes?"

"Are you all right?"

"You tell me," he answered. "How did I get to Fairbanks? Why am I in this hospital?"

"You're fine, Trent."

"All I know is I have to get back to San Francisco before morning. I promised Darcey she can go with me when I return to Alaska. If she finds out I came up here without her, she won't be happy," he said, with conviction. "And if there's nothing wrong with me, then discharge me from this hospital."

"It's all arranged, Trent," she said, cooperatively. "I've taken care of your discharge. Come lie down. By the time you wake up you'll be back in San Francisco. Darcey will never know you went to Fairbanks."

"I'll probably tell her," he mumbled, as he calmly climbed back into bed. "I don't like to keep secrets from her."

Trent had coffee ready at six o'clock when Darcey stumbled sleepily into the kitchen.

"Good morning, sleepyhead," he said cheerfully, kissing her and handing her a cup, already doctored with a little cream.

"Good morning," she replied, warily, looking him over. "Where are we?"

"We're in San Francisco," he said, puzzled. "Where else would we be?"

"We're not in Alaska? Not in Fairbanks?"

"Another hallucination?"

"Just a small one," she said. "You were quite amusing. And thanks for not wanting to go back to Alaska without me and not wanting to keep secrets from me."

"No problem," he said. "Sounds like it was fun. Sorry I missed it."

At seven o'clock Christopher started the team's day.

"After getting some eyes on the street in a few defensive positions, your assignments yesterday were to search your files for any open cases involving Spitting Cobra, the Barons of Lucifer and the Scourge. Anything we can move on. We don't have to have enough evidence to convict. In fact, we don't want to take them to court. We want enough to get warrants and bust a few of them, even if we hold them for only a few hours. This is poker, folks, not jurisprudence."

There was a ripple of laughter through the room.

"So what have we come up with?"

Lieutenant Mitchum was the first to speak up.

"We can bust Spitting Cobra for prostitution most any time. Can't ever make it stick against any of the big guys but at least we free up some women being held as sex slaves. Some of them are only 12 or 13 years old.

"We should be able to disrupt their business temporarily," Mitchum continued, "if Chief Marvin can help us get a couple of warrants. We've been watching a building on the edge of Little Saigon where we think they're holding some girls."

"OK. Let's get on it. Anybody have anything on the Barons of Lucifer?"

Nancy was the first to speak up.

"They're headquartered in Richmond. We know them well. Murder for hire is one of their biggest illicit money makers. And it's the one they enjoy most. We're working the Alexis Brandt murders. We're sure Steve Burgess was the trigger man on those killings. But then two Barons tried to take Burgess out. It's the only connection to the murders in Richmond. No way to bring a case. But it might be enough to haul a few of the leaders in for a few hours for questioning."

"Who's their head guy?"

"He calls himself the Mad Dutchman. His real name is Lin Winters. Woe unto anyone who calls him Lin. He thinks it's a sissy name. If you want to call him by his first name, call him Mad."

More laughter.

"See if Chief Dundee can help us with a warrant. What about the Scourge?"

Joseph Brady from the FBI spoke up.

"We're probably best positioned to take them on," he said.

"Do you have anything on'em?" Christopher asked.

"No, but if we can get a warrant we can bring in Abdul Rahman, their leader, for questioning. The charge can be a general one. Aiding and abetting interstate criminal activities."

"What criminal activities?" Christopher asked.

"I'll make a list," Brady said.

Still more laughter.

"Sounds like we're right on schedule. One more thing. Rossi has two men each watching Darcey Anderson's office building and Mr. Douglas' home. We scared them off Trent and Darcey's condo. But I want those four busted. When we make the raids tomorrow morning, I want one of the Mafioso clearly visible in the back seat of a black and white at both the Spitting Cobra and the Barons of Lucifer headquarters. And let's have two Mafioso on the scene when we hit the Scourge."

"What do we charge them with?" came the question from one of the team members.

"Stalking," Christopher said, drawing the most laughter yet.

"Now let's get busy and round up some warrants. Chiefs Marvin and Dundee, SAiC Harris, are ready to run interference for us. I'd like to hit all three groups simultaneously tomorrow, early in the morning, if possible. While they're still waking up."

Team members spread out to meet with their respective leaders. To get the warrants they needed, Marvin, Dundee, and Harris carefully selected the judges to approach. They avoided judges known to be soft on crime. They especially avoided judges suspected of being on someone's payroll. Though those judges would have been surprised to learn it, their unsavory connections were generally no secret in the law enforcement community.

Trent spent most of his day talking with Ross Brown. Scott was again available by Internet video link to answer questions. Trent and Ross participated in a conference call with law enforcement personnel in London, Paris, Lyon, and Rome. When Ross' computer game was finished and ready to play, coordination with the seven European police agencies was critical.

At three o'clock Christopher directed two black and whites each to the Marina condo building and the California Street office. The four men Rossi had assigned to watch the two buildings were taken into custody. At first they thought it was funny that they were being arrested for stalking. Then one of the arresting officers explained to them how serious a crime stalking is in today's world. They didn't think it amusing when they learned that such a charge could get their names listed on the sex offenders' registry.

The four were allowed the attorney Rossi sent to represent them. But they were rushed before a judge not of Rossi's choosing. Bail was denied. They were returned to jail. The attorneys promised to appeal.

At four o'clock the action began to move in the opposite direction. The plan Rossi had directed the night before was put into action.

Two men who at first appeared to be casually strolling down California Street stopped behind the officers watching Darcey's building. Each man produced a sound suppressed hand gun, firing two shots into his target. The shooters continued their walk.

A black van drove rapidly up California Street. Tires squealed as the driver slammed the brakes on to stop the vehicle in front of Darcey's office. The driver remained behind the wheel with an armed man beside him in the passenger seat. Four other armed men piled out of the rear of the vehicle and rushed the building. All six men wore ski masks.

Darcey was looking out her window. She was shocked to see the policemen across the street shot. Even more shocked to see the van and the men rushing into her building. She heard them running up the stairs. She heard Miles' emotional cries as they dragged him from his office. She reached for her phone and hit speed dial.

"Four armed men just raided my building. They're dragging Miles out. I can hear them coming down the hall for me," she said when Trent answered. She tried to remain as calm as possible.

"Where are the cops guarding your building?" he asked, dreading to hear the answer.

Darcey looked out her window at the two bodies lying across the street.

"They're both down. I don't know if they're alive or dead. They're coming for me, Trent."

Suddenly Trent felt biting cold sweep the room as he listened. He struggled for words.

"Don't fight, Darcey," he said. "Go with them. I'll find you. I WILL FIND YOU."

"I love you, Trent," he heard her say. In the background he could hear the shuffle and scuffle of the men taking hold of her.

"I love you, Darcey," he shouted into the phone.

The room got even colder as he heard a heavily accented voice speaking in his ear.

"How romantic, Mr. Marshall," the voice said. "If you want to see your wife alive again, tell Mr. Douglas to carry out his orders. Otherwise...." The voice left the other possible outcome hanging.

Trent sat staring into empty air when the call was ended. He felt uncharacteristically frozen. He was, in effect, on the verge of a post-traumatic stress reaction. He struggled to bring himself under control. Darcey was in danger. Now was not the time to freeze. Now was the time for action. White hot action.

As the adrenaline began to flow, bringing him out of the temporary trance, he motioned for Christopher.

"We have officers down at Darcey's office. We need Scott Douglas here. Now," he said as the big cop stepped to his side. "And have him bring his laptop with him."

Without question, Booth called for EMTs and back up to the California Street office. He directed the officers guarding Scott's condo to bring him to headquarters immediately.

"Douglas will be here in ten minutes," Christopher said. "What's going on?"

"Rossi has Darcey and Miles," he said. He repeated the little information Darcey had been able to pass along as well as the threat delivered by one of the abductors.

"Where do we go from here?" Christopher asked. "We have no idea where Rossi will be holding them."

"We'll find them," Trent said, with determination. "We'll find them and we'll bring them home safely. Meanwhile, I need to do something that you probably should not be a part of, Christopher."

Christopher raised his eyebrows.

"And it would be best if you asked no questions," Trent added.

Christopher looked at Trent, a meditative expression in his eyes. He said nothing.

When Douglas arrived, Christopher brought him directly to Trent. He asked Christopher to give them a minute alone. The big cop stepped away.

"Rossi's men have taken Darcey and Miles," Trent said bluntly.

"Oh, no! Please, God," Douglas said, his eyes closing as he tried to block out what he was hearing.

"It's too late for prayer," Trent said, callously. "If we're going to get them back alive we have to be more devil than saint."

"I don't know what I can do." Douglas was completely deflated

Trent was having none of it. He grabbed Douglas by the shirt, pulling the financier's face close to his.

"Listen to me, Douglas," Trent hissed. "Hear me well. My wife and Miles are in danger of dying because of you. And you're going to do everything you can to help me save them. If you don't, then I promise you Jonathan Rossi will be the least of your problems. Do you understand me?"

"I…I understand," Scott said. "What do you want me to do?"

"Have you ever been to Rossi's home?"

"Yes, I was there once."

"How many security guards does he keep on the property?"

"Usually six."

"He told you he was taking his wife to the theater this evening, didn't he? Will he take any of the security guards with him?"

"When I have met with him he has always had two security men with him."

"Write down the address for me."

"I really can't tell you much else about the house or neighborhood," Douglas said, as he wrote the address on a notepad.

"I just want the address," Trent said. "I'll take it from there."

"Oh, wait. There is one thing I remember about Rossi's home, Trent," Scott said. "It is surrounded by an electric security fence."

Trent's grin bordered on the sinful. "That's not a problem. Those fences are false security for the people living inside them."

He motioned for Christopher to join him again for the next instructions Trent planned to give Douglas.

"Your job this afternoon, Scott, is to find where they're holding Darcey and Miles" he said.

Douglas was stunned. "I have no way to know that."

"Don't make me threaten you again, Scott," Trent warned. "You know as much about Rossi's real estate holdings in the Bay area as anyone other than Rossi himself. Go through all your files. Look for likely places. Secluded places. Places where someone screaming wouldn't attract attention.

"Warehouses are common. But most any abandoned buildings set away from other properties would be possibilities. Old motels, office buildings. Any place where you would hold someone if you kidnapped them."

While Christopher left for Darcey's office to see if he could find any clues to where she and Miles might have been taken, Trent appropriated a laptop from the team. He spent the next hour looking at old maps and current satellite images of the expensive homes in the hills of Atherton. He hoped to find an old logging or mining road. But before it became an enclave for the extraordinarily wealthy it was ranch land.

The early mansions were built on very large plots. Some were in the hundreds of acres. In recent decades those land holdings had mostly been subdivided. The lots were still a minimum of an acre. Some were multiple acres, including Rossi's home. Trent was betting there would be a service road winding among the homes of the privileged. He was right.

He also studied the trees in the area. Another lucky break. The land around Rossi's home was studded with large oak trees. Trent was placing another bet. He bet there would be one along the fence with large limbs.

Christopher came back from the scene of the kidnapping. He reported that one of the officers shot at the scene was dead. The other was clinging to life. Barely.

"I need a four wheel drive vehicle, Christopher. Preferably an old beater."

"Take my truck. Nancy refuses to be seen in it. Is that beater enough for you?"

He took the keys and gave Christopher the Bentley's remote.

"Report your truck stolen before you leave for home today," Trent told him, "in case I don't make it back tonight."

"What if you do make it back?"

"Then tomorrow morning tell'em you remembered where you parked it."

Trent stopped by a store that sold supplies for construction workers. He took only two of his purchases to the 15th floor with him. The rest he left in the truck when he rode the elevator to the 15th floor. In the condo, he exchanged his jeans for a pair of black work pants. He kicked off his shoes and pulled on a pair of black, knee high work boots with insulated rubber shells and soles. He retrieved two extra magazines for the Desert Eagle.

Trent assumed the curtain would go up to open the show the Rossi family was attending at eight o'clock. Assuming the show would run two to three hours, the Rossi family would be returning home sometime after midnight.

Trent wanted to be inside the Rossi compound at ten o'clock. Half an hour should give him plenty of time to do what he planned. Plotting the route by his phone's GPS, he figured it would take him two hours to make the drive. Giving himself an extra 15 minutes for an unexpected contingency, he would plan on leaving at a quarter to eight. He looked at his watch. It was half past seven.

He took a couple of minutes to make a sandwich. It wouldn't do to have a lapse in energy. He ate the sandwich on the ride down to the garage.

Another minute to scoop up some dirt from the garage floor to rub across the truck's license plates. He didn't want Christopher's truck to be identified if he could avoid it.

Two hours later Trent was guiding the truck along the unpaved service road that wound among the mansions in the hills of Atherton. He had printed out a satellite image of Rossi's house. It lay beside him to consult as he steered the truck among the trees. The house he was seeking would be on his left.

He saw the fence that looked like the one in the satellite image. This was it. He drove slowly along the fence. When he had reached what he judged to be halfway down the property, he braked the truck to a stop. Luck was with him. There was a large oak tree standing between the dirt road and the fence. A thick limb extended from the trunk over the fence. Trent thought Rossi and his security people put way too much faith in their fancy fence and not near enough thought into staying alive.

He pulled on a pair of surgical gloves before exiting the truck. Once outside the truck's cab, he stepped to the edge of the service road. The dirt there was soft and black. He scooped some up and rubbed it over his face. Satisfied that his light skin wouldn't give him away in the moonlight, he strapped a set of climbing poles to his boots.

He wrapped a cloth around the hammer he had purchased and used it to pound a metal stake into the ground near the electric security fence. Placing the hammer into the small knapsack that was among his purchases, he wrapped a piece of copper wire around first the metal stake, then a length of the charged wire, effectively shorting it out.

Strapping the knapsack onto his back, he doubled the rope, then redoubled it. With his climbing poles gripping the sides of the tree, he used the rope like a lineman's belt to move rapidly up the large tree trunk. Once he was straddling the large limb, he visually surveyed the compound. He saw no one moving about. Draping the rope over the limb, he used it to lower himself softly to the ground inside the fence.

Trent removed the climbing poles and laid them with the knapsack under a small pile of oak leaves. He had been quiet so far. He wanted quiet for a while longer. Then he planned on chaos.

The Rossi home had just become an infernal region.

Trent judged it to be two hundred fifty yards to the large main house. There was a smaller house, a guest house he assumed, a hundred yards closer. Staying low, the Desert Eagle in his hand, he sprinted as best he could in the work boots, to the rear of the guest house. He paused there leaning against the wall with the corner of the building on his right, to catch his breath.

He heard the guard coming down the side of the building. Trent's respect for Rossi and his security, in fact for his entire operation, was declining rapidly. He had to guard against that. They were still very dangerous people.

That was confirmed when the guard came into view. Though the armed man blithely walked right past him without noticing, Trent was impressed with what he saw. He was carrying a short submachine gun, which Trent thought was a German-made Heckler & Koch, one of the most effective automatic weapons in the world. There was a long magazine protruding below the weapon. Trent thought it probably held thirty rounds that, if the man saw him and fired first, would come at Trent at a rate of nine hundred rounds per minute. It wouldn't take anywhere near thirty rounds to kill Trent. He didn't intend to let that happen.

Trent didn't want to kill anyone if he could avoid it. He wanted to put them out of action. Painfully out of action.

He tapped lightly on the side of the building with the Desert Eagle. The guard turned lazily in his direction. Not expecting to see an unauthorized, armed man in the compound, the guard was slow to react. Before he could raise his weapon, Trent fired one .50 caliber round that smashed into his opponent's left shoulder.

It wasn't a killing wound but was enough to make it impossible for him to use the H&K. As Trent expected, the guard tried to fire his submachine gun. He did fire it, but being unable to hold it steady with the neck of the humerus, the upper arm bone, in his left shoulder shattered, three rounds went wild into the air. Trent took two quick steps forward, pulled the weapon from the man's one good hand, and brought the heavy Desert Eagle down on his head. The guard collapsed, dazed, clutching his left arm, which would never be the same. Trent doubted if he had much of a medical retirement plan with his job.

"Gideon? What's all the shooting about?"

Trent heard the call from the same direction. This could wind up being something like a carnival shooting gallery, he thought. He might get lucky and stand here shooting them down one by one.

The second man saw his companion lying on the ground. This guard was even more foolish than the first. He looked right and left but never looked behind him. Instead of becoming more alert, he knelt beside his colleague, laying his own Heckler & Koch the ground. Commendable friendship. Foolish security.

The second guard knelt on his knee, exposing the sole of his left foot. A foot was an even better target for a non-lethal takedown than was a shoulder, Trent thought. He fired three rounds from the commandeered H&K into the man's left foot, sending metatarsal bones in all directions and bringing a howl from the target as he rolled to his side, again being foolish. He couldn't reach his own submachine gun. Trent could.

He used the Desert Eagle as a club again. Two down.

Trent didn't think he'd be so lucky a third time. He holstered the Desert Eagle, slung the weapon taken from the second guard over his shoulder, and held the first in combat position as he jogged toward the opposite corner of the building's back wall.

Trent thought the first Heckler & Koch he had taken had twenty-four rounds remaining in the magazine. Should be enough, he thought.

It was darker on this corner of the house. It was the darkness that saved him. The third guard was smarter than the first two. As Trent approached the corner, the man leaped into view, weapon in a two-handed firing position. No submachine gun for this guy. Trent was staring at a semiautomatic handgun.

Trent saw the muzzle flash as he fell and rolled to his right. The first and second shots both went over his head. Trent didn't think he'd be lucky with the man's third shot. He held up the H&K he had taken from the first guard and fired off another three round burst.

The small but powerful submachine gun shredded the guard's lower right leg. Trent had no doubt both the man's tibia and fibula would be found to be beyond repair. He leaped to his feet before his target could recover and took the weapon from his opponent's hand. It was a Sig Sauer, a very effective .40 caliber weapon developed for the army and favored by the Seals and Texas Rangers as well as other military and police units. Trent stuck it in his belt.

He didn't think it necessary to use the Desert Eagle as a club again. The man lay on the ground, crying, clutching his destroyed leg.

Trent edged his way around the corner and down the wall toward the front of the building. Before he reached the front of the building he saw the fourth man through a window. The last guard had heard one loud, booming shot, followed by three separate three round bursts from the automatic weapons two of his colleagues carried, two shots from a .40 caliber handgun, then another three round burst from a Heckler & Koch.

He didn't know what was going on. He had switched off the lights inside the guest house and was crouched in the darkened room, using both hands to steady his own semiautomatic handgun, which he had aimed at the front door.

Trent tapped on the window with the barrel of the H&K. The man turned, panic in his eyes as he saw Trent in the window behind him. He turned, already firing but wildly so. Trent triggered another three round burst from the submachine gun.

He hurried the last round of firing. His shots went high. He was sorry to see blood gushing from the last guard's face. Trent sincerely hoped he had not killed the man.

Moving quickly now, he jogged back to where the third man lay, still crying and clutching his useless leg. Grabbing him by the shirt, he dragged him to the front of the building. A swimming pool separated the guest house from the main building. He made the wounded man as comfortable as he could on a chaise lounge.

He went through the unlocked door into the guest house. The fourth man was still alive but seriously wounded. If he lived he would probably lose at least one eye.

Another Sig Sauer lay beside him. Trent stuck it in his belt along with the first one. He would leave here with a boost to his personal armory.

He pushed himself to move faster now as he returned to where the first two guards lay moaning. He forced Gideon, the first guard whose shoulder he had ruined with a single .50 caliber cartridge, to drag the second guard, whose left foot was shattered, to the front, placing each in his own chaise.

Moving quickly back into the guest house, he dragged the unconscious man out to where his three colleagues lay, placing him on a fourth chaise.

He spoke to the first man, the one with the wounded shoulder. "Is anyone else here?"

The man shook his head in the negative. Trent pointed the man's own weapon at him.

"No," the man said, panic in his voice. "I swear there's no one else here. Don Rossi gave the house servants the night off."

"Come with me," Trent ordered. He motioned for the man to walk in front of him. The guard still had one good arm. Trent was taking no chance that he had a hideout weapon. He pushed him around the corner of the building, out of sight of his comrades, far enough away that they could hear the two of them talking but not make out what they were saying.

"Where is Rossi holding Miles Diaz-Douglas and Darcey Anderson Marshall?"

"I don't know," Gideon whined. "I swear I don't."

Trent again pointed the Heckler & Koch at him.

"Some place on the water. South of the city. That's all I know, mister. I swear." The guard was crying, whether from fear or pain Trent didn't know. He didn't care. He motioned for the man to join his three friends.

Gideon sat on the edge of the chaise lounge. Trent handed him a small notepad and pen.

"Write what I tell you," he directed.

The man took the pen in his still usable right hand, held it poised over the notepad.

"Rossi," Trent dictated, remembering the words used to threaten Scott, "it's good to do things pleasing to your spouse. Think about your spouse tonight, Rossi. Think about her tomorrow as you do everything in your power to be sure Darcey Anderson Marshall and Miles Diaz-Douglas are alive when I get there to take them home. Your men have been very helpful."

The long, black Mercedes Pullman Deluxe limousine idled in front of the gate. Rossi lowered the privacy window.

"What's the problem? Why isn't the gate open?"

"It's not responding to the remote, Don Rossi," the driver replied.

"Why not?"

"I don't know. The remote works off the car battery so it's not that. Maybe the fence got short-circuited somehow."

You pay a small fortune for an electric security fence and it doesn't work because it short-circuited itself, he thought. At the moment, his thought continued, it's nothing but a very expensive boundary marker.

"Well, get out and see if there's any juice in it," he directed. "If not, open the gate manually."

The driver stared straight ahead. The man in the passenger seat looked at him. The driver made no move to get out of the vehicle. The man in the passenger seat swallowed hard. He hated this. He knew he would have to touch the fence. If it wasn't short-circuited, it wouldn't kill him but it would hurt.

He got out of the limo and approached the fence. He tentatively extended his hand toward the fence. Closing his eyes, he touched the wire. The man sighed with relief. Nothing.

"It's short-circuited, Don Rossi," he called out as he started to pull the gate open.

While his wife and children went upstairs to bed on entering their home, Rossi went to the bar. He mixed a martini, planning to sit at his desk and fantasize about what he might do to Miles Diaz-Douglas and Darcey Anderson Marshall if Scott Douglas remained recalcitrant.

Rossi enjoyed playing God. He enjoyed the power of deciding whether another human would live or die. He didn't often get the chance. Now he had two. He sipped his martini, contented.

Until his driver burst into the office.

"Don Rossi, I think you need to come outside. You need to see this," the man said, sounding out of breath. If Rossi didn't know better he would think the man was frightened.

"Whatever it is can wait until morning," Rossi said, taking another sip of his martini.

"No, sir, I don't think so," his driver insisted.

Rossi reluctantly set the cocktail on his desk and slowly rose from his chair.

"This had better be important," he warned.

He followed his driver to the pool. There he stopped to stare with disbelief. Each of the four guards he had left to keep his home secure lay on his own chaise lounge around the pool. Three of them were conscious, in pain and fearful of their fate. The fourth was still alive but not conscious. Blood covered his face.

When he regained his composure sufficiently to allow him to speak with authority, he turned to Gideon, the first of the guards attacked.

"What happened here, Gideon? Who did this?"

"We don't know who he was, Don Rossi. He just appeared out of the dark. He shot me with a very large hand gun. My shoulder is smashed. I won't ever be able to use it again."

"He? One man? Are you telling me one man did this? One man with one hand gun?"

"Not exactly, Don Rossi," the second guard said, hoping to let Gideon incur all their boss' wrath. "He shot the rest of us with Gideon's gun."

"And none of you managed to get a shot at him? Where are your guns now?"

"He took them all," the second guard said, the anguish of knowing his attempt to shift blame solely onto Gideon had failed.

"Let me be sure I understand this," Rossi said, speaking slowly, deliberately. "One man somehow gets over the security fence, which apparently is useless in defending my home. This one man, armed with only one hand gun, takes out the four men whose job it is to protect me and my family, and leaves with all your weapons. At least he was kind enough to lay you all out comfortably on my pool furniture."

The four guards were silent.

"Do I understand the situation correctly?" Rossi asked. "Is there anything else I should know?"

"Uh…He left a note for you, Don Rossi," Gideon said, holding slip of paper out in his one usable albeit trembling hand.

Rossi looked at the man with contempt as he took the note from him. He struggled to keep his emotions concealed as he read the note. To control his rage. And something more. Something he seldom felt. Fear. He wouldn't speak until he was sure his voice would be level.

"He talked to Gideon privately, Don Rossi," the second guard said, making another attempt to save himself. "We don't know what they talked about."

Ross looked at Gideon. "So? What did you talk about?"

"He wanted to know where you're holding those two people."

"And what did you tell him?"

"I told him I don't know. That's all, Don Rossi. I swear."

"Yes, I should think you would. Do something with these things," he told his driver, indicating with his hand the four wounded guards.

Returning to his desk, he took another sip of the cocktail waiting there. It was no longer ice cold. Martinis should be ice cold. Warm gin isn't pleasing to the palate. He sipped it anyway as he considered the options.

He began to develop a plan.

First, he would send his wife and children to visit her family in Virginia on the first flight he could find.

Second, he opened the door to a small storage closet. He ignored the printer and various office supplies that occupied most of the space. He found what he was looking for leaning in a far back corner.

He laid the ArmaLite AR-18 on his desk. One man managed to abrogate the contracts of four of his security team. The thirty round magazine extending below this rifle would not be so easily overcome.

Capable of selective fire, the rifle was popular with the Irish Republican Army in the days when the streets of Northern Ireland often ran red. It was the IRA's use of the weapon that led to it being called the "Widow Maker." An appropriate nickname, Rossi thought, for surely when he found whoever was responsible for this night's devastation, and if that man had a wife, he would force her to watch as he made her a widow.

Only then did he reach for his phone and dial a number.

"We have a problem, Peter," Rossi said when the man answered.

On the other end of the line, Peter listened to his don. Peter was both Rossi's underboss, or second in command, and his consigliere, his advisor. He lived in a more modest house a short distance from the Rossi compound. Rossi wanted Peter close by at all times.

When the call was ended, Peter made other calls carrying out Rossi's orders.

Then he sat at his own desk for a while. Thinking. Rossi was correct. They had to come up with a response to this unexpected development.

Peter needed a plan.

Wednesday, August 3rd

Trent awoke and lay still for a few minutes. He felt no pain. Nothing unusual. He didn't remember having any hallucinations but then he probably would have no memory if one had occurred. He thought it would be a symptom-free day. He was grateful.

He had managed to sleep for three hours before leaving to meet Christopher and his team at SFPD headquarters. Christopher was already in the conference room when Trent arrived at five o'clock. Other members of the team were there as well, preparing to execute their plan.

Trent tossed the truck keys to Christopher. The cop caught them and reluctantly returned the keys to the Bentley in return.

"I don't know what you did last night and don't want to know," Christopher said. "But I wouldn't mind driving that car for a few days more."

Trent laughed. "Maybe we can work something out. By the way, I left a little present under the seat." The "present" consisted of one of the H&Ks and one of the semiautomatic handguns. Their twins were safely stowed in Trent's duffel in his closet.

"No one was killed," Trent said in reply to the question he could see in Christopher's eyes. "Four of Rossi's security team won't be working for a while but they're alive."

The SFPD and FBI teams were assembled and ready. Over in Richmond Nancy's team was also ready. At 5:30 Christopher gave the order to go.

In a luxury apartment on the top floor of a building on Ellis Street in Little Saigon, one of very few homes in this part of the city that could be so described, Kiettisuk Jetjirawat was sitting down to breakfast. He sighed happily as he gazed at his favorite morning meal, khao neow moo ping. The grilled pork skewers were seasoned with cilantro root, garlic, and white pepper, among other things. It was accompanied, of course, with sticky rice. An excellent way, Kiettisuk thought, to begin the day.

He was not in the least concerned with his personal safety. He owned the building, though that would be hard to prove unless someone managed to weave a path through the various corporations between him personally and the title to the apartment building.

He had armed his personal security guards with Springfield M1A SOCOM-16 rifles. He had personally selected the weapon for his men. The relatively small, semiautomatic rifle packed a very powerful punch. No other rifle had ever been able to put that much power into such a lightweight weapon.

He took the first bite of the pork, perfectly prepared as always. He was feeling much younger than his 67 years. He was thinking about the new shipment of girls that had been delivered to his hotel over on Eddy Street. One in particular had caught his eye. She looked to be perhaps 15 years old. Well developed for her age. Beautiful, long dark hair. He would have her sent over tonight.

As he took the first bite of pork, there was a sound from the street. Much like two cars smashing into each other. Or one vehicle crashing into something else. The sound had nothing to do with him but it interfered with the quiet that Kiettisuk preferred in the morning.

He could have looked out one of the two bay windows in his apartment to see what caused the noise. But he found the view of the street below and the buildings surrounding his to be unprepossessing. He motioned for the security guard standing by the door to investigate.

Had he looked through one of the bay windows he would have been surprised to see the noise was caused by an armored SWAT vehicle belonging to the San Francisco Police Department smashing through the gate. Cops in bullet proof vests poured out of it as a string of black and whites, filled with more combat-ready cops, followed it onto the grounds of his building.

He would have been even more surprised to see his security force laying down their high-powered rifles as they surrendered to the assault team led by Lieutenant Billy Mitchum. Kiettisuk's guards wisely determined their rifles were no match for the SA80 L85 selective fire assault weapons with which Mitchum had armed his team. The SA 80s, with a fully automatic fire option, were popular with the British army. The lightweight, semiautomatic rifles with which Kiettisuk had armed his private soldiers were no match.

Kiettisuk didn't look up from his breakfast when the man returned to his apartment.

"Well?"

"Good morning, Kiet."

Kiettisuk was immediately enraged with the informal greeting. When he looked toward the door he saw not the man who had been sent to investigate the disturbance downstairs but a smiling Lieutenant Billy Mitchum backed by three other police officers, all four of whom held the wicked-looking assault weapons.

"What is the meaning of this? How dare you invade my privacy?" Kiettisuk raged. "Do you have a warrant permitting this atrocity?"

"Sure do," Mitchum replied, cheerfully, as he handed over the warrant. "Now you're going downtown with us for questioning. It's a little matter of operating a prostitution ring. You haven't had time to hear of it yet but your hotel over on Eddy Street is shut down. Your crew in charge of it is in custody. Some of those girls were only 12 years old. You make me sick, Kiet."

"I have nothing to do with any of that. You have no proof of such a thing nor will you find any."

"We'll see about that, Kiet," Mitchum replied. "Meanwhile you're going with us for some questioning. Cuff him," the lieutenant directed.

Kiettisuk was outraged. He wasn't even allowed to get dressed. He was taken into public view dressed only in pajama pants, slippers, and an undershirt. His hands were cuffed behind his back.

Two black and whites were parked in front of the apartment building. The rear door of one was being held open for him. As he was guided into the vehicle his head was turned toward the other. He didn't allow his facial expression to change but he was surprised to see one of Jonathan Rossi's men in the back seat of the second vehicle.

He was being personally insulted by being dragged out in public in handcuffs. He had lost a large sum of money with the shutting down of the Eddy Street hotel and the loss of the young talent he had only last week imported. And now one of Rossi's men was sitting in an SFPD car. He would have to give some thought to what it all means.

At the same time, Sergeant Nancy Patrick's team was moving in on the warehouse that was the headquarters of the Barons of Lucifer. Located in the Iron Triangle district of Richmond, near the interstate, luxurious would be the last word to describe the building.

There were no guards outside. There was an entry on either side of the large garage door leading into the warehouse. At Nancy's direction, four of her biggest colleagues smashed through them.

Nancy led her team into the garage, startling two men playing poker. Both men went for the semiautomatic handguns lying on the table. One of the men stood, swinging around to get into firing position. Nancy's Ruger barked twice. One nine millimeter slug smashed into the upper part of the biker's femur, near where it connected to the pubic structure. The second man dropped to the floor and managed to fire his weapon three times with no hits. A hail of bullets chewed up the concrete floor all around him. He dropped his weapon, pushing it away.

Two of Nancy's team quickly cuffed the two Barons taken on the main floor while she led the way across the warehouse to the stairs leading to the second floor. It was there that the Barons kept a series of rooms, not unlike a dormitory. Gang members could use the rooms for the night or for an hour.

At one end of the second floor was the club house. There was a bar and pool tables. Another Baron was passed out, his head lying on one of the tables. He was quickly awakened and subdued. Doors to a few of the rooms along the hall were opening. Barons were stumbling out, half asleep and still drunk from the night before. None offered serious resistance.

Nancy and two other officers moved toward the other end of the building. The Mad Dutchman's apartment was there. The noise woke him. He was hungover and feeling mean. The naked, tattooed blonde he had taken to share his bed the night before woke up, too.

"What's going on?" she asked, her voice still slurred from the booze and coke.

"Shut up," the Dutchman said, slapping her.

He reached for the half full jug of red wine sitting on the floor by the bed. Turning it up, he took three deep swallows, hoping the wine would stop the pounding in his head.

The pounding only got worse as the door to his room was kicked in. He looked up to see three cops, one of them a woman, holding guns pointed at him.

His own weapon, another Sig Sauer, cousin to the semiautomatic handguns Trent had taken from two of Rossi's men, lay on a table near his bed. He liked the weapon. It was in a batch intended for the Immigration and Customs Enforcement agency that the Dutchman had hijacked.

Nancy saw him look at the gun. She smiled, her own weapon held steady, her aim dead on the Dutchman.

"Go ahead, Lin," she taunted. "Try for it. Let's see if your hand can move faster than my bullet."

As hungover as he was, Winters wasn't entirely slow-witted. He held up his hands.

"What's this all about?" he asked.

"We had a double murder in our town a few days ago," she said. "We have reason to believe you might be involved in it. I'm taking you in for questioning. And, before you ask, yes, I have a warrant. We'll be searching this lovely home you have here."

"This is harassment," Winters said, as two officers cuffed his hands behind his back. Nancy kept her Ruger aimed at the Barons of Lucifer leader.

"We'll see. Take him to the cars," she directed the officers.

As they passed through the building she counted fourteen Barons and seven women, most of them severely hungover or still high from the night's activities. An interesting assortment of weapons was being assembled as the rooms were searched.

Outside the warehouse, as at the apartment building in Little Saigon, there were two black and whites. As Winters was being helped into the second vehicle, he saw one of Rossi's men in the first.

The vehicle he was in pulled out first, passing the vehicle with Rossi's man in it. The Mad Dutchman looked hard at the Mafia soldier as they drove slowly by. The fire in his eyes gave proof to why he was called Mad.

Abdul Rahman completed his morning prayer at 5:30. He was enjoying a cup of tea on the terrace outside his bedroom. He had purchased this home in the affluent city of Pleasanton because of its architecture.

The large house was over a century old. Most thought it to be Spanish. And so it was, in a roundabout way. The architecture showed the influence of the Moors in the centuries they dominated significant portions of the Iberian Peninsula, of which Spain is the largest part.

Abdul had been precocious as a child in the study of Islam. He was a devoted follower of the religion from his earliest years. His very name pronounced him as a servant of God.

Now he enjoyed his public persona as a successful venture capitalist. He enjoyed even more his private life as the leader of the Scourge, an organization dedicated to overthrowing this silly republic known as the United States and bringing it under Islamic control.

He kept a few of his followers on the grounds of his estate in the guise of servants and assistants. Some were relatives. He considered it a sign of his intelligence that none, including himself, were armed. He knew the xenophobic forces among the government, as well as throughout the general population, were constantly on the lookout for armed Muslims. He refused to give anyone the satisfaction of coming into his home and finding anything that could be described as supportive of revolution.

It wasn't that he didn't have an army or arms for them. He had both. Most worked at his warehouses on the coast. It was in one of them that he kept his armory. He was prepared to act on the orders of Al Dawla al-Islamyia fil Iraq wa'al Sham. That which is called ISIL, or ISIS, in the United States and the hated acronym Da'ish in Great Britain.

For the time being he was content moving among the elite of the Bay area and sitting on his terrace, sipping tea.

He was shocked, then, when he saw the black SUVs speed up the driveway. He was more shocked as he watched the black-clad, armed men and women emptying from the vehicles.

With great irritation, he went downstairs to meet the armed force invading his home. Abdul knew Agent Joseph Brady. There had been confrontations between them in the past. Abdul was not concerned about the outcome of this latest attempt by the FBI to intimidate him.

Agent Brady handed the warrant to Abdul.

"This is our authority to enter and search these premises, Abdul," Brady said. "And we will take you to our office for questioning."

"Questioning for what?" Abdul demanded to know. "This is racial discrimination. Harassment. Nothing more. I am a respectable and successful businessman."

"Yes, it would seem so," Brady agreed as he looked around at the lavishly furnished house. "You're also the leader of the Scourge, one of the groups funding ISIL through several illegal activities, which cross state lines."

"Ridiculous!" Abdul said. He kept his face expressionless but he was surprised that Brady had information connecting him to the Scourge. He had thought that was known only to his four partners in Rossi's fiduciaria.

He was outraged when his hands were cuffed behind his back and he was led to an SUV. One of the SUVs they passed had all the windows open. His rage was even more enflamed when he saw two of Rossi's men sitting inside. They were not cuffed.

In the hills of Atherton, Rossi's wife and children were driven to the airport to catch an early flight to Virginia. His wife had been part of the Rossi family long enough to know better than to ask why.

When they were gone, he sat at his desk staring straight ahead. Trying to control the fury raging within. He wasn't sure who had penetrated his defenses and taken out his security team. He suspected it was Marshall.

He had eight men patrolling the grounds now. But Marshall, or whoever it was, moved like a ghost. Rossi thought he could have twenty men around him and he still wouldn't be safe. Without thinking about it, his hand reached out to caress the weapon lying on his desk.

It was a hard decision to make. But until he had worked out a new plan and put it into motion, he had no choice but to heed the warning. Reaching for another burner, he dialed a number. He gave new orders to the man who answered.

The man who answered the phone and got the new orders was younger than most of Rossi's soldiers. And one of the meanest. At birth he was given the name Gaetano. He hated it. It sounded too old country. Other kids made fun of it. When he was old enough to get away with it, he began calling himself Guy.

He thought the new name would help him fit in with others. It didn't. He wasn't like others. He was one of those people who enjoyed the suffering of others. Marshall had called it by the German word. Schadenfreude. Guy's own people would have called him "sadico." The English word was more direct. Sadist.

He might have become a serial killer had he not met some of Rossi's security team. They introduced him to their boss. Something about him interested Rossi. He couldn't put his finger on it. He had the feeling Guy would carry out any order he was given, no matter how vicious or messy it might be.

Guy was disappointed at the new orders he had just been given. He stepped into the large room that had once housed an illegal casino. He stared regretfully at the man and woman. Each was bound to a chair.

Miles' was without a shirt. His face and thin chest showed signs of being beaten. None of Darcey's clothes had been removed. There was only one red mark on her left cheek. Guy had felt obligated to show her who was boss. He was disappointed that she hadn't fought back. There wasn't much fun in a single slap to the face.

He began to untie the knots binding Miles to the chair.

"I don't like doing this," the thug said, "but I have to follow orders. If I don't, I'll be sitting in your chair." He laughed, thinking that a funny joke.

"But I'm disappointed," he continued. "The boss told me I could do anything I wanted to you if your boyfriend didn't do what he was told. I could exsanguinate you if I wanted. I didn't know what that meant. But I Googled it. It sounded like fun. Do you know what it means?"

Miles weakly shook his head, indicating the negative.

Guy laughed. "It means to drain the blood from your body. I was looking forward to seeing that. But orders are orders. I guess the boss has decided to give your boyfriend another chance."

"He's not my boyfriend," Miles said, his voice barely above a whisper. "He's my husband."

Guy laughed again. "Your husband? Then I guess that makes you the wifey, doesn't it? Well, I'll tell you what, wifey, the boss is sending out some groceries. When they get here, you can get your skinny self in the kitchen and do the cooking. She can help you," he said, as he began releasing Darcey from her bonds.

By nine o'clock the team leaders, Lieutenant Mitchum, Sergeant Patrick, and Special Agent Brady were back in the headquarters conference room. All three reported their assignments had gone off without a hitch. Nancy was the only one who reported resistance, weak though it was.

Each of the leaders reported the presence of Rossi's men had been noted by the targets of their raids. Christopher had raised the bet to Rossi.

Scott Douglas arrived at the team's headquarters shortly after nine o'clock. Trent wanted to give Christopher time for the raids to be conducted and team members to report before launching the next part of their plan. In Trent's mind, it was the most important of all. Scott would not disagree.

Only Trent, Christopher, and Nancy would be participating. The original plan was to include only Christopher and Trent. That was until Nancy told them that if they thought they could exclude her they were dumber than they appeared.

The three of them now huddled with Scott, who had brought a handful of documents and maps with him.

"These documents list all of Rossi's real estate holdings in the area. At least all that I know about. I can't imagine there would be more that I'm not aware of," Scott said. "I've marked them all on this map of the Bay area."

"There are a lot of x's on the map, Scott," Trent pointed out. "Do any of them stand out to you as a place they might use to hold Darcey and Miles?"

"I'm not used to this sort of thing, Trent," Scott replied, nervously, "so I'm not really sure what to look for."

Trent glared at him.

"But there is one place that seems to me a logical choice. It's here." Scott had a red marker among the items he had brought with him. He drew a circle around one of the x's on the coast south of San Francisco

"The location matches the description that Rossi's security guard gave me. What do you know about it?" Trent asked.

"It sits right on the ocean about twenty-five miles south of San Francisco. Rossi's grandfather and great grandfather used it for smuggling. It also was a bar and illegal casino at various times. It has a few rooms on the upper floors so it was probably used for prostitution as well. It's been abandoned for years. I'm not sure why Rossi has let it sit unused. It's valuable property. It's not like him to pass up the opportunity for profit."

"Unless you need a place to stash stolen goods or maybe a few hostages every now and then," Christopher suggested.

Trent and Christopher drove past the dilapidated building without slowing or demonstrating any interest in it. Two miles farther south on the Coast Highway they parked the truck at a scenic vista site. They hiked through the hills and rocks on the west side of the highway until they were adjacent to and above the old hotel.

The building was a quarter mile off the highway and built directly above the water. Approach was via an unpaved road over hard-packed sand.

They found a place among the rocks where they could lie concealed to watch the building, each with his own binoculars. For the first hour they saw nothing.

The building looked to be roughly square. Approximately one hundred feet per side. That would make it 10,000 square feet on the ground floor. There were two upper floors. 30,000 square feet. A lot of area to search.

The windows had been painted over. Any lights on the inside couldn't be seen from the outside.

They agreed that most of the action would be on the first floor. It seemed logical that the men holding Darcey and Miles wouldn't want to get too spread out. There would probably be bedrooms on the upper floors. Rossi's men on site would no doubt take turns sleeping.

Darcey and Miles would probably be restrained and not comfortable. The kidnappers wouldn't be concerned about how well their captives were sleeping. To the contrary. The more sleep-deprived the captives were the easier it would be to control them.

Trent studied approaches to the old building, which sat on a small cove. He pointed out to Christopher that a jumble of rocks similar to those in which they lay concealed came almost to the walls on both sides of the building. The rocks would provide cover for the team as they moved in.

They were beginning to wonder if Scott had guessed wrong when a dark sedan drove up. Three men got out and went to the rear of the vehicle. When the driver popped the trunk open, each man took a box and carried it to the building, the last man closing the trunk.

The door that looked like the main entrance into the old building opened, held by a fifth man. The men carrying the boxes entered the building. The door closed. The driver of the car drove to the far end of the building, disappearing behind it. It almost appeared as though the vehicle had driven into the inlet.

"This building isn't abandoned," Trent said. "Those men were carrying groceries. Rossi has kept up the appearance of an abandoned building. I'll bet he's found many uses for it."

"Groceries are a good sign," Christopher added. "There was a lot of food in those boxes. I think that means Miles and Darcey are still alive and are being fed."

"Right," Trent agreed. "Let's get out of here. We need a plan to get them out."

They met Nancy and Scott at the Nob Hill condo.

"Look at this," Christopher said as he made a rough drawing of the building. "The car we saw today drove back here and disappeared. There has to be an approach into the building from the water. It's the only reason it would ever have been useful for smuggling.

"I'd bet that car drove into a space that was used as a loading dock during Prohibition when booze was smuggled in by water. The goods could be either taken into the building or loaded onto trucks for delivery elsewhere."

"I think we have to enter from the north side," Trent observed. "We can deduce that there is some sort of driveway on the north side since we saw the car drive into it. But the inlet has to be L-shaped. If the building opened directly onto the ocean, wave action would make entry almost impossible. By utilizing the shape of this small inlet, the waves are broken, providing a relatively smooth entry."

"But what if entry into the building from the water is sealed off?" Nancy asked.

"I doubt if it is," Trent said. "This building is still very much in use. That probably includes entry from the water. Besides, the driver of the car never reappeared after he turned in behind the building. He must have entered the building from the ocean level. I think it's worth a try. But we need a diversion. Something to attract their attention away from the water."

"That's my job."

Scott's announcement was a surprise to all three of them.

"That's a very dangerous offer, Scott," Christopher said. "You might not survive it."

"I'm the one who got us into this mess. It's only fair that I do whatever I can to get us out."

"You being dead does us no good, Scott," Christopher argued.

"Believe me, I'm in no hurry to die. But if that happens, I have provided you all the financial details of Rossi and his fiduciaria. You'll have no problem convicting all four organizations in court."

"If our plan works, we won't need to go to court. The four partners will destroy each other. Remember the den of snakes," Trent said.

"We have to be prepared for whatever direction this thing takes, Trent," Christopher said. "All right, Scott, but at least let me get you a gun."

"No," Scott said. "No gun. I wouldn't know what to do with it. Besides, if I'm your diversion the first thing they'll do is search me. I would be safer unarmed."

The other three would be armed. Trent with the Desert Eagle; Christopher with his Smith & Wesson; Nancy with her Ruger. Trent went to the bedroom he shared with Darcey, returning with the pink and black gym bag.

They made sandwiches while they waited for night. Trent wanted everyone to have plenty of energy but wanted no one to eat so much as to feel sluggish

He and Christopher discussed how many of Rossi's men they could expect to encounter. They had seen four enter the building earlier in the day. A fifth was seen opening the door for them. They thought two or three must have been out of sight. They decided the logical number would be eight.

With surprise on their side they thought they could handle eight. The difficulty would be to do so while keeping Scott, Miles, and Darcey alive.

Ordinarily they would have scheduled this type of operation in the early hours of the morning. That's when people were most vulnerable. But they didn't think they could wait. Trent's penetration of Rossi's compound had gained them a little time. A few hours. No more than that. Once Rossi realized another day had passed and Scott still hadn't followed orders, there was no way to know what he would do.

It was fully dark when they parked at another pullout, this one a mile north of the building. Trent rode with Christopher in his truck. Nancy followed them in her car, a non-descript, three year old sedan. The Bentley was left behind. It would attract too much attention.

They waited in their vehicles until Christopher's phone rang. Scott was calling to say he would be there in an hour. The call was prearranged. It was part of the plan.

They had an hour to work their way through the rocks bordering the ocean. Fortunately, the roar of the surf meant any noise they made wouldn't be heard.

They had to be in place when Scott arrived. They didn't know what would happen when he was inside. They only knew it was critical that they get into the building soon after he arrived.

They made two stops on their way to the coast. The first was to the conference room serving as headquarters for Christopher's team. There he retrieved several sets of handcuffs.

The second stop was to the store Trent had used before. They bought three lights with elastic head bands. They would have to be careful in using them but they would at least come in handy when they were underneath the building alongside the small inlet. They wouldn't use the lights on their approach.

They were surprised to find the store sold combat face paint. They didn't ask why. They used it to darken the backs of their hands and their faces.

The trek through the rocks was difficult. Nancy held her own with the men. If anything, she had an easier time than Christopher. His large size made it harder for him to navigate through the natural maze of boulders. Trent was hampered by weaponry. In addition to the Desert Eagle, a large handgun itself, he carried the pink and black gym bag.

They made it to the edge of the rocks bordering the old building with ten minutes to spare. They would have to cross twenty-five yards of hard-packed sand in the open before reaching the vehicle entry, which they could now see at the rear of the building. So far their deductions were correct. Their luck was holding. Trent was confident they would find entry into the building itself once they were below it at the water level.

Exactly ten minutes later, Scott's gray Mercedes pulled up to the main entrance. They watched him walk up to the door and knock loudly. There was silence.

He knocked again. Finally the door was opened.

They heard him speak to whoever opened the door.

"I'm Scott Douglas."

They couldn't hear what was said in return.

"I'm the reason you're holding two people. Jonathan Rossi is mad at me. Not them."

They heard nothing from whoever Scott was addressing. He did see an arm reach out to grab Scott's shirt and pull him into the building. They watched as a man stepped outside, holding a strange looking rifle in his hands.

"That's interesting," Trent said, speaking softly, the roar of the surf muffling the sound of his voice. "A small rifle. Looks like one of those survival weapons. Probably a .22. Not very powerful but a sneaky little weapon at close range. It's not a threat to us out here. Inside is another matter."

They stayed low among the rocks as the man looked around. He opened the door to Scott's car to look inside. He walked around the parking area, looking in all directions. As he turned his face toward them, they remained motionless.

When he was satisfied that Scott had come alone he went back inside. Trent, Christopher, and Nancy waited a full five minutes to be sure he was gone.

Under different circumstances they would have waited another five or ten minutes. But Scott's entry into the building was another shot fired into the den of snakes. They had to get Darcey, Miles, and Scott out now. When the snakes started striking it was important that they hit each other. No one else.

Christopher led his team, with weapons drawn, to the driveway leading down to water level. They reached the building without hearing any alarms. Still they pressed themselves against the wall as they side-stepped down the slanted driveway. At the bottom, Christopher was the first to look around the corner. As they had deduced, the water was relatively free from wave action thanks to the L shaped inlet. There was a concrete loading dock along their side, wide enough for trucks.

As they turned into the darkness of the water entry, all three switched on their head-mounted lights. The concrete landing extended all the way under the building. The car they had seen arrive earlier in the day was parked there, along with two other sedans and the dark-colored van used to kidnap Darcey and Miles.

A highly polished wooden runabout was tied alongside the loading dock. It was meant for speed rather than hauling freight. It was there for a quick getaway on the water.

At the end of the dock was a door with glass panels on the top side. The way in.

They moved quickly, carefully, and quietly down the loading dock, keeping close to the wall. It was dark inside. They could see nothing through the glass panes. Not surprisingly, the door was locked.

Christopher was preparing to risk the noise of smashing the glass when Nancy put her hand on his arm, stopping him. Holstering her Ruger, she knelt by door. With a set of picks produced from her pocket she quickly released the two locks that ineffectively secured the door.

Christopher looked at her with a mixture of respect and fear. He lived with this woman and didn't know about this skill. He wondered what other skills she had unknown to him. But there was no time to consider that now.

They were in a basement hallway leading off the loading dock. Doors lined the hallway on both sides. Storage rooms, probably from the days when the Rossi Family ran an illegal casino and prostitutes upstairs.

They could see light spilling through a doorway at the end of the hall, about fifty feet away. That would be under the main entrance. The doorway where they had seen people moving in and out. Where Scott Douglas had entered.

They heard the man before they saw him, giving them time to switch off their head lamps. Each of them found a doorway to press as deeply into as possible.

More light spilled into the dark hallway as the door opened. The man who had looked around outside after Scott arrived put in an appearance. The lightweight rifle was still in his hands.

"I hate that jerk," he was mumbling. "'You screwed up, Ietro. You left the door open when you parked the car.' I did not leave the door open, Guy," he said, turning and speaking louder. Just a little louder. He didn't really want whoever Guy was to hear him. He was scared of Guy.

"And your name isn't Guy," Ietro continued. "It's Gaetano. You should be proud of your heritage." He was back to mumbling.

There must have been a silent alarm system they had tripped when Nancy picked the lock. The kidnappers would be on the alert. No matter. The team's attack was fully committed.

Nancy and Christopher were pressed into doorways on the man's left; Trent was on his right. He would pass Nancy first. Christopher didn't like it but he nodded to her, indicating that she should take him out.

Nancy let him take one step past her before stepping out of the doorway and bringing her semiautomatic down on the back of his head like a hammer. Trent stepped up and caught him before he fell. Christopher grabbed the rifle before it clattered to the floor.

Nancy quickly cuffed the man's hands behind his back. Trent ripped a strip of cloth off the Mafia soldier's shirt, which he used to gag him. He ripped off another strip to bind his ankles.

Christopher held up one finger. "One down," he indicated.

They didn't think the other Mafioso would go down as easily.

Scott felt sick when he looked at Miles, bruised and bloody. It was all his fault. He knew that. Darcey had only one red mark on her cheek, as though she had been slapped. Miles had been the focus of punishment.

They were in the first floor's large main room. Miles and Darcey were sitting side by side on an old sofa. Neither was bound. In addition to the one who called himself Guy, there were four other armed men in the room.

"So you're the husband," Guy taunted. "Your wifey has been telling us about you."

"I doubt that," Scott replied, with as much confidence as he could muster. "Our relationship isn't something Miles would choose to discuss with scum like you."

"He's just lucky Don Rossi gave me orders to lay off. I was planning to have a lot of fun with him. And when I had him worn out, then I was going to start on her," Guy said, wrapping his hand in Darcey's hair and jerking her head back.

Scott said nothing. He wouldn't give the man the satisfaction of an emotional response.

"So are you crazy or what?" Guy asked, releasing Darcey's hair. "What are you doing here? Did you think you would just come in here and leave with these two? Does Don Rossi know you're here?"

"No, he doesn't know I'm here," Scott answered. "And yes, I do plan to leave here with Miles and Darcey."

Guy picked up his FN Herstal P90, pointing the strange but highly effective personal defense weapon at Scott.

"Maybe I should just blow you away right now."

"Your boss might not like that," Scott said, struggling to keep his fear hidden. "He might be angry at me now but he still needs me."

Guy was obviously uncertain about the situation.

"Then maybe I should shoot your wifey," he said, swinging the short weapon in Miles' direction.

"If you do that, then you might as well shoot me, too. That's the worst thing you could do."

Guy's uncertainty was intensifying. He found his phone in his pocket. "I'd better call the boss."

"Are you sure you want to do that?" Scott questioned. "Rossi might be curious about why you let the first person to knock on the door come right in."

Guy laughed nervously. "How did you know where to find us? Did someone talk? Who was it? I'll take care of him right now."

"No one told me anything. It wasn't hard to find you. And if I found you, you can be sure others will as well."

Climbing the stairs as noiselessly as they could, Christopher, Nancy, and Trent found themselves in a large lobby.

To the left was a long front desk. The place had never been a hotel. The front desk would have been used as a coat room or a place where customers would check in to affirm their desires for the evening

Tonight it was manned by a guard carrying a large assault rifle. Bulky and heavy. Trent thought it didn't look especially effective. It still could be a nasty weapon.

"Hey...what the ...?" the guard said, rising from the chair, coming around the end of the front desk as he attempted to bring his rifle into play.

"Freeze," Christopher ordered.

The guard ignored him. Nancy wasn't waiting. Her weapon fired once. The bullet slammed into his left knee, crushing the patella. With his kneecap gone, his tibia and femur were left connected only by shreds of tendon. He fell to the ground, out of action. Trent grabbed his rifle, tossing it down the stairs.

Behind them were stairs going to the upper floors. To their right, a double set of swinging doors led into another room. Judging by the size of the doors, Trent guessed it was a large room. Most likely where the casino was once located.

The sound of a shot coming from the lobby froze all activity in the main room.

"Guglielo, Barnaba, Martino. Go see what that's all about," Guy ordered.

With the surprise element gone, Christopher and Trent focused on the double swinging doors. Nancy kept an eye on the stairs.

Suddenly three men charged through the swinging doors. Two carried assault rifles. The third man carried a the same futuristic appearing personal defense weapon that Guy had flaunted to Scott.

Two of the men came out firing their weapons. Christopher, Nancy, and Trent hit the floor simultaneously.

Trent's Desert Eagle roared, a .50 caliber slug ripping into the first man's upper right arm, wrecking the humerus bone. He dropped his rifle as he stumbled toward the front desk, seeking a place to escape the fight.

The next round from the Desert Eagle missed the second man, striking the wall no more than an inch from his head. Close enough to cost the would-be gunman what little nerve he had. He dropped his weapon, his hands clawing for the ceiling.

"On the floor, face down, spread eagle," Trent ordered. The unnerved gunman hastened to do as he was told.

"Barnaba, you coward," the one called Martino shouted as he watched his companion surrender.

The man with the small, personal defense weapon, was distracted as he unwisely berated his companion. Christopher took the opportunity to fire his Smith & Wesson, striking the gunman squarely in the crotch.

The weapon dropped from his hand as the injured man fell to the floor, screaming in agony, hands between his legs. His face reflected the horror of his recent transition from healthy manhood to no manhood at all. His screams rose and fell in multiple levels, ranging from agonized wailing to pathetic whimpering.

"First time I ever heard multi-syllabic whining," Nancy said as she cuffed Barnaba's hands behind his back. Trent picked up the two assault rifles and the personal defense weapon. He tossed them downstairs to join the rifle already there.

"You ruined me!" Martino whined.

"Uh oh," Christopher replied, unsympathetically.

The five people in the main room listened to the rattle of gunfire. Then the silence. Each of them wondered what was going on. Guy heard a man crying out in pain. Cursing in Italian. One of his men was down.

"Guglielo! Barnaba! Martino!" Guy called out. "What's going on out there?"

There was no reply. Just the wailing of a badly wounded man.

Guy clutched his weapon. One of his men remained in the room with him. Guy liked Brock best. He had an American name. Like Guy. Not the old world names of the rest of his crew.

"That's it," he said to Brock. "Shoot the wifey."

Brock didn't question the order. That was another reason Guy was partial to him. The man turned his own personal defense weapon toward Miles.

"NO!" Scott shouted, hurling himself in front of Miles just as Brock pulled the trigger. A three round burst traced a path from Scott's shoulder diagonally across his chest. His clavicle was broken. There was no way to know the extent of internal damage.

Seeing the man he loved viciously shot down roused Miles from the lethargy of the arduous experience of the past few days.

"Oh no. Scott! Scott!" Miles threw his own battered body over his husband's in an attempt to protect him from any continued assault. Darcey quickly jumped behind the sofa.

Miles and Scott were ignored for the moment as Brock turned to the double swinging doors to see Trent flinging himself into the room. Don Rossi's man fired another three round burst that went high as Trent dropped to the floor.

He had unzipped the gym bag before entering the room, extracting the M16. He slid it across the floor to Darcey before firing two wild shots in the general direction of the two remaining kidnappers.

"Shoot them! Kill them all!" Guy shouted as he shoved Brock forward.

Brock lowered the barrel of his weapon to where Trent lay on the floor. Before he could pull the trigger again, Darcey put the M16 into action. It was hard to reach her target from where she had taken cover. She hit her target just above his foot. The powerful M16 rounds turned the talus of Brock's left ankle into shards of bone. He would likely lose his foot.

Guy found himself alone. He felt the tingle of fear travel through his body. He fired a burst over his shoulder as he ran for a door at the far corner of the room.

Trent and Darcey both fired their weapons in his direction. But he got through the door unscathed.

"Where does that door go?" Trent shouted.

"I'm not sure. I think it might be a back way down to the water." Darcey said. "I heard them mention something about that."

"Do what you can for Scott and Miles," he shouted as he ran back through the swinging doors.

"There's another one down in there," he said as he ran past Christopher. "The leader is headed to the water." He heard the big cop behind him as he ran down the stairs, taking them two at a time.

They heard the roar of a boat motor as they ran down the lower hallway. By the time they reached the door leading to the loading dock, they saw the runabout making the turn of the L-shaped inlet, heading for open water. Trent fired the last two rounds from the Desert Eagle. To no effect.

Returning to the hallway, they released the feet of the first guard they had taken out. He preceded them, with the occasional encouragement from Christopher's Smith & Wesson prodding his back.

Two more Mafioso were upstairs. They called down to say they were surrendering. Nancy had them toss down their weapons. Another assault rifle and a lightweight Glock .40 caliber handgun clattered down the stairs.

Christopher and Trent returned to the main room where Darcey was attempting to console Miles and do what she could to help his wounded husband. Scott was barely breathing.

"Oh, Scott, Scott, don't leave me," Miles cried.

Scott raised his hand, trying to touch Miles' tear-stained face. He didn't have the strength. His hand fell away. He closed his eyes. His breathing was shallow, red-tinged bubbles floated on his lips each time he exhaled. Not a good sign.

Christopher dragged Brock, who was unable to walk, to the lobby to join his comrades.

Trent knelt by Darcey, putting his arms around her. She let him hold her.

"Are you all right?" he asked

She nodded. He kissed her.

"What took you so long?" she said.

He smiled. Darcey would be fine.

He wasn't sure about Scott and Miles.

Within half an hour the packed sand leading to the old building was jammed with ambulances and police vehicles. The first ambulance took Scott, who was clinging to life. Miles rode with him, refusing to leave his husband's side.

Armed police officers accompanied the wounded kidnappers as they were loaded into ambulances. The officers would accompany their prisoners, each of whom was handcuffed to the gurney he was on, to the hospital. They would remain on guard as the men were treated.

Chief Marvin himself was on the scene. Darcey told him how she and Miles were kidnapped. She described their treatment as hostages.

"It was awful, Chief Marvin," Darcey said. "But they treated Miles far worse than they did me. They ripped his shirt off when we first got here, taunting him. The one who was in charge, Guy he called himself, enjoyed beating poor Miles. He hit me only once," she added, touching the red spot on her cheek, "when I tried to intervene."

"Can you definitely say Jonathan Rossi was behind this?" the chief asked.

"Only to the extent that I heard them mention 'Don Rossi' a few times," she replied. "Guy got a phone call this morning that displeased him. He was ordered to lay off any mistreatment and to feed us well. He didn't like that at all. Guy is a sadist, Chief. He told Miles he had planned to drain all the blood from his body. He was disappointed that Rossi, or whoever called, ordered him to make sure we were well treated."

"So, Sergeant Booth," Marvin said, turning to Christopher, "you and Sergeant Patrick, assisted by our consultant, Mr. Marshall, created quite a bit of carnage. Don't you think bringing in the rest of our department would have been appropriate?"

"Uh...Yes, Sir," Christopher stammered. "But we didn't have a lot of time."

"You say Mr. Douglas called to tell you where he was going and what he planned to do. Is that correct?"

"Yes, sir," Christopher answered. "Nancy...Uh...Sergeant Patrick, Mr. Marshall, and I decided we could best help him by getting into the building undetected as quickly as possible. Frankly, sir, it's likely that a fleet of black and whites with lights flashing and sirens blaring would probably have resulted in the three innocent civilians being killed."

"And you always carry combat face paint with you?" the chief questioned.

"Never leave home without it, sir," Christopher answered, keeping a straight face.

"I see," the chief replied. "How did you get here? I see only Mr. Douglas' car."

"We parked in a pullout about a mile north of here. We came down through the rocks and found the ramp leading down to the water underneath the building. We were able to get in there and take them by surprise."

"And one, this Guy fellow who was in charge, escaped. Right?"

"Yes, there might have been others that got away," Christopher said, "but he did for sure. There was a door leading down to the water that we didn't know about. He managed to get to the boat that was moored down there and out to open water."

"I see," the chief said before turning to Trent. "And now, Mr. Marshall, what do I do about you? I'm starting to wonder if bringing you on board as a consultant to the department was a good idea."

"Trent's participation has been invaluable in the operation we put into action," Christopher said. "Operation Den of Snakes was his concept. He was intimately involved in developing the strategy and planning its execution. It has worked without a hitch so far, Chief. It has the potential to cripple four of the city's major crime organizations for a generation or more."

Nancy chimed in to support Christopher. "I agree with Sergeant Booth completely, Chief. Mr. Marshall is playing a critical role. And, if I might point out, at considerable personal risk. One of the kidnap victims is his wife, sir."

"Yes, I'm aware of that," the chief said, glancing at Darcey who had returned after helping Miles into the ambulance with Scott. "And I agree that Operation Den of Snakes is a brilliant plan, which I endorse without reservation."

"Thank you, Sir," Christopher said.

"Now if we're done with our encomia," Chief Marvin said, looking at the Desert Eagle holstered on Trent's hip, "I will assume that weapon is a legal .44 caliber. And that," pointing to the M16 Darcey had retrieved, "is an AR-15."

His sarcasm did not go unnoticed.

Christopher spoke up. "You approved the permits and waivers for Trent and Darcey yourself, Sir."

"So I did," Marvin agreed, with a hint of a smile. "So I did."

There was silence.

"Well, it's all a bit irregular," Marvin said, "and the media will be all over us when they get wind of it, but good work."

"Thank you, sir," Christopher said.

The ache in Rossi's head was approaching unbearable. He feared his head might explode. Or he might have a stroke. How many disasters could he endure?

Guy had called to report to him on the attack that had cost him eight more soldiers and his hostages. He would have felt better had his soldiers been killed. None were. One wasn't even injured. He surrendered when the first shot was fired. And how was it, Rossi asked Guy, that he was the only one to escape? He got no satisfactory reply.

Rossi was glad his father and grandfather weren't around to see how poorly Rossi Family solders were performing. He would be ashamed to face them.

He blamed Trent Marshall for his mounting problems. The man seemed invincible. Rossi was sure Marshall was the one who invaded his home and took out his entire security team. The eight men he had guarding Douglas' boyfriend and Marshall's wife couldn't stop him.

Now without the hostages, he had no hold over Douglas and Marshall. None at all.

To add to the paranoia Rossi was beginning to feel, Jimmy Shadow hadn't responded to his last message requesting assistance. Rossi was starting to consider taking Marshall out himself. He stroked the rifle lying on his desk.

The slim, bald man wearing horn-rimmed glasses turned his van into the parking lot of the warehouse on the Oakland waterfront. His cousin walked swiftly from the warehouse to climb into the passenger seat.

"What has happened this time, Gaetano?" the driver asked. Even though they were cousins, he was several years older than Guy. He had been called many times on nights like this when the younger man was in trouble.

"It's nothing, Filippo," Guy said. "Don't worry about it. I just need to get out of town and lay low for a while."

"Where do you want to go now?" Filippo asked.

"Can I spend the night at your house? In the morning I can get some cash and hit the road."

"Yes, of course you're welcome to stay with me," Filippo said. "I owe your dead father that much."

Filippo drove to the area in San Francisco's North Beach known as Little Italy. Guy hated it that his cousin still lived in the old neighborhood. Filippo lived in his parents' house. It was the only house he had ever inhabited.

Filippo didn't know that before the night was over he would die in that same house.

Thursday, August 4th

The magic hour. Time for Trent's symptoms, if there were to be any, to appear.

He was standing silently in their bedroom when she awoke. The Desert Eagle was in his hand.

"Trent," she said softly, "are you all right?"

He motioned for her to be quiet. He was listening to something.

At last he spoke in a whisper.

"There's someone here," he said. "A voice. It's speaking to me."

"What is it saying, Trent?"

"I can't quite make it out."

He moved down the hall to the living room. Darcey got out of bed and followed him, moving as quietly as she could. She didn't want to startle him.

"Turn what on?" he heard him say. "You want the lights on?"

Darcey didn't hear anyone else talking.

"I don't have a lantern," Trent said. "Might find a flashlight somewhere around here."

Darcey still heard no one else speaking.

"I understand. We're being careful," she heard Trent say. "I know they might bring the fight to us. They've already tried that without success."

Darcey eased into the living room. Trent was standing near the entry door, looking around, the Desert Eagle still in his hand.

"Where are you going?" he asked. "I'm going with you."

Darcey watched as Trent opened the door and stepped into the hallway. She was alarmed. He was wandering around with a high-powered gun in his hand, listening to voices that no one else could hear

She followed him into the hall. He was standing still. Listening.

"This hall has bad exposure," Darcey heard him say.

He was speaking loudly. Darcey was becoming more concerned. She feared he would awaken her neighbors.

"Get out of here!" Trent unexpectedly exclaimed, loudly.

Darcey's worst fear was confirmed when Preston Johnson opened his door and stepped into the hall, his ever-present cane in hand.

"Darcey, is everything all right?" the old man asked. He was watching Trent closely.

"Oh, Preston, I'm so sorry if we woke you," Darcey said. "No, everything's not all right. Trent is hearing voices. I'm really worried about him."

"Yes, I can see why you would be. And that's a very large weapon in his hand."

"I have a great phone," Trent said, making no sense whatsoever. "Great coverage."

He felt in the pockets of his pajama pants.

"Can't seem to find it right now," he said.

"Maybe this is an opportunity to help him, Darcey," Preston suggested. "I don't think he would hurt either one of us even if he's not fully conscious. Perhaps we could offer to help him find his phone."

Darcey nodded. She approached him slowly, quietly.

"Sweetheart, you left your phone in the bedroom," she said, speaking softly. "Let me help you find it."

The sound of her voice seemed to draw him out of whatever trance he was in. She reached out for the Desert Eagle. Meekly, he let her take it from his hand.

Preston stepped up at that point and took Trent by the arm.

"Let me help you, young man," he offered.

Trent looked at him blankly but didn't pull away. Together they led Trent back into the condo. Leaving the Desert Eagle with Preston, she guided Trent back to their bedroom.

Once he was safely in bed and had gone back to sleep, she joined Preston in the living room.

"I'm really sorry that we disturbed you so early in the morning, Preston," she said.

"You didn't disturb me," he said. "I'm a very old man, Darcey. At my age sleeping through the night is a rare luxury. I was awake. But I'm concerned about Trent.

And with that, Darcey unloaded the stress they had been under since their return from Europe. The horrible insect that had transmitted a previously unknown spirochete to Trent; the numbness in his hands and feet; the hallucinations; the kidnapping; the violent, bloody rescue Trent, Christopher, and Nancy had accomplished just a few hours earlier.

"Hearing voices is one of the possible symptoms the doctors warned us about," Darcey said.

"I had no idea what you were going through, Darcey," Preston sympathized. "Remember you're not alone. I'm just across the hall anytime you need me."

"Thank you, Preston. You're a dear friend. I might very well call on you."

The old man rose and walked slowly to the door. When Darcey reached to open the door for him, he put his arms around her in a fatherly hug.

"I have come to think of you as a daughter, Darcey," he said. "And I think very highly of your choice in a husband. I wouldn't want anything to happen to either of you. Please know that. And please allow me to help in whatever way I can."

"Thank you, Preston. Thank you so much."

Back inside his own condo, Preston made a pot of coffee. He sat wrapped in a heavy robe to keep him warm in the chilled air on his terrace. Sipping his coffee. Watching the sun rise.

He was worried.

Christopher had directed his team to release Rossi's men the day before once Kiettisuk Jetjirawat, Lin Winters, and Abdul Rahman were booked and out of sight. He had also ordered that Abdul Rahman be allowed freedom for all his prayers, including the one usually delivered at 5:30 a.m.

The three gang leaders were to be released simultaneously after Abdul completed his prayers.

It was the Thai who took the initiative.

Kiettisuk Jetjirawat was pleased on his return to his Little Saigon penthouse. There was a crew already replacing the damaged gate leading onto his property. At least some things were being done properly, he reflected.

His night in jail and the questioning was absurd. Yes, they had shut down one of his prostitution dens. Yes, they had released twenty fresh, young beauties. Yes, they had cost him money. But they could not connect him to the operation.

Had they harmed him? No, they had not.

He had other hotels scattered through the area where he kept girls he imported. And, yes, he could easily import more. And the amount of money this travesty had cost him was relatively trivial.

What, then, was the point? And what role did Jonathan Rossi play in the events of the past twenty-four hours? One of Rossi's men was accompanying Lieutenant Mitchum. That man didn't seem to be a prisoner. He seemed more like a collaborator.

He reached for his telephone.

The Mad Dutchman returned to his Richmond warehouse apartment in a foul mood. The same slut who had been in his bed when the cops broke in was still in his apartment. She was dressed now but he'd change that. Slap her around. Use her. That would put him in a better mood.

The bottle of red wine was still sitting on the table near his bed. He upended the bottle and drank deeply. It wasn't enough.

He, too, was thinking about Rossi's man who accompanied the cops when they raided him yesterday. That man didn't seem to be a prisoner.

He opened the small wooden box resting on the table near the wine bottle. The bag of white powder wasn't there.

"Where's my stash?" he demanded. "You'd better not have done it all."

"It's right here, baby," she whined, producing the bag from the pocket of her jeans. "You know I wouldn't do that. I only did a line because I was so scared."

The Dutchman spilled a little of the white powder onto a small mirror. Using a razor blade, he shaped it into two straight lines, each about two inches long. He used a rolled up hundred dollar bill that he kept close at hand for just this purpose.

He refused to freebase coke or do crack. He enjoyed the rush from the cocaine but had no intention of becoming a crackhead. And he didn't want any crackheads around him. They weren't reliable.

He snorted a line of coke into each of his nostrils. He closed his eyes to feel the drug take effect. Then another deep slug of wine.

"Get your clothes off," he growled. "Time for you to pay for the coke you snorted."

Then his phone rang.

Darcey drove them to the hospital to which Scott and Miles had been taken. They heard Miles before they saw him.

When they entered Scott's room, they found Miles lying across Scott's lifeless body. Sobbing.

The tending physician met them halfway.

"I take it you're friends of Scott and Miles?" he said. When Darcey nodded, he continued. "I'm Doctor Bilko. I'm very sorry but Mr. Douglas has passed away. Only minutes before you arrived. He fought hard but his wounds were too great."

"How is Miles?" Darcey asked.

"Physically he's fine. His wounds were superficial. No broken bones. Bruises and minor contusions only," the doctor answered. "Emotionally… well, he's going to need every friend he has."

"He has friends, Doctor," Darcey said. "Good friends. We'll take care of him."

"I can write a prescription for something to help him with the stress…help him sleep. And for something to help with the depression I'm sure he will experience. But, frankly, I'm concerned about giving him a lot of pills. His emotional stability right now is…well…"

"We'll take him home with us," Trent volunteered. "We can monitor his medications."

Kiettisuk Jetjirawat didn't like talking to Lin Winters. Or the Mad Dutchman, as the man insisted on being called. At least his other three partners, vicious as they could be in business, were civilized in appearance and lifestyle. Winters was an animal.

"You got busted yesterday?" Winters responded when his partner described his experience of the day before. "I did, too. The cops came crashing in here before I was even out of bed. Shot one of my men. And for nothing. Questioned me about a couple of hits I had nothing to do with and released me this morning."

"Yes," Kiettisuk said, "much the same as my experience."

He saw no need to let the biker know that one of his operations had also been raided and shut down.

"If you and I got rousted, I wonder if our other partners got hit, too," Winters said.

Kiettisuk was pleased that Winters was the one to raise the issue.

"I don't know about Abdul," he replied in his buttery manner of speaking. "Interestingly enough, I saw one of Rossi's men accompanying the police."

"Yeah, so did I," Winters said. "And it didn't look like he was a prisoner."

"I had the same impression."

"I'm gonna call Rossi and ask him what's going on," Winters thundered.

"Perhaps it would be wiser," Kiettisuk said, speaking calmly, "to speak with Abdul before we contact Don Rossi. I will call him now, if you have no objection."

"That's a good idea," the Dutchman said, glad to avoid the chore. He would much rather spend the time with the now naked blonde waiting in his bed.

Abdul went straight to his shower when he arrived home. He would cleanse himself of the foul odors of the jail. While he was bathing, his chef would prepare his breakfast. In the Middle Eastern world breakfast was a favored meal.

He entered his dining room clean and fresh to find his table laden with freshly baked flat bread, salty white goat cheese, olives, both black and green, and labnah, that Middle Eastern favorite. Thick cream cheese drizzled with olive oil.

He was enjoying his meal, again secure within the serene walls of his home. The image of Rossi's two men, sitting comfortably in the SUV as he was led by them, his hands cuffed behind his back, remained fresh in his mind. He intended to think about that later. After breakfast.

Then his phone rang.

Darcey gently led Miles to the guest room where he would stay until he had recovered from the shock of losing Scott. They had stopped by the home that Miles and Scott had shared so Miles could get some clothes and personal items.

Being in their home brought on another breakdown. Darcey held him for almost an hour as grief overflowed the banks of his emotional reservoir.

Trent occupied the time with finding a suitcase and beginning to pack things that Miles might need. The grieving man identified his closet. Trent began to pack, interrupted by the occasional, "No, not that." Even in the darkest moment of his life Miles remained committed to fashion.

The unseen voices Trent had heard earlier that morning had not reappeared. He was, however, cautious. Each time he heard "No, not that," he asked Miles to repeat it. He wanted to be certain a real person was directing his movements; not an unknown voice in his head.

In a guest room in the Nob Hill condo, Darcey helped Miles put things away. It was not yet noon. Darcey couldn't remember the last time she saw Miles eat. But, he told her, he wasn't hungry.

He wanted to take a hot bath, he told her. He felt so dirty. Then he would like to sleep but didn't think he could.

"I can give you something to help you sleep, Miles," she said. "The doctor prescribed it for you."

When he had changed into the long, pink night shirt he favored for sleeping, Darcey brought him a glass of water and a pill. He swallowed the pill and was asleep within minutes. Darcey left the water at his bedside.

Abdul was not pleased when he received the call from his Thai partner. He was already concerned with the message from Iraq, received while he was being held incommunicado in a federal jail. The $10 million he had directed Rossi to transfer in a quick burst to a recipient in Iraq had not been received. Abdul had made the request almost a week ago. It was another thing he intended to consider after breakfast.

But now Kiettisuk was saying he was rousted by local police at the same time that Abdul was being humiliated by the FBI, paraded publicly in handcuffs. And, he was being told, their ruffian partner, the so-called Mad Dutchman, received the same treatment.

Was Rossi also taken in? Abdul wondered. Kiettisuk didn't know the answer to that question but noted the presence of one of Rossi's men accompanying the local police.

"Interesting," Abdul said. "Two of Rossi's men were with the FBI agents who came for me. Neither of them was cuffed."

"Something is going on, Abdul," Kiettisuk warned, unnecessarily. "Is our friend Rossi up to something? What would he gain by teaming up with American law enforcement?"

"Nothing I can think of," Abdul replied, "unless it has more to do with keeping us occupied. I can think of no other reason."

"Yes, there are several reasons why Rossi might want to divert our attention," Kiettisuk carried on. "None of them bode well for us. I think perhaps one of us should call Rossi."

"I have reason to speak with him on another matter," Abdul said. "Would you trust me to make that call and raise this latest issue with him as well?"

"Certainly. You have proved yourself to be a trustworthy partner. Three of us seem to be targets of someone for reasons unknown. It's important, therefore, that we trust each other. Whatever is happening, whoever is behind it, has the potential to crush us. We must not let that happen."

Guy drove east in his cousin's van. Filippo had gone to bed as soon as they got to his house. Guy found a bottle of Prosecco in the refrigerator. He switched through the tv channels until he found a movie about a man with amnesia who kept killing people he thought were criminals. Turned out they were innocent. Just people who came across his path. The man with amnesia was the criminal. Guy thought the movie was hilarious.

When he heard Filippo snoring, he went quietly into the bedroom, his personal defense weapon in hand. He put a pillow over Filippo's face, wrapping the barrel in it to muffle the sound. He pulled the trigger. What was left of Filippo's face didn't appear human.

He took Filippo's wallet and ransacked the house looking for money. He found a little over eight hundred dollars. He took that and Filippo's credit cards. He also found his cousin's ATM card and, amazingly, Filippo kept the PIN on a small piece of paper in his wallet. Filippo wasn't too smart, Guy knew. He probably couldn't remember the PIN.

He would stop at an ATM machine on the way out of town. Knowing Filippo, his cousin had probably saved every dime he ever made. He might have enough money in his account for Guy to live on for quite a while.

His plan now was to drive toward Sacramento. He would find a cheap motel. There he would stay until he could figure out his next move. He was afraid of what Don Rossi might do to him when he found out that Scott Douglas had been shot.

Rossi was having a ham sandwich at the table overlooking his garden. He couldn't taste the food. Even the sight of his garden wasn't particularly pleasing today. There had been nothing but one disaster after another for almost a week. He didn't know how much more he could take.

His phone rang. The private phone to which only his three partners had access.

It was Abdul Rahman calling. As was their procedure, Rossi was quickly given another number to call. A burner phone. Hanging up his private line, he dialed the new number on his own throwaway phone. Burner to burner.

He was about to learn how much worse his life could become.

"Hello, Abdul," he said, a syrupy greeting. "How nice to hear from you. I trust all is well."

"No, Jonathan, all is definitely not well," Abdul said. "By chance did you have a visit from any law enforcement agency yesterday?"

"No," Rossi said, suspecting that this call would not go well. "I was visited by someone in the middle of the night recently who wiped out my entire security detail. Fortunately my family and I weren't here at the time. But I have had no visits from any law enforcement agency. Why do you ask?"

"Merely because Kiettisuk, the Mad Dutchman, and I were all taken in handcuffs for questioning," Abdul said, a thought beginning to nag at the back of his mind. "We were held overnight in stinking jail cells. And for no reason. They had no charges against any of us. Do you know anything about that, Jonathan?"

"No, nothing," Rossi said, his hands beginning to shake. "Why would I know anything about that?"

"You were the only one of us not rousted by police," Abdul said, speaking slowly, deliberately. "All three of your partners found it an interesting coincidence that each of us saw one of your men accompanying the police. In my case, two of your men were with the FBI."

Rossi felt the blood drain from his head. He thought he might faint. So that's what happened to the four men he had watching Douglas' condo and Darcey's office.

"I assure you, Abdul, I know nothing about that. I do know that four men I had keeping an eye on some people were picked up."

"The men we saw weren't in handcuffs. I should say they appeared more as collaborators than prisoners."

Sweat was now rolling down Rossi's face. How could this be happening?

"I have no idea what those men might have done. I assure you, Abdul, if the cops turned them I will make them pay. I promise you that. And I apologize for the inconvenience they might have caused you. How can I make this right?"

"We'll talk about that, Jonathan," Abdul said, a sly smile splitting his usually stern visage.

"As you wish, Abdul."

"Now, Jonathan, tell me, what has happened to the $10 million of my funds that I directed be transferred via quick burst? I gave you that direction almost a week ago. I received word that the transaction has not been completed."

Rossi closed his eyes. He had been praying Abdul wouldn't ask about the transfer.

"I don't know, Abdul," he said, stammering more than he wanted. "I'll look into it immediately. I will make it happen."

"See that you do," Abdul said as he ended the call.

Rossi stared at the phone. Abdul had hung up on him. He had never done that before. Never. Their relationship had always been cordial. It was necessary to have a strong, positive relationship in order for their fiduciaria to succeed.

The ancient system of hawala on which the fiduciaria was based depended on trust. Without hawala the fiduciaria would collapse. If that occurred before he chose the timing to exercise the tontine, all would be lost.

He went into his office and sat at his desk. He ran his hands yet again over his rifle. Someone had taken out four of his security guards. What if it was not Marshall? Could it have been one of his partners? But why?

He called for Peter, his most trusted man. He was born Pietro. He anglicized his name without hesitation when Jonathan suggested it. Peter showed his loyalty in many ways.

"How many men do we have patrolling the grounds, Peter?" Rossi asked.

"I had eight brought in after the invasion we suffered."

"Double it," Rossi ordered.

"Yes, Don Rossi." Peter didn't question his orders. He obeyed. When asked, he advised. Rossi wasn't asking.

He made a mental note to keep his own weapon close, at least until whatever was going on had worked itself out. Peter favored a larger version of the Heckler & Koch submachine guns with which two of the ill-fated security men had been armed. With this weapon, Peter feared nothing.

Abdul was surprised when Rossi told him that an unknown assailant had taken out his security guards. That was something else to think about. Clearly someone was playing games. He had assumed it was Rossi. Perhaps more than one player had stepped onto the field.

Now it was time to talk to his other partners. Abdul called Kiettisuk Jetjirawat first.

"I think we have a problem," the Middle Easterner reported to his Southeast Asian ally.

"Yes, there is no doubt about that. The questions are, 'What, exactly, is the problem?' and 'What do we do about it?'"

"I think you and I should meet face to face with Winters. This is serious, Kiettisuk, and requires serious discussion and coordination."

"May I offer to host the meeting?" Kiettisuk offered, diplomatically. "I know your hospitality to be unparalleled. However, our less cultured ally might bring with him companions and substances that would be offensive in your devout home."

"Your offer is kind, and graciously accepted."

Rossi used another burner to dial Scott Douglas. It was not Douglas who answered.

"I'm calling for Scott Douglas," Rossi said. "Have I dialed a wrong number?"

"No, this is Scott Douglas' number," Christopher answered. "Unfortunately Mr. Douglas can't come to the phone."

"Please tell him this is an urgent call," Rossi insisted.

"Scott Douglas is dead, Mr. Rossi," Christopher said, correctly guessing who was calling. "He died trying to protect Miles Diaz-Douglas from your thugs."

Rossi ended the call. Again he felt the blood rushing from his face, leaving him pale.

Douglas dead? The idiot Gaetano hadn't mentioned that in his report of last night's disaster.

Douglas was the key to Rossi's money laundering operation. An attorney on Rossi's payroll had enough knowledge of the system to continue it in partial operation temporarily. But he didn't have the detailed records. Douglas kept that information himself. Without him the ability to continue the operation indefinitely was compromised.

With Douglas' death his successor at the firm would order an audit. That was normal procedure. It was imperative that the right person was chosen to succeed Douglas. Rossi was certain he could arrange that.

But what of the records that Douglas must have kept hidden away? Of course Douglas would have kept them on his computer. That's the way finance was done these days.

He had to get his hands on Douglas' computer. He would have a lap top, Rossi guessed. A machine he could take home with him. He knew Douglas often worked from home.

He had to get a man into Douglas' home to find that computer. He called for Peter again.

Kiettisuk Jetjirawat entered through the front door of the modest Thai restaurant not far from his penthouse apartment in Little Saigon. The Mad Dutchman and Abdul Rahman would enter through the rear door. He couldn't care less if the Dutchman was offended. He did regret that Abdul should be subjected to such a rude requirement. It was necessary to avoid, to the extent possible, the wrong eyes seeing them together.

The private room arranged for them was more than adequate. It approached the elegant. He had selected the menu himself.

His partners would be served Pla Muek Yang, grilled squid in a tangy sauce with peanuts and cilantro; Som Tum, green papaya salad with dried shrimp, fish sauce, tamarind juice and chiles; and yellow beef curry with potatoes.

All were Thai specialties. He thought Abdul would enjoy them.

The Middle Easterner was the first to arrive. He slid noiselessly into the room. Kiettisuk rose as Abdul entered, pressing his hands together, fingers extended upward in the traditional wai greeting.

"Welcome," he said, with a slight bow.

"As-Salam-u-Alaikum," Abdul intoned, honoring Kiettisuk with the greeting usually reserved for fellow Muslims. "Peace be unto you."

As the two men sat at the table, a pretty young Thai woman brought warm jasmine tea.

"This tea is excellent, Kiettisuk."

"I am glad it pleases you, Abdul," he replied, modestly. "I suspect our third party will find it less pleasing."

With perfect timing they heard the distinctive roar of a motorcycle at the rear of the building. Seconds after the sound died the Mad Dutchman entered the room, dressed in jeans, leather boots, denim jacket with his gang colors over a black tee shirt. His long, unkempt hair and beard gave him the wild look of a man barely in control of himself.

"Good evening, Dutchman. Welcome," Kiettisuk said. "May I offer you a cup of jasmine tea?"

"Tea?" Winters laughed. "No, I don't want no tea. I'll have a beer."

"A Hoegaarden, please," Kiettisuk said to the young waitress.

"Make it two," Winters growled.

After serving the beer, the waitress set a bowl of steaming rice by each of the men. She quickly returned with large plates of the steamed squid, green papaya salad, and green curried beef.

Kiettisuk and Abdul helped themselves to all three dishes. Abdul complimented Kiettisuk on his choice of restaurants.

Winters pushed the squid and papaya aside.

"What's this green stuff?" he asked, gruffly.

"It's beef curry with potatoes," Kiettisuk replied, controlling his irritation at the biker's rudeness.

"Guess I'll have some of that," he said. "At least it's American."

As the meal came to an end, Abdul reported on his conversation with Rossi. Rossi, he said, had not been bothered by any law enforcement. He also, Abdul told his partners, denied any knowledge of his men collaborating with any of the agencies. Rossi said they had disappeared. He told Abdul he didn't know what had happened to them until the Middle Easterner told him about seeing them with the cops.

Winters slammed his fist down on the table.

"I don't believe it. Rossi's up to something. He's messing with us."

"It gets worse," Abdul said calmly.

"How could it get worse?" Winters demanded.

Kiettisuk just looked at Abdul.

"I am concerned that games are being played with our money," Abdul responded. "A transfer I ordered almost a week ago has yet to be accomplished."

"That's it," Winters said, rising and drawing his Sig Sauer handgun. "The time for talking is over. Let's get him."

"We should not act rashly," Kiettisuk calmly suggested. "We can't just shoot Rossi. He controls the fiduciaria. If we do away with him we would have difficulty accessing our funds. We must proceed cautiously. And we must have more information."

Abdul looked at Kiettisuk thoughtfully.

"By any chance, my friend," he asked, "do you have a contact within the Rossi Family?"

"One would be foolish to play a dangerous game without taking all precautions," Kiettisuk replied with a small smile.

Miles slept through the afternoon. At 6:30 he walked unsteadily out of his bedroom.

Darcey and Trent were dining on spaghetti with meat sauce and garlic bread that she had made. Trent helped Miles into a chair at the table while Darcey prepared a plate for him. He took only a few bites before telling them he was going back to bed.

Later, Trent made gin and tonics for himself and Darcey. They sipped their cocktails in silence. Both feared Miles might not recover.

Friday, August 5th

Darcey woke at 4 o'clock. It was the hour she had come to dread.

She was relieved to find Trent sleeping peacefully beside her. Perhaps it would be a day without symptoms. They could use one of those.

She rolled over, gently laying one arm over his chest, one leg over his. He shifted slightly in his sleep, his hand coming up to cover hers.

It would be a good day.

At least for Trent's illness.

At eight o'clock Ross Brown called to say he had completed the computer game they asked him to develop. He told them he had loaded the data Scott provided. It was ready to do its work. All he had to do was touch one button when they gave him the word.

Christopher and Trent again followed a circuitous route using the power of the Bentley for the short trip to Brown's house. They had not identified Ross Brown or revealed this part of their plan to any of the other law enforcement agencies working with them.

So far they had encountered no interference from moles. But they weren't naïve. Criminal organizations at the level of the four they were confronting would have officials on their payrolls. Some in high positions. Thanks to Captain Albright they already knew about Deputy Chief Amanda Justice. No action had been taken against her yet. Not yet.

Once again in Brown's historic basement he showed them the "game" he had created. It was impressive. He lit it up for them on a dry run. It looked to Trent like one of those ant hills encased in plastic with thousands of small creatures moving through a maze of tunnels.

Except there were no animals. There were only lights. And the lights connected banks, investment firms, and other businesses in six Caribbean island nations, four scattered across the Pacific, two in Latin America, three in the Middle East, three in Africa, two in Asia. All were countries with few or no laws controlling the movement of money. Or countries that didn't enthusiastically enforce the laws that were on their books.

Surprisingly, three banks in France were included, as were one bank and three investment firms in Great Britain. In Italy there was only one bank. A bank, they suspected, controlled by Jonathan Rossi. In the case of those three countries, it meant high level employees were simply turning their heads. Failing to report transfers of funds.

"Mr. Douglas gave us all the information we needed to identify the businesses he was using to launder the funds of Rossi's fiduciaria," Brown said. "The fun for me was figuring out how to link them up, aim them all to one location, and program them to transfer funds in short bursts when I push this button." His finger hovered over a silver button.

"Not yet," Christopher said, anxiously.

Brown laughed. "No worries. I'm anxious to see it work but I won't get ahead of the game."

"So we can assume that in each of these circles along the electronic pathways you've connected up you have all the account numbers and which organizations are connected to them?"

"Absolutely," Ross said. "Mr. Douglas kept detailed records. For instance, Rossi has accounts in these two Caribbean countries, one here in the Pacific, one in Africa, two banks in France, one in Great Britain, and, of course, this one in Rome. There are also two banks in the U.S. One in New Orleans and another in Washington, D.C. And there's an investment firm in Shreveport." He lit up each small circle along the tiny electronic highway he had built each time he called out one of Rossi's interests.

"When you hit that button, Ross," Trent asked, how long will it take for the accounts to be emptied and the money sent on its way?"

"It will be instantaneous. If a banker, say here," he said, pointing to a Middle Eastern country, "was looking at an account belonging to the Scourge, it would simply show a zero balance when I hit the button. He would have no idea what happened. The account to which we were sending the funds would reflect the deposit just as quickly."

"We need to get on the phone with our friends in Great Britain, Paris, and Rome so they can be prepared. We also need to talk to FinCEN and the FBI. They should be ready to step into the offices of these firms as soon as you hit the button. We'll let Interpol be responsible for contacting the other governments. They'll have a better idea of which of them will take action against these rogue banks and which won't."

They spent the next hour on the phone, talking to their European allies, FinCEN and the FBI. They said they could be ready in three hours. It was agreed that at one o'clock Pacific Standard Time Ross would hit the button.

Other than those in the United States, the banks would be closed by then. They would reopen for full service Saturday morning in London and for drive through only in Paris. The bank in Rome was one of the very few Italian banks open on Saturday. The investment firms would be open at varying times, as would the banks and firms in the Caribbean, the Pacific, Latin America, Africa, the Middle East and Asia. Many of them had staff on duty twenty-four hours a day to accommodate large customers.

They would all be stunned to discover that huge accounts were emptied, the funds transferred to a single account in the Rome bank. In those countries serious about enforcing laws against money laundering, the staffs on duty would be further surprised to find members of their country's police as well as Interpol at their doors.

At exactly one o'clock, Ross pressed the magic button. Pressed it gleefully, Trent thought. Ross really did create, at least in his mind, a new game.

On the screen resembling a plastic-enclosed ant hill, the light began rapidly moving along the lines linking the round dots. As each dot was reached, it went dark. The signal that an account had been emptied.

In less than a minute, all the dots were dark but one. The bank in Rome, controlled by Jonathan Rossi, glowed brightly. So it should. Its coffers had been increased by more than $200 million dollars.

Peter was surprised to receive new orders. He didn't think it was time to put the tontine into motion. He didn't think Don Rossi was sufficiently in control. He decided to make some changes in the orders he had received. He made a few calls of his own. He would take twenty men with him and an eighteen wheeler.

He fitted his Heckler & Koch with its sound suppressor. His men, armed with the smaller H&K submachine guns and Sig Sauer semiautomatic handguns, were ordered to attach their sound suppressors as well. While the target was relatively secluded it wouldn't do to have the sound of gunfire rolling across the community.

Though he was unaware of it, Peter and his men arrived at the Richmond warehouse at the exact moment Ross Brown touched his magic game button. Five cars and a large truck. As the truck driver was backing up to the loading dock under Peter's direction, one of the warehouse doors rolled up. Two Barons of Lucifer stepped out of the dim indoor lighting.

"What's this?" one of them asked, tersely. His eyes focused on the nasty-looking rifle Peter was holding.

"Just conducting a little business," Peter replied with a smile. "Business is always good, right?" He put his arm around one of the Barons and led him back into the building. The other one stared at the truck for a few seconds, then followed.

Inside the warehouse were two stacks of recently arrived crates. One stack was marked "Furniture." Peter knew it contained Glock 40s, powerful handguns. Peter had heard the Glock 40 was capable of taking down vicious feral hogs.

The guns were intended for the FBI. The Barons had thought hijacking the shipment was a huge joke. The weapons would sell quickly on the black market for a healthy profit.

The second, smaller crates, marked "Candles," contained drugs. Heroin. Cocaine. Prescription painkillers. And Ecstasy, the party drug. Peter couldn't keep up with the various names for this one. It was Molly for a while. Now he was hearing it called Strawberries or Candy. It was all money to him.

"I'd better get the Dutchman," the first Baron said.

"Oh, don't worry about that," Peter said. "I'll take care of him."

With that he lowered his submachine gun and, with hardly any noise, left a trail of bullet holes beginning at the first man's right shoulder and moving across his chest. The second man took all three bullets in the belly.

As previously ordered, his twenty men spread out through the building, killing any Baron of Lucifer who showed his head. Thanks to the sound suppressors, Peter could hardly hear any noise, except for the occasional lucky shot a Baron got off before falling in a hail of bullets.

Peter followed in the wake of his soldiers to the second floor. While they broke into every room looking for Barons, he walked purposely down the hall. He kicked in the door of the Mad Dutchman's apartment and wasn't surprised to see the naked leader of the Barons aiming his semiautomatic handgun at the door.

The Dutchman made a fatal mistake. He let his surprise at seeing Peter leading the attack force slow him for a second. No more. Time enough for Peter to let loose with a burst that blasted the weapon from his opponent's hand.

"Oh, I've ruined your pretty little pistol, Lin," Peter said, with an evil laugh.

The Dutchman was overcome with rage. He charged Peter completely unarmed. Before he took three steps Peter riddled him with bullets. The Mad Dutchman was mad no more.

Nor was the unfortunate naked woman cowering in the bed behind him. Peter couldn't afford to leave her alive.

Two of Peter's men had been wounded. One was shot in the foot; the second in the neck. Peter shot them both in the head. He left their bodies on the warehouse floor.

No witnesses.

They were in and out within fifteen minutes. No Baron of Lucifer unfortunate enough to be at their headquarters was left alive.

The truck drove away with cargo worth millions.

Peter thought it had been a good day.

Darcey worked from home. She didn't want to leave Miles alone just yet. He continued to sleep. When he woke briefly that morning, she managed to get him to eat a few bites of scrambled eggs. She gave him one of the anti-depressants. He didn't need another pill to go back to sleep. He spent a second day in bed.

Trent came home at five o'clock. He seemed buoyant. Mixing martinis for both of them, he led her out onto the terrace to tell her about Ross Brown's game. How effectively it had worked.

When his phone rang, he was not surprised to see Christopher's name show up. They had fired yet another round into the den of snakes. He assumed the cop wanted to discuss the next step.

He was mistaken.

"Someone hit the Barons of Lucifer headquarters in Richmond today," Christopher said. "Nancy says not one Baron was left alive, including the Mad Dutchman. And any goods, whatever they might have had on hand, are gone. The ware house is full of nothing but dead bodies now."

Trent was taken aback. He hadn't expected that.

"Well, when you get the snakes snapping at each other, you don't know what will happen next," he said. "But I have to admit I didn't expect this. And the timing. This operation was carried out before it was known that Brown sent all the fiduciaria's funds to Rossi's bank in Rome. Does Nancy have any idea who might have done it?"

"We might have a pretty good clue. Two of Rossi's men were found dead on the scene."

"Maybe Rossi decided one or more of his partners were out to get him so he decided to strike first," Trent said. "Or maybe someone recruited a couple of Rossi's men just to set him up. Either way, our snakes are striking at each other. And that's exactly what we want them to do."

Trent and Darcey dined on Hunters stew, redolent with mushrooms, onions, and Louisiana spices. After dinner, Trent made them each a second martini.

"From now on events are going to be unpredictable, Darcey," he said. "I would appreciate it if you and Miles would stay here in the condo. It's a secure building."

"No argument from me," Darcey agreed. "One kidnapping a week is my limit."

"And keep the M16 right near."

Abdul was temporarily stupefied when a government official on his payroll called to tell him that the warehouse headquarters of the Barons of Lucifer had been attacked. He was told that all the Barons who were on site were dead. That included Lin Winters, aka the Mad Dutchman

When asked if the police had any idea who carried out the massacre, he was told only that they were guessing two of the dead worked for Jonathan Rossi.

Abdul immediately called Kiettisuk Jetjirawak who hadn't yet heard.

"Our partner has turned against us, Kiettisuk," Abdul said, barely able to control his already bad mood. "The question is now, 'What do we do about him?'"

"Yes, what indeed?" Kiettisuk replied. "We must plan carefully, Abdul. Let's think about it and talk later in the day."

Kiettisuk smiled as he ended the call.

Saturday, August 6th

Phones began ringing early.

Kiettisuk Jetjirawak received calls from banks and investment managers on two Caribbean islands, one Pacific island, two Asian nations, London and Paris. The message was all the same. The message was electrifying. Terrifying.

All Kiettisuk's accounts, even those under other names, had been emptied. Transferred electronically by burst transmissions.

Abdul Rahman received the same calls from one Caribbean island, one Pacific island, one Latin American nation, three Middle Eastern countries, and one investment firm in Paris. The message was the same. All accounts now reflected zero balances.

When the calling agents were asked, both men were told the funds were directed to a bank in Rome. When the accounts of Lin Winters, the Mad Dutchman, were included, more than $200 million had just been diverted to a bank controlled by Jonathan Rossi.

While Kiettisuk Jetjirawak had not seemed overly concerned when Abdul called with the news of the demise of the Barons of Lucifer, he was highly agitated when he called Abdul.

"We were foolish to delay moving against Rossi," Kiettisuk admitted. "He has ruined us."

"He has stolen many millions from us, Kiettisuk," Abdul replied. "But he has not destroyed us. We still control lines of business that are highly profitable. We will recover the millions we have lost. But we must eliminate Rossi now. Immediately."

"We trusted too much in allowing Rossi to administer the fiduciaria," Kiettisuk said. "We don't know enough about the process to reverse it."

"Perhaps our administrator can be convinced to reverse his actions," Abdul replied, "with the proper techniques of persuasion."

"I'm told that Rossi enjoys martinis," Kiettisuk said. "I'm also told that recent stress has led him to enjoy multiple martinis in the evening."

"The perfect time to discuss the situation with him," Abdul agreed with the implication. "But how do we get into his compound."

"I can arrange that," Kiettisuk said, with confidence.

"Then by all means, my friend, please do so. As soon as possible."

Abdul thought Kiettisuk was more confident than he would have expected. That was something worth thinking about.

Darcey had turned off all the lights and drew the drapes on all windows. Still Trent wore dark glasses. It was barely enough.

Another of the symptoms about which they had been warned. Dilated pupils. Light, even dim light, was painful to him. Darcey hoped this symptom, as had the others, would be of short duration.

Fortunately, he was in no pain. He could see well enough with the dark glasses. When he took them off, he was blinded by the light.

He was lying on the couch when Miles came in.

"Well, good morning, sunshine," Darcey said, trying to sound as cheerful as possible given the circumstances.

"Please, I'm up but not feeling like sunshine," Miles said. "And speaking of sunshine, why is there none in this room? It's as dark as night in here."

"I guess you might as well know, Miles," Darcey said, as she poured him a cup of coffee. "Trent is suffering a symptom of an illness he has contracted. There are several symptoms. Today his eyes are completely dilated. The least bit of light is blinding to him. Hence, even with no light in the room, the darkened glasses are a neccesity."

"How awful!" Miles exclaimed. "What happened? How did he get this disease?"

Darcey told him the whole story. He shuddered when she described the nasty little bug. Trent himself broke the tension in the room when he exuberantly described the hallucinations, the belief that they were in the Witness Protection Program and his early morning visit to Fairbanks.

That gave them all permission to laugh. Laughter was medicinal for all of them.

"I would be happy to make you a big breakfast, Miles, but I don't want to turn the lights on. Is there something I can get you that won't require me to be able to see well?"

"I'm not very hungry. Maybe a piece of toast? Would that be OK?"

"I think I can handle that. I had planned to make calas, another wonderful New Orleans treat that Ivy taught me to make. One of Trent's favorites. We'll do it another day."

Kiettisuk Jetjirawak called Rossi once again. He said he and Abdul Rahman would like to visit Rossi at his home on Sunday. Would eleven o'clock Sunday morning be convenient?

Rossi said of course he would be happy to see his two partners. He asked if the Mad Dutchman would be accompanying them. Kiettisuk said the Dutchman would not be available.

Rossi called again for Peter. He instructed him to send two men to Scott Douglas' condo in the Marina district. Have them search the place for his laptop and for any financial records related to the fiduciaria. He wanted it done that night.

"What if Mr. Douglas is there, Don Rossi? What are your instructions?"

"Don't worry about that. He won't be there," Rossi replied, not looking at Peter.

Peter left his boss' office wondering. This seemed unusual. He knew they were holding Douglas' boyfriend and her boss. Why would they need to burglarize Douglas' home? With his boyfriend in danger surely he would do as Rossi directed. Something wasn't right. He suspected Rossi hadn't told him everything.

Peter was correct. Rossi hadn't told Peter or anyone else about the rescue of the hostages the night before.

He certainly would not mention the death of Douglas. That was a tragedy that might bring down Rossi's fiduciara, the tontine he had planned, and perhaps the Rossi Family itself.

He had to think. He had to come up with a plan. When he had a plan, of course he would share it with Peter. He relied on Peter completely and would trust him to carry out the plan.

Think, Rossi. Think. What would your father do? What would your grandfather do?

The usual cocktail hour at the Nob Hill condo was canceled this evening. There was no way they would let Miles have a drink given the medications he was taking. And they didn't think it hospitable for them to indulge while denying him.

Darcey prepared a light dinner of grilled cheese sandwiches. Miles seemed to have recovered his appetite. He ate one whole sandwich and half of another.

"I think I'd like to go to our condo this evening, if it's not too much trouble," he requested.

"No trouble at all," Darcey said. "I'll be happy to drive you."

"You can drive him, Darcey," Trent piped up, "but I'll be with you."

"Do you feel up to it?" she asked.

"I feel fine. I just can't see in bright light. As long as I have these dark glasses I can see just fine. And with all the lights off I don't even need the glasses. If we run into trouble, this might be the best night for it," he said, with some amusement.

"We'll wait until full darkness falls before driving to the Marina."

"And I want you to keep your commitment," Trent said. "Bring your gym bag."

The two men Peter sent also waited for darkness. The condo Scott and Miles had occupied was not in a secure building. It was a simple matter to slip the lock on the door leading into the condo.

They immediately spotted the desk at which Scott had worked from home. There was no computer of any type on it. They went through each drawer of the desk, looking through every file, every sheet of paper. Trying to find anything remotely connected to Don Rossi, any of his partners, or the fiduciaria.

They searched the house. Every room. Emptying drawers.

Nothing.

They took down every painting, every wall hanging looking for a hidden safe.

Nothing.

They slit all the cushions on the furniture, all the mattresses.

Nothing.

They were ready to give up and leave when they heard someone at the door. They quickly switched off the lights. It seemed a reasonable thing to do.

It was a mistake.

Darcey had seen the strip of light under the door. She was surprised since to her knowledge no one had been in the condo since they had brought Miles there to pick up some clothes for him.

Then the lights were switched off. She grabbed both Trent and Miles by their arms and quietly pulled them away from the door, whispering so that only the two of them could hear.

Inside Rossi's burglars drew their handguns and found cover, one at the end of a large couch, the other behind a Queen Anne chair. He didn't know it was a Queen Anne chair. He only knew he could hide behind it and it might stop a bullet.

Outside, Trent asked Miles if there was a way to switch off the lights in the hallway. Miles said there was a fuse box near the elevator.

Trent directed Miles to flip the switch in the fuse box to darken the entire floor. Then lie down on the floor in the hallway, away from the front door. He told him to stay there and make not a sound.

He told Darcey to prepare her M16. He wanted her to get on the floor. When he opened the door he wanted her to crawl into the room on her belly.

He said with the lights in the condo and the hallway out, whoever was inside couldn't see him but he would be able to see them as though they were in a spotlight.

If they started shooting, Darcey should look for the flash of their gunshots and fire at those.

When Miles had extinguished the hallway lights, Trent removed the dark glasses and quietly opened the door. It was black as tar for everyone but Trent. He could see one man behind the Queen Anne chair; the other at the end of the couch. Both were armed only with handguns, not the submachine guns he had encountered at the Rossi compound.

"You, at the end of the couch. And you, behind the chair. Drop your guns and stand up."

As soon as he spoke, he stepped forward and to his right. He had guessed right.

The burglars were taken by surprise. They could see no one. But the voice was real.

The man behind the couch fired at the direction he thought Trent's voice had come from. But Trent had moved. All he did was give Darcey her target. She fired a three round burst from the M16. The powerful weapon

NEIGHBORS AND OTHER STRANGERS

smashed through the arm of the couch and made a mess of the burglar's left femur. He wouldn't be walking with that thigh wound for a while.

Trent didn't have to wait for the man behind the chair to fire. He could see him clearly. One .50 caliber round punched through the chair, striking the would-be gunman's left hand. His gun hand. He dropped the weapon and leaped to his feet, his hands up.

"Please, I give up," he bawled. "Don't shoot."

"Me, too," they heard from the end of the couch. "But I can't stand up."

"Kick your guns out into the middle of the floor," Trent ordered. "Keep your hands where I can see them."

Putting the dark glasses on again, he told Miles to restore the lighting on the floor. Darcey turned on the lights inside the condo.

Miles was furious when he saw the condition of his home.

"What have you done to our home?" he shouted. "It's ruined. You have destroyed it."

The two men said nothing. Trent dragged the man Darcey had wounded in the thigh out into the middle of the room.

Darcey called 9-1-1 requesting two ambulances. She told the operator one burglar had a relatively minor injury. The second man's wound was more severe. She said he would survive but needed immediate medical attention.

Trent called Christopher and quickly told him what had happened. He said it would be helpful if Christopher himself could get to the condo and make sure they didn't get thrown in jail.

That's exactly what the first two uniformed officers had in mind when they arrived. They arrived at the same time as the EMTs. While the medics tended to the wounded, the officers confronted Trent, Darcey, and Miles.

All the two uniforms knew was there were two men wounded by two citizens armed with illegal weapons. Trent and Darcey both produced the papers showing them to be consultants to the SFPD and the permits and waivers authorizing them to be in possession of the weapons. Miles showed them his identification and told them this was his home. He didn't know why, he said, the two wounded men had ransacked the condo.

The two young officers weren't sure enough of themselves to accept what seemed to them to be a very unusual situation.

They took the guns away from Trent and Darcey. Handcuffs were out and ready to be applied. Then one of the young officers looked suspiciously at Trent.

"Take off those shades," he ordered.

"I can't. I'll be blinded if I take them off."

"I said take off the shades," the officer repeated.

At that point Darcey spoke up. "He's suffering from an illness that has his eyes completely dilated. If you force him to remove the glasses he will not only be unable to see, he will be in pain."

"That's his problem, lady," the officer said.

"No, officer, it's your problem," said a deep, rumbling voice from behind the group.

They turned to see Sergeant Christopher Booth.

"If you want a career with this police department, officer, with any police department for that matter, you'd better learn judgment. You'd better learn when to listen and when to speak."

"You know these people, Sergeant?" a suddenly nervous young officer asked.

"I do. They are exactly who they say they are. Who those papers, signed by Chief Charles Marvin, which you ignored, say they are. They are assigned to me as part of a special operation about which you know nothing and should know nothing. Furthermore, unless you take this as a learning opportunity, you will never know anything about such things."

The young officer quickly returned their weapons. He had the good sense, and the grace, to apologize for his behavior. He was also smart enough to find other tasks needing his attention.

"What is this all about, Trent?" Christopher asked.

"We were taken by surprise. We brought Miles over here to pick up a few things he needs and walked in on a burglary. We called on them to surrender and they opened fire."

"Trent's eyes are completely dilated, Christopher," Darcey said.

She explained that, while the dilation caused Trent some discomfort through the day, it had proved an advantage in the confrontation with the burglars. When Miles put the floor in total darkness, Trent could see clearly. The bad guys were shooting in the blind.

"That's not going to be permanent, is it?" Christopher asked.

"I sure hope not," Trent answered. "All the symptoms so far have been very short lived. Hopefully this one will be also."

More police officers, including a scattering of detectives were on the scene. Christopher said he would hang around for a while but they were free to go. He said they would need to make a statement but they could do that later.

Detective Harry Sherman recognized the burglars as Don Rossi's men. He was anxious to report to Rossi.

As soon as he could get away for a few minutes, he went downstairs and stepped around the corner of the building. He thought he would have privacy there.

The phone rang four times before Rossi answered. His voice sounded slightly slurred. Sherman thought he had awakened him.

"This is Harry Sherman, Don Rossi," the crooked cop said. He went on to report the disaster.

"Are the two men alive?" was Rossi's only question.

"Yes, Sir," Sherman answered. "One of them has only a minor wound. The other's wound is more serious but not fatal."

"Pity," was Rossi's only comment before ending the call.

Sherman was surprised at Rossi's response. It was unnerving to know that the man had such little regard for his employees.

He was even more surprised when he turned to see Sergeant Booth standing behind him.

"Interesting conversation, Sherman," Christopher said, pulling a handkerchief from his pocket. "I'll take that phone."

"You have no right to confiscate my private property," Sherman said, the shakiness of his voice invalidating his pretense of confidence.

"Give me the phone, Sherman," Christopher repeated. "Don't make me take it from you. It won't be hard."

Sherman handed the phone to the sergeant who was careful not to touch it except with the handkerchief.

"At eight o'clock Monday morning, you and I will meet with Captain Albright," Christopher directed. "Be there. If you're not, we'll find you. You still might be able to save yourself. But if you try to run, you're dead. If we don't get you, Rossi will. Now get out of my sight."

Christopher made Sherman leave first. There was no way he would turn his back on the cowardly crooked cop.

In the hills at Atherton, Rossi mixed a fourth cocktail.

Another disaster.

Another martini.

Sunday, August 7th

Trent awakened at seven o'clock. He was hesitant to open his eyes. He lay in self-imposed darkness for a few minutes.

Might as well get it over with, he thought.

He opened his eyes.

They were no longer dilated. His vision had returned to normal.

He lay in bed for minutes longer. There had been so many symptoms. This morning there seemed to be none.

No hallucinations. At least none that he knew about.

No voices speaking only to him.

Vision normal.

It was starting out to be a good day.

He made it better. He put his arms around Darcey, pulling her to him. She was only half awake but she returned his kiss when she felt his lips touching hers. They lay for long minutes in each other's arms.

Later, she lay with her head on his shoulder, his arm around her.

"Can I assume there are none of those pesky symptoms this morning?"

"None. The world looks normal. Did I tell you any wild stories in the middle of the night?" he asked, referring to the earlier hallucinations.

"Not that I recall."

They wandered into the kitchen, Darcey in her robe, Trent in the long sleeve tee shirt and black pajama pants he always slept in.

They were surprised to find Miles, still in the tight-fitting, pink tee shirt covering him halfway to his knees, flitting about the kitchen. He had found lox and cream cheese in the refrigerator. Capers and bagels and a red onion in the pantry. He had chopped the onions, and laid out a breakfast feast on the kitchen island.

"Girl, I thought you were going to kill that poor man from the noises I heard coming from your bedroom," he teased, sounding more like his old self.

"Oh no, there's been nothing the least bit unpleasant this morning," Trent intervened. "It's a beautiful day."

"And you look like the Miles I used to know," Darcey added.

"I feel more like myself," he replied. "Scott died because he loved me. He was the only person in this world who ever loved me. I'll be grieving his death for a long time. I have been feeling like something inside me died with him. But those men destroying our home last night brought whatever that was back to life."

"That's great news, Miles," Darcey said, giving him a hug.

Trent poured coffee for both of them. Darcey joined him on a stool at the kitchen island.

"They killed Scott. I won't let them kill his memory," Miles continued. "Darcey, I want to make arrangements to get all the damaged furniture out and new furniture brought in. I want to clean up the mess and restore our home."

"Let's do it," Darcey replied, enthusiastically. "I'll get a cleanup crew over there to clear out the old stuff. And let's go shopping."

"Trent, I know I have things to take care of. I have to meet with the funeral home. Scott and I agreed we will both be cremated and our ashes mixed together," Miles said with a whimsical smile. "And I have to meet with our lawyer about the will and such. That's for tomorrow. For today, do you mind if we have a girls' day out?" Miles asked.

"You two go for it. It's time."

He didn't want to spoil the mood by reminding Darcey to take her gym bag. He trusted her to remember her commitment.

In the hills of Atherton Rossi slept until well past eight o'clock. He rang down to the kitchen for coffee. There was no answer.

Putting a red silk robe on over his blue silk pajamas, sliding his feet into leather, sheepskin-lined slippers, he walked on unsteady legs downstairs. There were no servants in sight.

"What's going on?" he said aloud.

In the kitchen he made his own coffee. With a cup in hand, he walked outside, seeing no one. He walked around the pool to the guest house. There was no one there either.

He checked all the bedrooms. Empty.

He was alarmed. His hand was shaking enough to slosh coffee over the rim of the cup.

He returned to his office. The assault rifle lay on his desk. He took it upstairs to his bedroom.

Trent volunteered to clean up the kitchen while Darcey and Miles got dressed, preparing for their girls' day out.

The doorbell rang just as he finished wiping down the kitchen island. Preston Johnson was at the door. Trent welcomed him in. The old man accepted the offer of coffee. Trent filled mugs for both of them.

"How are you feeling today, my boy?" Preston inquired. "Any more symptoms?"

"Today is a good day," Trent responded. "Yesterday not so much, though it turned out well."

"Oh? More symptoms yesterday?"

"Yes, my pupils were fully dilated. I had to stay in a darkened room or wear heavily darkened glasses if I went outside. It was uncomfortable. Not especially painful as long as I stayed in the dark."

"I see," Preston said. "Well, I'm pleased that you're having a better time of it today."

Though he tried to make light of it, the old man was concerned.

Darcey and Miles went first to their office building. They had catalogues there with furnishings from all the suppliers with whom they did business. Darcey brewed tea for them to sip as they flipped through the pages.

"I'm thinking clean. Modern. Sleek silhouettes. Sexy. Like me!" Miles pronounced dramatically.

"Yes, just like you," Darcey agreed, glad to see him showing some life again. "And don't forget that brass is back. Brass is very in this year. Burnished brass."

They giggled their way through living room, dining room, and bedrooms. By the time they were out of tea, they had furnished Miles' condo. At least on paper.

"How in the world will I pay for all this?" he worried.

"Well, we'll get the firm's discount, which will lower the price significantly. If necessary, I'll have it billed to the firm and you can pay it back. I'll get a cleaning crew out there tomorrow. We can order the furniture to be delivered after they've finished their work."

"Oh, thank you, girlfriend," Miles gushed. "You're the best."

"Just taking care of my Chief Operating Officer," Darcey quipped. "Got to have you happy so I can go play."

"I'm not sure I'll ever be happy again," Miles said, turning serious. "But at least I'll recover enough to take care of business, Darcey."

"You'll be happy again, Miles. You won't ever forget Scott, nor should you. But you will be happy."

"I don't think I'll ever get married again," he said.

"Maybe. Maybe not. You don't have to be married to be happy."

"No, but it helps," Miles insisted.

"Some days, yes; some days no."

"I heard those noises from your bedroom this morning, girl. This definitely started as a 'yes' day."

"Oh, yes, it most assuredly did!" Darcey laughed.

The day wasn't going as well at the Rossi compound in the hills at Atherton. By 10:30 Rossi had dressed and was in his office. He was expecting Kiettisuk Jetjirawak and Abdul Rahman to arrive soon.

He still had found no one on the grounds. He didn't even know how they would get in. He would have to use the gate remote to buzz them in.

Since he discovered he was alone, he had kept the rifle with him. Now sitting at his desk, he had secured the weapon, barrel down, next to his right leg in the well of his desk. It would be out of sight of his visitors but he could reach it easily.

At exactly eleven o'clock, Peter stepped into his office. He held his own Heckler & Koch submachine gun in his hands. He was followed by Kiettisuk Jetjirawat and Abdul Rahman. Curiously, Abdul was dressed in traditional Arab robes rather than his usual western business suit. Rossi had never seen him wear the robes.

"Good morning," Rossi said, forcing a smile to his face. "Welcome. I would offer you refreshments but I find that my kitchen staff has taken a day off."

"That's quite all right, Jonathan," Kiettisuk said. "We're here on business. Serious business."

"Oh? Well, then let's get down to business. What can I do for you?"

"You can return the $200 million you took from your three partners," Abdul calmly demanded.

"$200 million that I took?" Rossi started to stand but didn't think his legs would hold him up. "I didn't take any money from you. I don't know what you're talking about."

"It's simple, Jonathan. All the accounts of your three partners in the fiduciara have been reduced to zero. All the funds were directed to the bank you control in Rome," Kiettisuk repeated, as if explaining it to a slow-witted child. "Only you could have done that. Or ordered it done."

"I assure you I gave no such order. I don't know anything about this. Let me get Giovanni Costa, the manager of the bank in Rome, on the phone. We'll get this straightened out. I can reach Giovanni at his home."

"Put your phone on speaker, Jonathan," Abdul said. It was not a request.

Rossi dialed the international number. After several rings, a voice answered.

"Ciao."

"Hello, Giovanni. English, please," Rossi said.

"Certainly, Don Rossi. How may I help you?" Costa inquired.

"Help me figure out what is going on. I'm told that over $200 million was transferred to the bank electronically. How could that have happened?"

"I assumed you ordered it, Don Rossi," Costa answered.

"I issued no such orders, Giovanni. I want that money returned to the rightful owners' accounts immediately."

"I'm sorry, Don Rossi, I can't do that."

"What do you mean you can't do that? I'm ordering you to do it!" Rossi was shouting into the phone.

"Please, Don Rossi. Certainly I would obey your orders if I could. I can't reverse the transactions because I don't have the account numbers, the banks or firms where the accounts are located. I don't have all the necessary details and I don't know the process you use for such transfers. I mean I physically can't do it. Only your Signor Douglas can do that."

"I see. Thank you, Giovanni. I'll get back to you."

Rossi ended the call. He was silent. He didn't know what to say.

Giovanni Costa laid the phone down on the desk in his home office when Rossi ended the call. He looked around the room. The representatives of the Direzione Investigativa Antimafia, the Guardia di Finanza, and the Arma dei Carabinieri stared back at him.

There was no warmth in their eyes. But at least he had done as he was told. It gave him no comfort as they led him from the room in handcuffs.

A similar scene was being enacted in the homes of officials of at least three banks in Paris; one bank and three investment firms in London. In the United States, the FBI was escorting bankers from their homes in New Orleans and Washington, D.C., as well as the head of an investment firm in Shreveport.

Miles and Darcey stopped for salads at one of their favorite cafes for lunch near their office. After the light lunch, they spent the next three hours going from one small shop to another. Looking for small decorative items. Little things that would make Miles feel at home.

"I want to keep Scott in the home with me," he told Darcey, "but I want a few new things to help me begin a new life."

Rossi wasn't thinking about starting a new life. He didn't know what to think. He was being truthful when he told his partners he didn't know what happened to their money. That he had not issued any orders, except for Abdul's instructions to transfer $10 million. The order that Douglas refused to carry out.

He looked blankly around the room. He knew Kiettisuk Jetjirawat and Abdul Rahman didn't believe him. Neither would the Mad Dutchman when he finally showed up.

He let his right hand slide under his desk, intending to grasp the weapon concealed there. Before he could do so, Kiettisuk produced a small Ruger hideout gun from his pocket.

"Put both your hands on the desk, Jonathan," he ordered.

It was then that Rossi learned why Abdul Rahman had chosen to wear his ancestral robes. He produced an M4 rifle, the smaller, modernized version of the M16.

Jonathan had no choice but to obey. He looked at Peter, expecting him to come to his defense.

Peter didn't move.

"Call Douglas," Abdul ordered. "If he did this, he can undo it."

"I can't call Douglas," Rossi said, misery in his voice.

"Why not?" Kiettisuk inquired.

"Scott Douglas is dead."

"Douglas is dead? How did that happen?"

"One of the dummies who works for me took it upon himself to shoot Douglas' boyfriend. Douglas threw himself between them to save the boyfriend's life by giving his own." There was no energy in Rossi's voice. None.

"Surely there's someone else who can manipulate the system. Did Douglas have an assistant?"

"Yes," Rossi replied in his lifeless voice. "But we can't find Douglas' files. Without those files, no one can operate the system."

"This smells of something rotten," Abdul said. "How convenient it is that just as over $200 million in our money is transferred to your bank, apparently the only man who could have done it, and who could have undone it, is killed by one of your men."

"If this is true, Jonathan," Kiettisuk added, "of what use to us are you?"

"He has holdings here," Abdul reminded Kiettisuk. "If he turns those holdings over to us at least a portion of our losses would be reimbursed. This house alone is worth perhaps $30 million."

"Yes, Abdul," Kiettisuk nodded. "Of course, you're quite correct. No matter how we determine the final solution that would certainly partially satisfy our claims against this man."

"NO!" Rossi shouted. "You can't do this to me. I'm the Don of the Rossi family. You can't treat me like a common worker!"

Kiettisuk Jetjirawat smiled.

"Are you quite done with your little snit?" he asked. "Look around you. Do you see anyone on the grounds? Do you see your once efficient security team? There is no more Rossi Family, Jonathan."

Rossi made no reply. He looked at Peter for support but saw none. He dropped his eyes to stare at his desk.

"Peter, help me," Rossi pleaded, begging for the first time in his life.

"My name is Pietro, you pompous, vain fool," was the reply, fully packed with the frustration of the years enduring Rossi's arrogance.

"Pietro, please keep Jonathan here while Abdul and I take the necessary steps to pursue this plan."

"Please watch him closely, Pietro," Abdul added.

Steve Burgess had stayed out of sight as much as possible since the night of the failed assassination by the two Barons of Lucifer. He had left his cheap hotel only to get food and booze. It was Sunday afternoon. He didn't think he could bear one more day staring at the dingy walls around him. It was time to take a chance.

Since he went into hiding he had stopped shaving and let his hair grow. With his shaggy, gray hair and matching whiskers, he thought he looked like just another San Francisco character. He was confident he wouldn't be easily recognized.

He found a dimly lit bar not far from his hotel. There were only a few customers. He sat at the bar and ordered a shot of tequila. The bartender was talking to another customer. It felt good to hear men's voices again.

After a second shot, he noticed the woman sitting alone at the far end of the bar. Probably a hooker. It had been a long time since he had been with a woman. Maybe it was time to risk that as well.

But then something the bartender said caught his ear. He ordered a third shot of tequila.

"Couldn't help but hear what you were talking about," Burgess said when the bartender was pouring the shot. "What was that about the Barons of Lucifer?"

"They're wiped out," the bartender answered. "Somebody hit them at their warehouse in Richmond. Killed every one there. Cleaned out everything in the warehouse. They even killed the Mad Dutchman, the gang's leader. The word is they caught him naked in bed with some woman. Fully loaded but blown away before he could get a shot off."

The bartender and Burgess both laughed at the joke.

Burgess thought that was good news. So much so that he ordered a fourth shot and told the bartender to pour one for himself.

"Here's to the memory of the Mad Dutchman," Burgess said, clinking glasses with the bartender.

With four shots of tequila under his belt, Burgess was feeling bold. He decided to stroll by the Nob Hill condo. He was curious how Marshall was faring with the little gift the former New Orleans cop had left for him. In his imagination, Marshall was suffering terribly. Maybe he was even dead by now. Burgess was ever hopeful.

By the time he reached the condo building he was puffing hard from the hike up the hill. Pausing for a few minutes to catch his breath, he used the time to look over the building. He saw nothing helpful.

He didn't want to hang around the front of the building too long. Once his breathing returned to normal, he walked on. At the corner of the next intersection, there was a bench. He found an old newspaper in a nearby trash can. He sat on the bench, pretending to read the paper while he kept an eye on the building.

It was a good cover. Lots of people out on a nice Sunday afternoon. Burgess was certain he would attract no attention.

Upstairs Trent was also feeling a bit hemmed in. Since Darcey had discovered that ugly little bug attached to him he had not been working out. He was starting to miss the exercise.

There were no symptoms today. He felt good. He decided to go for a run. He changed into a tee shirt and shorts and put on his running shoes.

Burgess couldn't believe what he was seeing. Trent Marshall came out of the building, ran up the hill toward Huntington Park.

Running! He was running! Burgess feared he would have a stroke. His brain might explode. He could not believe that Marshall showed no sign of illness. None.

He had no way of knowing the symptoms Trent had suffered or how serious his condition was. The doctors had said there would be good days and bad days. This was a good day. Burgess didn't know that.

He went back to the bar. He spent the rest of the afternoon there, kicking back shot after shot of tequila. He wanted to be drunk. He wanted to drink the vision of a healthy Trent Marshall from his memory.

With the altered state of his inebriated brain, he decided he could wait no longer. Obviously the nasty little bug had failed to do its job. He would have to kill Marshall himself.

He still had the electronic keys he had forced Piper to give him. He could get onto the secured floor and into their condo. He had the French revolver he had taken from the dead biker. He could do it.

The only question in his besotted mind was when.

It was in the late afternoon by the time Darcey and Miles returned. Trent had showered after his run. He spent the rest of the afternoon in the kitchen. He had meatballs in a spicy tomato sauce with pasta ready for them.

Miles told them to go out on the terrace. It was cocktail hour.

"No, Miles," Darcey said. "You can't drink with the medications you're taking. And it wouldn't be fair for us to enjoy a cocktail if you can't join us. That would be rude."

"Girl, for once will you please do as you're told?" Miles insisted. "I don't intend to have a drink. But you're doing so much for me. I don't want to be any more disruptive to your life together than I have already been."

"I'm not arguing," Trent spoke up. "I'll have bourbon on the rocks. You'll find a bottle of Rebel Yell in the liquor cabinet."

Darcey surrendered. "All right then. I'll have the same."

She thought Miles was going to be all right. It would take time. But he was going to survive.

Monday, August 8th

It was a day of appointments.

Harry Sherman was late for his. He wasn't at the precinct at eight o'clock. He came in just as Christopher was ready to ask the captain's permission to seek a warrant for his arrest. He looked like he hadn't slept.

Christopher told Captain Albright about the conversation he had overheard the night before. At least Sherman's part of the conversation. Sherman had mentioned Rossi's name but apparently Rossi had little to say.

"Has this phone been dusted for prints?" Albright asked.

"Yes, Sir," Christopher said. "I had that done as soon as I got in this morning. Only one set of prints. No doubt Sherman's."

Albright was feeling much better about himself since he had approved Christopher's operation. He had turned his head a few times in his career but never did anything definitively illegal. He despised crooked cops, especially since he realized how close he had come to being one.

"So what are we going to do with you, Officer Sherman?" the captain pondered.

Sherman sat silently. Head down. Eyes on the floor.

"First, put your badge and gun on my desk. Now!" the captain ordered.

Sherman unclipped the holstered Model 1911. He laid it on the captain's desk along with his badge.

"And the Glock in your ankle holster," the observant Christopher added.

Sherman unwrapped the strap holding the holster on his lower leg. He added that to the pile on his desk.

"Maybe we'll just do nothing," the captain mused. "Just kick you off the force. I wouldn't give a dime for your life if Rossi decides you're of no more use to him."

Sherman went pale. The captain was right. The crooked cop would be a dead former cop by the end of the day.

"You can't do that, Captain," Sherman pleaded.

"Of course I can. You're a disgrace, Sherman. You took money to sell out your colleagues. You put every officer on the force in danger. I can set you up for Rossi to take out and not lose a minute's sleep over it. You disgust me."

"I can help you, Captain," Sherman rushed to offer, now in a panic. "I'll turn state's evidence. I can tell you a lot about Rossi's operation. And about some of his partners."

Albright said nothing. He stared at Sherman. Finally he spoke

"I'm not sure how much help you can be. We already know a lot more about them than either you or they realize. But it never hurts to have another witness," he concluded. "Sergeant Booth, book this man into protective custody. We can hold him for a couple of days while we figure out what to do with him."

Trent, Darcey, and Miles decided they would all go together. It was a day for friends to support each other.

They would begin at the funeral home at 9:30 as Miles arranged for Scott's cremation. Scott was always insistent that he wanted no service. Perhaps only a few of their best friends gathering to toast his memory.

They decided to schedule the cremation for Thursday, August 11th. Miles asked Trent and Darcey to be there with him. He said he would then like to host a small gathering at the home he and Scott had shared, if the new furnishings were delivered by then. He would invite Mandy Rillard and Preston Johnson, the core of the group of friends, to toast Scott's memory.

A few tears flowed when they discussed the timing and the process. But Miles held up well. He was showing more signs of recovery each day.

The day's appointments started differently for Kiettisuk Jetjirawat and Abdul Rahman.

They agreed to meet at Abdul's home. Each summoned their teams of attorneys. Pietro accompanied Kiettisuk Jetjirawat.

The attorneys were instructed to work around the clock to prepare the necessary paperwork to transfer all holdings of the Rossi family to a new partnership between Spitting Cobra and the Scourge.

Rossi had reluctantly provided detailed lists of properties owned directly under his name, that of his family, and those registered in the names of numerous interlocking holding companies. Ironically, the list included the old building south of the city once used as a casino and for prostitution, still occasionally used for smuggling, and most recently the scene of a gun fight resulting in the release of two hostages as well as the death of the one man who could have saved Rossi.

The attorneys were told that the paperwork must be ready for signing in twenty-four hours. When the attorneys said they didn't know if they could meet that deadline, the response was not reassuring.

"See that it is done," Abdul warned. "If not...well, lawyers are expendable."

The attorneys left the meeting pale-faced and sweating. More than one regretted the decision to represent these deadly clients.

At eleven o'clock Trent and Darcey met with Doctor Slim and Doctor Raymond. Miles stayed in the waiting room thumbing through two month old celebrity magazines.

The doctors listened closely to Trent's description of the symptoms he had experienced. He described the hallucinations in a humorous manner, giving them permission to laugh with him. Doctor Raymond was especially impressed, she told him with an impish grin, that he was insistent on returning from Fairbanks before Darcey woke up in San Francisco.

They, too, were relieved to learn that each symptom had lasted only a matter of hours. Some even less. That, they agreed, was a very good sign. They were also pleased when he told them that he had taken none of the pain medication they had prescribed. So far he hadn't needed pain relief.

They said they were making some progress in their study of the spirochete causing the chaos in Trent's blood. They had not found a cure yet but they were hopeful. Meanwhile, they told him to continue with the antibiotics.

After lunch, they accompanied Miles to the office of the attorney who had prepared Scott's will. Robert Tracy was the consummate professional, striking the proper balance between sympathy and business.

"Miles, I can't tell you how sorry I was to hear of Scott's death. He was a good client, a good man, a good friend. I shall miss him, though I know you will feel his loss much deeper than will I," the attorney said.

"Thank you, Robert," Miles said, his eyes misting. "I know Scott thought highly of you. He had the utmost confidence in your ability to handle our affairs. And now I'm here for your guidance. What happens now?"

"Well, first you should know that you are the sole beneficiary of all Scott's holdings."

Miles nodded. "I thought that was probably so. But I'm not sure what all is included."

"To begin with," Tracy explained, "Scott had a fully paid up whole life insurance policy in the amount of $1 million. That, of course, is not subject to taxation."

Miles eyes grew wide, his face flushed as he realized the attorney had just told him he was now a millionaire.

"You know that all Scott's bank accounts and investments are joint accounts. As such, they are yours to draw on. You will simply be required to present a copy of the death certificate to each bank or investment firm in order to draw on the funds. Scott had prepared a Revocable Living Will so taxation will be minimal."

"I vaguely remember signing some papers but didn't really pay much attention. I trusted Scott to handle all our business," Miles said, awe in his voice.

"Additionally, you might not be aware Scott transferred the condo you shared to you. You are, and have been for some time, the sole owner of the property, which is unencumbered. That will not be affected by Scott's death. The same, by the way, with the Mercedes he purchased last year. Six months ago he transferred the title to you."

Miles was feeling faint. He fanned his face with one hand.

"I had no idea," he said.

"For whatever reason, Scott felt he wanted to be sure you would not suffer financially if something happened to him," Tracy said. "Perhaps he had a premonition. In any event, Miles, he took very good care of you."

"How good?" Miles asked, his voice trembling.

"Including bank accounts, investments, and the condo, you are worth in the neighborhood of $15 million, depending, of course, on what taxes might be levied."

Miles could barely speak.

"$15 million? Are you sure?" Miles really thought he was going to faint.

"Well, subject to settling the tax issue, yes, that's approximately your current net worth."

Miles turned to Darcey.

"I was a kid living on the streets when he found me," he said. "He was the first person who ever treated me decently. But I had no idea…" His voice trailed off as the tears began to flow.

Darcey held him in her arms.

It was a long and emotional day for Miles, as well as for Trent and Darcey. They were all too internally drained to worry about dinner.

Miles opened a Merlot for Trent; a Chardonnay for Darcey. For himself, he stayed with mineral water, his drink of choice for the past few days.

Darcey made a pan of nachos, layered heavily with melted, browned cheese and handfuls of sliced jalapenos. That was good enough for dinner.

Tuesday, August 9th

The day started with a scream from Trent's side of the bed.

Darcey was shocked awake. It wasn't a good sign.

Trent was sitting on the edge of the bed. His hands were over his ears. He was moaning. Another symptom the doctors had predicted.

Moving as quietly as possible, she withdrew the behind-the-head ear muffs from the drawer in her bedside stand. They had purchased them for just such an occasion.

Gently she placed them over Trent's ears. They would block all loud, sudden sounds. They could also be adjusted to the level of voice allowed. She let Trent make the adjustment. She noted that he turned the allowable decibel level down to almost zero. He would be able to hear and respond to voices but louder sounds would not penetrate the protective muffs.

"Better?" she asked, speaking as softly as she could.

He nodded.

She realized their bedroom door was open. Miles was standing in the doorway, looking frightened.

She got out of bed and led him into the living room, closing the door behind them.

She whispered to Miles to make as little noise as possible. This was another symptom about which they had been warned. She said Trent would be wearing sound-suppressing earmuffs but they still must endeavor to make as little noise as possible. All phones were to be put on vibrate only.

Miles returned to his en suite bathroom to wash his face, clearing it of the creams and lotions he put on before going to bed each night, and to get dressed.

Darcey went back to the bedroom she shared with Trent. She held his hand. She kissed him.

"Is it painful, sweetheart?" she asked, softly.

"Not really painful," he replied in the same way. "The sound suppression on these muffs is very effective. It makes me feel a little nauseous though."

"I think this might be a good day for you to stay in bed."

Trent didn't argue.

Darcey felt her phone vibrate in her pocket. She went back to the living room before answering.

It was her office calling. The clean-up crew had completed its work. Her staff wanted to know if they should have the furniture delivered. Darcey told them to get the trucks rolling. She and Miles would meet them at the condo.

She crossed the hall and rang Preston Johnson's doorbell. The old man opened the door, dressed casually but elegantly, as always.

She quickly explained the symptom Trent was suffering today. She said he would be staying in bed but she needed to accompany Miles to his condo. She asked if Preston could possibly stay with Trent. He wouldn't have to do anything but stay in the living room. She just didn't want to leave him completely alone.

"Of course, my dear. I would be happy to help."

Kiettisuk Jetjirawat and Abdul Rahman returned to the Rossi compound in mid-morning accompanied by their teams of attorneys. The lawyers, unshaven and looking haggard, carried briefcases full of documents they had worked all day Monday and through the night to prepare. They feared disappointing their clients.

They were welcomed by Pietro, who opened the gate for them and then led them into Rossi's office.

Rossi looked even worse than the overworked and frightened accountants. He was half drunk from the martinis of the previous evening. He was having difficulty accepting the loss of his empire, much of which he had inherited from his father and grandfather and great grandfather. All his scheming, in the end, had resulted in a grand failure.

The attorneys began stacking piles of documents on his desk, all marked with small pieces of red tape indicating where he should sign. He looked at the documents, then at Kiettisuk Jetjirawat and Abdul Rahman.

"This isn't right," he said in one final attempt to save himself. "I didn't take your money. We have always had trust among us."

"Yes, Jonathan," Kiettisuk Jetjerawat agreed, "'had' would be the proper word."

"What about the Dutchman?" Rossi asked. "I don't see mention of him here."

"That's something else we suspect you know more about than we do," Abdul answered.

Rossi didn't pursue the issue. He had a sickening feeling that the Dutchman's fate preceded his own. He didn't know who was responsible for that either.

He spent the next two hours signing whatever document was placed before him. He didn't argue. He didn't even bother to read what he was signing. He had lived in this world long enough to know it didn't matter. Nothing mattered.

Abdul asked if he and Kiettisuk Jetjirawat should be signing as well. Kiettisuk said they could add their signatures later. At the moment, it was important for Rossi to sign.

"In such situations," Kiettisuk Jetjirawat said, "one never knows what the future will bring."

In Miles' Marina district condo, the cleanup crew had done a good job. All the damaged furniture had been removed. Paintings rehung. Files and papers straightened and returned to the desk, which Miles had decided to keep.

He had asked them to remove Scott's clothing from his closet and take them to the Salvation Army. He even wanted all the bedclothes removed. While he didn't want to erase Scott from the home they had shared, he didn't think he could bear looking at his clothing every day. He didn't think he could sleep on the sheets they once slept on together.

The first trucks arrived soon after Darcey and Miles got there. They spent the next several hours directing the placement of furniture. They unpacked the new bedclothes and decorative items they had picked out on their shopping trip.

By late afternoon, the home looked livable again. There were pictures of Scott and Miles. Other mementos from their life together.

"I love the new things we've picked out, Darcey," he said, "but I also love the memories of Scott. The pictures of us together are especially comforting to me. Is that weird?"

"Certainly not, Miles. It's normal. It's healthy. It's all part of the grieving process."

"It's like he's still here with me somehow."

"He is, Miles. He will always be with you. I still feel my dad's presence and he's been gone for almost five years. Be open to Scott, Miles, and you'll feel him with you."

There were fewer tears today.

At last Rossi signed the final document. The attorneys picked up the piles of papers and filed out.

Kiettisuk Jetjirawat and Abdul Rahman stared at Rossi. Neither showed sympathy or encouragement.

"This is all regrettable, Jonathan," Kiettisuk Jetjirawat said, "and so unnecessary."

He and Abdul left Rossi alone with Pietro.

It was quiet in the room after Rossi's former partners left.

"Why?" Rossi asked. "Why did you turn against me?"

"Your arrogance became unbearable," Pietro replied. "But more than that, it became apparent to me you weren't a good business partner. I saw things. I saw you double-crossing your partners. If I could see it, eventually they would, too. I had to protect myself."

"The Dutchman," Rossi said. "What happened to the Dutchman?"

"Apparently you ordered a hit on him."

Once again, Rossi was caught by surprise.

"I ordered no hit on the Dutchman," he protested. "You would have known if I had. I didn't order any funds transferred to my bank. Someone set me up. I don't know who or how. But someone set me up."

"As Kiettisuk Jetjirawat said, that's regrettable. Sogni d'oto," Pietro added. "Sweet dreams, Don Rossi."

He raised the Heckler & Kock, with the sound suppressor still attached. He pulled the trigger and traced a line of bullet holes beginning with Rossi's left hip, continuing upward diagonally across his body to his right shoulder. Rossi's body jumped like a puppet on a string as each piece of lead struck home.

He slid down in his chair. Half sitting; half lying. His eyes were open but beginning to glaze over. He was struggling to take shallow breaths. Pietro let him struggle.

Then he fired a single shot into Rossi's head.

After a century of ruling a criminal empire, the Rossi Family ceased to exist.

In the Nob Hill condo, Trent got out of bed and joined Preston Johnson in the living room. Preston was careful to speak very softly when he asked if there was anything he could get for Trent, or do for him. Trent shook his head no.

Suddenly, Trent turned to the entry door. Preston heard nothing. With his finger to his lips, he motioned to Preston to be silent. He stepped to the door, jerking it quickly open.

Jean Philby was walking by carrying a small bag. She ignored him. He assumed the slight noise he had heard even with the sound suppressing muffs was the elderly woman shuffling down the hallway. He stepped back inside and closed the door.

The face in the small glass pane of the emergency stairs alongside the elevator watched. Fortunately, Burgess had heard the elevator stopping at the 15th floor in time to get out of sight.

He had managed to get on the elevator to the secure floor without being seen when the concierge took a bathroom break. It wouldn't do for anyone to remember seeing him in the building, especially on this floor, when he carried out his plan to take his own revenge on Trent Marshall.

Trent returned to bed.

Preston Johnson sat quietly, holding the ever present cane. He was thinking about how he had spent his life. For the first time in his memory he was beginning to have regrets.

After a while, he quietly opened the door to Trent and Darcey's bedroom to check on his charge. He found Trent sleeping soundly.

As he watched his ailing friend sleep, his concern deepened.

There was no cocktail hour.

Darcey scrambled some eggs and crisped up some bacon when she and Miles returned. Trent ate some of the eggs but declined the bacon. He went back to bed after the meager dinner.

Miles told Darcey he thought he would move back to his condo the next day.

"Are you sure you're ready, Miles?" Darcey questioned. "You know you can stay here as long as you need to."

"I'm ready," he said. "I need to be alone there with the memory of Scott. And don't worry. I'll be fine. I won't drink. I won't do anything stupid."

Darcey nodded. She understood.

"If you don't mind, I would like to take some more time off work. I need to get through this process before I can focus on the job."

"Take as much time as you need, Miles," Darcey said.

Wednesday, August 10th

The day dawned peacefully.

Darcey was awakened by her husband bringing her coffee with a kiss. She enthusiastically, and gratefully, accepted both. She raised her eyebrows questioningly before speaking.

"It's ok," Trent said in a normal voice. "My hearing is back to normal. These symptoms seem to last no more than a few hours."

"The doctors say that's a good sign," Darcey noted, optimistically.

"They're still unpleasant though," Trent said. "So far we've been lucky. Nothing debilitating has shown up at a critical time. In fact, the dilated pupils helped us capture the men who trashed Miles' home."

The day they had planned was uneventful.

Trent would take Miles to the police impound lot to retrieve Scott's Mercedes. Or as they learned the day before, Miles' Mercedes. Then he would accompany Miles home to be certain that all was well.

Darcey planned to spend at least part of the day in the office. With all the events of the past few days, neither she nor Miles had been able to tend to business. It was time for her, at least, to get back to work.

And, yes, she assured Trent, she would take the pink and black gym bag with her.

At ten o'clock Abdul Rahman appeared in Kiettisuk Jetjirawat's top floor apartment in Little Saigon. He was there at the Thai gangster's invitation. He believed they would be adding their signatures to the papers dividing the Rossi empire between them.

Abdul had become leery of recent events and who might be behind them. He had at first believed Rossi ordered the hit on the Mad Dutchman. That assumption was based on the bodies of two of Rossi's soldiers found at the scene. Since discovering that Kiettisuk Jetjirawat's source within the Rossi family was the don's underboss and consigiliere, Abdul was no longer sure that the Mafia leader had ordered the hit.

It was not clear to him who had attacked Rossi's compound. He was certain he had not ordered it. But the Mad Dutchman might have and Rossi could have ordered the outlaw biker gang wiped out in retaliation.

He didn't see how anyone else but Rossi had siphoned off $200 million of his partners' money. That was the one event for which he could think of no other possibility. Yet the question of the death of Scott Douglas remained. Why would one of Rossi's men kill Douglas? Unless Rossi wanted to be sure the transfer couldn't be undone.

Clearly there were many questions.

For that reason, Abdul again wore his ancestral robes to the day's meeting. The M4 was hidden within the folds. The rifle had a telescoping buttstock. Abdul folded the stock down, reducing the weapon to a size that allowed it to be easily strapped to his leg.

For the first time, he was accompanied by three of his men. He had armed them with USAS automatic shotguns, the powerful weapons designed in South Korea. Each of the weapons was fitted with a magazine containing ten 12-gauge shells.

Seeing no one but Kiettisuk Jetjirawat in the room when he entered, Abdul instructed his men to wait outside the door

The two surviving members of the fiduciaria first enjoyed a cup of jasmine tea. It was one of the things Abdul appreciated about doing business with Kiettisuk Jetjirawat. Their meetings were always very civilized occasions.

Abdul spoke as Kiettisuk poured each of them a second cup of tea.

"Shouldn't we begin the signing?" he asked, waving his hand at the stacks of documents lying on the table.

Kiettisuk Jetjirawat continued pouring.

"I don't think that will be necessary, Abdul."

Abdul was immediately alarmed. Alarm escalated to apprehension as Pietro entered the room, the Heckler & Kock submachine gun with sound suppressor still attached in his hands.

"I believe you know Pietro," Kiettisuk Jetjirawat said. "His full name, by the way, is Peter Greco. He is a most talented and useful man."

"Good morning, Abdul," Pietro said, pleasantly. He leaned against the wall near the door.

Abdul forced himself to turn back to Kiettisuk Jetjirawat.

"I don't understand. Why do you say no signatures are necessary?"

"Because these stacks of forms we forced Rossi to sign are worthless, Abdul."

"Worthless?" Abdul was taken aback. "How can they be worthless? How can we assume ownership of the Rossi properties without them?"

"Jonathan Rossi has met an unfortunate fate," Kiettisuk said. "The same fate the Mad Dutchman met a few days ago."

Abdul looked from the Thai to Pietro and back.

"Rossi didn't order the hit on the Dutchman," he concluded. "It was you. Pietro was working for you. He carried out the hit and left two of Rossi's men dead at the scene to make it appear it was done on Jonathan's orders."

"Perhaps," Kiettisuk Jetjirawat said.

"Maybe it was you who ordered the attack on Rossi's home also."

Kiettisuk only smiled.

"But what does all that have to do with our current situation?" Abdul asked. "I ask again. How do we assume ownership of the Rossi properties without formalizing the new arrangement with our signatures on these documents?"

"We already own them, Abdul."

"We own them? How can that be so?" Abdul's bewilderment showed clearly on his face.

"You didn't investigate thoroughly the terms of the fiduciaria the four of us entered into, Abdul."

"The fiduciaria? The fiduciaria no longer exists. We eliminated it when we required Rossi to sign these documents."

"That was done, Abdul, simply to get a complete inventory of the Rossi properties. These documents are worthless. To assure that they don't linger and complicate matters at some future date, I shall have them burned before the day is done."

"But...but..." Abdul was reduced to stammering mindlessly.

"The fiduciaria, Abdul. The fiduciaria is alive and well. Only it is much more than a fiduciaria."

Abdul sat dumbly, waiting for Kiettisuk Jetjirawat to explain.

"Rossi thought he was being extraordinarily clever in constructing the fiduciaria. He established it as a tontine."

"Tontine?" Abdul was unsure what meant.

"A tontine is an ancient legal device whereby partners in a business venture agree that as one partner dies the others inherit his interests. When all but one has died, that one remaining partner has legal ownership of all properties."

"Surely that can't be legal," Abdul objected.

"It is a vehicle seldom seen in business these days but I assure you it is quite legal. Since it is a rarely used device, Rossi was counting on his partners overlooking it."

Abdul again looked from Kiettisuk Jetjirawat to Pietro Greco and back.

"So now there are two of us," he said.

"For the moment, yes. We are the two surviving partners. Which reminds me, to commemorate the occasion I have a gift for you. I had it made especially for you. Pietro, if you would, please…"

Pietro laid his submachine gun against the wall. He stepped briefly into a side room, returning quickly with a strange appearing vest.

Abdul turned pale. It was not strange to him. He recognized a suicide vest when he saw one. He tried to access the rifle hidden in the folds of his robes. It was too late.

He felt the press of the barrel in his left ear. From the corner of his eye, he could see the subcompact but deadly Ruger in Kiettisuk Jetjirawat's hand. Pietro laid the vest on the table before Abdul. He reached into the robes worn by the leader of the Scourge and retrieved the weapon hidden there.

Pietro opened the door leading out of the room. Abdul's astonishment grew as he saw the three men who had accompanied him with their arms bound tightly to their bodies. Six of Kiettisuk Jetjirawat's men pointed their lightweight, heavy caliber rifles at the prisoners. One of the Thais tossed the three automatic shotguns into the room to join the M4 taken from Abdul.

"So you intend to eliminate me and then you will control all that I have."

"You're partially correct, Abdul," Kiettisuk Jetjirawat said. "I do intend to eliminate you. But you have nothing that I want. I already have a prominent position in all the lines of business you have pursued. You have siphoned your profits to the Middle East rather than investing them here."

"Then why is it necessary to eliminate me?" Abdul asked, in a last desperate attempt to save himself.

"While you possess nothing I want, Abdul, you do possess something that worries me. You have a warehouse on the Oakland waterfront that is filled with explosives. I don't know what you intend to do with that much firepower. But in this regard, I'm much like any other San Francisco businessman. It makes me nervous.

"Pietro, let's get Abdul fitted with his new vest," Kiettisuk Jetjirawat said. "Please stand up, Abdul."

"Why should I cooperate in my own assassination?" Abdul challenged.

"Pietro, please help Abdul understand."

The room went black just after Abdul felt the blow on the back of his head.

Trent followed Miles from the impound lot to the condo on Capra Way in the Marina District. They had first stopped at police headquarters where Miles was quickly granted a release.

Miles was solemn as he entered the condo in which he now lived alone. Trent wasn't sure what to do. He wished Darcey was there. He silently watched Miles wander from room to room. He thought Miles and Darcey had done a nice job of design, leaving memories of Scott scattered among the beginning of Miles' new life.

"Well, what do you think?" Miles asked.

"I think y'all did a great job, Miles. The more important question is, 'What do you think?'"

Miles looked around one more time.

"It feels good," he said. "It feels like home. It feels like Scott is still here with me on some level. I can live here with his memory."

"And that's all that's important," Trent said.

"Thanks for all you and Darcey have done for me, Trent. I don't know how I would have made it through this without you guys."

"Hey, Miles, that's what friends are for. You can call on us anytime. You know that."

"Yes," Miles agreed, "and I know the grieving process has a long way to go. I have no doubt I'll be calling. Now there's one more thing I'd like to ask you to do for me."

"Whatever you need."

"I want you to help me buy a gun and teach me to shoot."

"Whoa, Miles," Trent said, taken by surprise. "That's serious. What do you have in mind?"

"No worries, Trent. I'm not planning on doing anything foolish. Not to myself or to anyone else."

"That's good to know."

Tears were flowing from Miles' eyes. He took a moment to compose himself.

"Look at me, Trent," he said, struggling to keep his voice from breaking. "All my life I've been small. Effeminate. I've been called names. Faggot. Queer. I've been bullied and made to do things I didn't want to do. At least not with the people who made me do them."

He paused again, attempting to calm himself.

"Scott was the first person in my life who ever treated me with respect. He loved me unconditionally. He was proud to be my husband. And I just held him in my arms as his life drained away. He died trying to protect me. I could do nothing to protect him."

Miles paused again. He raised his face defiantly, looking directly at Trent.

"I might not appear very masculine but I don't intend to let that happen ever again."

Trent said nothing.

"Will you do it? Will you teach me to shoot?"

"I'll call Christopher. Maybe he can get us out to his friend's gun shop on Friday. We'll get you fixed up, Miles."

Four blocks away from Miles' condo, Captain Henry Place steered the eighty-two foot yacht out of the marina's West Harbor. Kiettisuk Jetjirawat had named her Ruthai, which Captain Place understood meant 'heart' in the language of Thailand.

She was a sturdy ship, well-constructed by Dutch master craftsmen. Though there was no firm distinction between a ship and a boat when it came to vessels of this size, the captain thought of Heart as a ship. Her twin inboard diesel engines gave her sufficient power to accomplish open sea cruising. He had personally selected her crew with regard to nothing other than seamanship and, of course, loyalty.

The master stateroom was in the stern with its own head. There were two en suite guest staterooms amidships. The crew quarters were located in the bow and included a separate crew galley. When Kiettisuk Jetjirawat came aboard, he brought his personal chef with him.

Yes, the captain thought, Heart was a fine ship. He was looking forward to taking her to sea. Today they would be cruising only across the bay to the Oakland waterfront.

Captain Place had the wheel. Though he had two competent helmsmen in the crew, he was taking her out of the harbor because he enjoyed it.

Pietro Greco stood beside him. Captain Place had also come to enjoy Pietro's company. He found him to be a pleasant companion aboard ship on their brief cruises together.

Today they talked amiably, keeping their voices low. The captain knew it was a deadly business in which they were involved today. He thought better days would be ahead for himself and for Heart.

Pietro left the bridge and entered the yacht's luxurious main salon. There he found Abdul conscious but not such pleasant company. He and his three men were securely bound, their arms tied to their bodies in such a manner as to prevent them from moving freely. Six Thais stood guard with their rifles.

The suicide vest was wrapped around Abdul's arms. There was no way he could maneuver out of it. He was helpless. He had briefly thought of attempting to detonate the bomb himself while aboard Kiettisuk Jetjirawat's yacht, which he knew cost the Thai almost $8 million. At least he would have the satisfaction of taking the beautiful vessel to heaven with him.

It was a hopeless thought. For the first time in his life, Abdul Rahman had no control over his fate.

"You can't move, can you, Abdul?" Pietro said, pleasantly as he strolled into the yacht's main salon. Stepping into the spacious gallery, he found a bottle of Italian lemon-flavored sparkling water in the refrigerator. Pulling the tab to open the can, he took a long drink of the refreshing beverage.

"I'm disappointed in you, Abdul," he said. "When I first discovered what Rossi was attempting, I thought you would be the final survivor. You let Kiettisuk Jetjirawat get the better of you."

"With your help," Abdul spat, contemptuously.

"Eventually, yes," Pietro agreed. "It didn't start out that way. I simply waited to see who was going to outlast the other three. Once I discovered the winning side, I did what I had to do to get on it."

"This vest will not accomplish what you want it to," Abdul remarked, in a gruesome change of topics. "It's too light. You didn't put enough ball bearings in it."

Pietro smiled.

"There are no ball bearings in it at all, Abdul," he replied. "We're not interested in murdering your men, though no doubt most will die. Your vest is filled with Semtex, which is the most explosive substance known to man. But, of course, you know that. We learned about Semtex from you."

"But why destroy my warehouse?" Abdul wondered. "It contains hundreds of weapons. Why not sell them and take the profit?"

"We have access to all the weapons we can move, Abdul. We don't need yours. Your warehouse contains more explosives than guns. Kiettisuk Jetjirawat was being honest with you when he told you he worries about your intentions. When he considers the potential uses of all that explosive material, he worries."

The weakest point of the human body is that space between the jaw and the neck. Since explosives literally "blow up" directionally, the bombers' heads quite often are taken off intact.

That's why the first responder on the scene of the explosion looked down to see Abdul's head rolling toward him. The first responder had been called on for many disasters. This was the first time he vomited.

Captain Place had taken Heart out into the bay, well away from the warehouse, before Pietro entered the code on his mobile phone to detonate the explosives wrapped around Abdul Rahman. The two men watched the destruction on the waterfront from the yacht's grand salon.

Abdul's warehouse was set apart from other buildings along the Oakland waterfront. It was one of the reasons Kiettisuk Jetjirawat had decided on this tactic. He had no desire to harm other buildings, including a few he owned himself.

Trent felt more than heard the explosion as he drove away from Miles' building. He first thought it was an earthquake. Then he saw the plume of smoke rising from across the bay. An industrial accident, he thought. A very serious industrial accident.

His phone rang before he reached the Nob Hill condo. He saw Christopher's name come up.

"Hey, buddy, where y'at?" he answered.

Christopher wasn't aware of the traditional greeting of New Orleans' Vieux Carre'. He took the question literally.

"On my way to the Oakland waterfront," he replied. "There's a new development in Operation Den of Snakes. Where are you? I'll come get you."

By the time Christopher and Trent arrived, Nancy was already on the scene. Lieutenant Mitchum and FBI agent Brady, the other members of Christopher's team, were also there.

Several local fire departments were attempting to get the flames under control. FBI agents were assisting Oakland police in securing the area.

"How do we know this explosion is related to Operation Den of Snakes?" Trent asked.

"This warehouse was owned by Abdul Rahman," Agent Brady responded.

"Do we know who set off the explosion?" Christopher asked.

Nancy looked pale.

"Abdul did it himself," she said.

"Why would he do that?" Christopher was mystified.

"He probably didn't do it intentionally," Brady said. "He was fitted with a suicide vest and locked in the building. Someone detonated the bomb remotely."

"How do you know that?" Christopher continued.

"Because Abdul's head is in that vehicle," Nancy said, a look of distaste on her face as she pointed to a nearby SUV, "and his body in that one," she added, pointing to a second ambulance.

"Do you want to see it?" Mitchum asked. Trent thought he seemed a little too cheerful for the occasion.

"We'll take your word for it," Christopher said. Trent nodded in agreement.

"But you're right," Trent added. "Operation Den of Snakes is having the impact we thought it would. Two down. Only Rossi and Kiettisuk Jetjirawat to go."

"The transfer of all fiduciaria funds to Rossi's bank in Rome is known by now," Christopher said. "The evidence is Rossi ordered the

196

hit on the Barons of Lucifer. Could he have done this also? A matter of self-protection?"

"Possibly," Trent said. "It's difficult to say. We set in motion a military-style operation. The problem with such things is you can never predict all the possible outcomes. Old soldiers say a plan begins to fall apart as soon as you implement it. If Rossi is behind all this, he's far more clever than I gave him credit for being."

Darcey was sautéing mushrooms and onions when he got home. She had two beef filets seasoned and ready for the fire.

He mixed martinis for them. Darcey joined him on the terrace for what had become their favored cocktail hour ritual. He told her about the day. She shivered at the mention of Abdul's head. Given the waiting steaks, Trent was glad he had passed on the offer to view the loathsome trophy.

Thursday, August 11th

Trent moaned in his sleep, waking Darcey. She put her arm over him, seeking to comfort him. What she felt brought her immediately awake. He was burning hot with fever. Another of the symptoms about which they had been warned.

She quickly went to the kitchen for a large bottle of water. She had aspirin in the drawer of her bedside table. She woke Trent and made him take two of the pills with a healthy drink of water.

It was almost seven o'clock, the time they had intended to awaken. She told Trent to rest and drink more water. She would make him some tea. He didn't feel like eating.

They were scheduled to meet Miles at the funeral home at ten o'clock for Scott's cremation.

"Do you feel up to going?" Darcey asked. "I'm sure Miles will understand if you don't."

"I'll make it. I don't feel great but I'm not in any pain. Might have to lean on you a little."

Darcey smiled.

"You can always lean on me, Trent. Lean on me forever." She kissed him.

Preston Johnson was riding with them. Mandy Rillard was going to pick up Miles. She thought Miles might become too emotional to drive.

Preston was alarmed as he watched Trent on the elevator as they descended to the garage. The younger man seemed weak. Enough so that Preston and Darcey each took an arm to help him into Darcey's BMW. They put him in the rear passenger seat of the spacious SUV. Preston climbed in to sit beside him.

By the time they reached the funeral home, Trent was sweating profusely. Preston used his own clean handkerchief to wipe Trent's face.

Seeing the action in the rear view mirror, Darcey reached into her purse for the wet wipes she had brought just for this purpose. She passed them back to Preston.

Preston tended to Trent as best he could.

The worried look in the old man's eyes became more pronounced.

There was something else in his eyes as he watched Trent.

Something indefinable.

The cremation itself took about two hours. Trent, Darcey, Preston, and Mandy had gone into the room with Miles to be with him as he said goodbye to Scott. They were joined by Christopher Booth and Nancy Patrick.

After the farewell, the friends sat with Miles as the funeral home staff carried out the cremation. It was done very professionally. The process was designed to place as little stress as possible on the grieving family.

Miles shed tears. They all did, to one degree or another. Christopher and Nancy hadn't known Scott. But they had come to like Miles in the few days they had known him.

Just after noon, the staff brought an elegant, burnished brass urn to Miles. It contained the earthly remains of Scott Lucas Douglas.

"You didn't know his middle name was Lucas, did you?" Miles said, with a sad smile. "He hated it. It was his grandfather's name. He didn't hate his grandfather. He loved him. But his grandfather was a farmer and Scott hated farming."

The group of friends couldn't help laughing at Miles' description. Miles looked around at his support group, giving a slight giggle of his own.

Miles had arranged for a caterer to prepare refreshments for the small group. His new dining table was laden with pulled pork sandwiches, potato salad, pickled okra, mac & cheese, deviled eggs, corn salad and Coleslaw.

"These are all Scott's favorite foods," Miles explained. He held up his glass of sparkling wine. "The only thing missing is the ribeye steak that Trent showed me how to make in a cast iron skillet." He pointed to the heavy pan sitting on the stove.

"Here's to my Scott. May he always be with me," Miles said, holding up his glass of sparkling wine.

His friends all touched glasses in response to the toast.

Darcey hugged Miles, whose eyes were tearing again.

"And he always will be, Miles. Always."

Christopher felt the vibration of his phone. Looking at the number, he excused himself and stepped into the next room to take the call. He returned within a few minutes. The look on his face alerted the group that something big had happened.

"Miles, I'm sorry but I'm going to have to take Trent and Nancy away," the big cop said, "If you're feeling up to it, that is, Trent."

By this time, the sweats had stopped. Trent was feeling a little stronger.

"I'll make it. What's up?"

"That was Joseph Brady calling," Christopher reported. "He's at Rossi's house in the Hills at Atherton with the local police. They just found Jonathan Rossi."

Darcey noted with surprise the look of shock on Preston's face.

"It was actually the pool service who found him," FBI Agent Brady briefed them. "They thought it unusual that no one was around. They went to knock on the door and found it standing open. They discovered Rossi as you see him now, behind his desk."

Once again, Trent, Christopher, and Nancy found themselves in a room with a body that had been going through the deterioration process for more than forty-eight hours. It was no more pleasant in the multi million mansion than it was at the humble cottage in Richmond.

"Shot multiple times diagonally across the body," Brady continued. "Then the coup de grace. A single shot to the head."

Though Trent was feeling better, he was still shaky. He found a chair and sat. He wiped his face with the wet wipes supplied by Darcey. He drank heavily from the bottle of water she insisted he keep with him. He was grateful to her.

From the angle at which he sat, Trent's line of sight showed him something not easily noticeable.

"Christopher, it looks like there's a safe behind that painting," he pointed out. "The big seascape."

Christopher pulled on the painting. It opened like a door. Behind it was a wall safe that was closed but not locked. Opening it, he found it empty.

"Looks like someone helped themselves after Rossi was taken out," Christopher said.

"I've been wondering where Peter Greco is," Brady added. "The underboss hasn't been seen in several days. Usually if you see Rossi you see Greco."

"Yeah, Rossi didn't do anything without Greco's advice and even approval," Christopher agreed. "He's either dead, too, or has taken over the Rossi Family and is in hiding."

Guy sat in his room in the cheap motel near Sacramento. The television was blaring a local news station. He didn't like watching the news. He was about to change it when the reporter said something that attracted his attention.

"Private services were held in San Francisco today for Scott Douglas, the Bay area financier who was killed trying to protect his spouse, Miles Diaz-Douglas. Diaz-Douglas had been kidnapped. Douglas was heroically attempting to rescue Diaz-Douglas when the kidnappers decided to kill their victim. Scott Douglas hurled his own body between the killers and his spouse."

Guy laughed.

"So the little wifey is all alone now," he said aloud. "What do you know about that?"

Filippo had a few thousand in the bank. Not as much as Guy had hoped. He had drained the account. It allowed him to eat well. But now the money was starting to run low.

He needed a new source of funds. He thought it a cinch that old Douglas would have a stash of cash at his house. At the very least, he would have jewelry or something valuable that could be sold.

Now only the wifey was there. That little wimp wouldn't give him any trouble.

And Guy had been assigned to keep an eye on Douglas' condo one day not long ago. He knew the address. He laughed again.

At the Nob Hill condo there was no cocktail hour on the terrace that evening.

No dinner.

Darcey put Trent to bed. She lay beside him.

Looking after him.

Friday, August 12th

Trent woke up feeling normal. He felt better than normal. He felt good.

"No symptoms today?" Darcey asked.

"Yes," he replied. "There is a symptom that needs your attention."

She laughed as he pulled her to him, loving the feel of his lips on hers, his hands touching her.

Later they made a hearty breakfast of steak and eggs and hash browns together. It was starting out as one of Darcey's "Yes!" days.

Trent and Miles met Christopher at Jess Hickok's gun shop and shooting range on the south side of the city at mid-morning. Hickok raised an eyebrow when Miles came prancing into the shop in his dramatic style.

"So you want to learn to shoot, young man?" Hickok questioned.

"Yes," was Miles determined reply.

Hickok sighed.

"All right, then. Come with me."

For the next half hour Miles blasted away with an assortment of semiautomatics and revolvers in various calibers. At the end of the half hour, Hickok was exasperated.

"I don't mean to appear parsimonious, young man," the gun shop owner said, "but you have gone through several boxes of ammunition. This stuff isn't cheap, you know."

"Don't worry," Miles said. "I can pay for it."

"That's actually not the point," Hickok said. "So far you haven't hit the target a single time."

"Not even once?" Miles questioned, disappointment evident in his voice.

"I'm not sure you've even hit the wall. Frankly, I don't know where the bullets have gone."

"I was so sure I could do it," Miles said, completely deflated. "Maybe I really am just a silly queen."

"Hold on, Miles," Trent said. "You're no such thing. There's more than one way to defend yourself."

He drew Christopher and Hickok into a whispered conversation. Eventually the group appeared to reach agreement. Hickok left the range.

"Trent, I don't know how I let you talk me into these things," Christopher said.

Trent cast an amused look at the big cop.

Hickok returned with a shotgun. Not just any shotgun. A Remington twelve gauge Model 870P.

"This is the shotgun used by the FBI," Hickok said, handing it over to Miles. "It has an eighteen-inch inch barrel, a pistol grip on the buttstock and a flashlight with a toggle switch. You can focus the light on an intruder and it will scare the pants off him. Just be sure to toggle it off quickly so he doesn't use it to sight in on you."

Miles held the weapon lovingly.

"Such a pretty toy," he crooned, stroking it.

"It's not a toy, Miles," Trent cautioned. "It's a very powerful weapon. The good thing about it is you don't have to aim carefully. Just point and shoot. But don't forget it's powerful. If you fire it inside your condo it can take out most of a wall along with any intruder."

Miles learned to load the weapon with four twelve gauge shells. Then Hickok demonstrated how he could pump one shell into the chamber and add a fifth to the magazine. He showed him how to fire the weapon without breaking his shoulder.

Miles was happy. He marched out of the gun shop with his new weapon over his shoulder looking much like a toy soldier from The Nutcracker.

"I think I might fear for the Marina district," Christopher said, under his breath.

He and Trent watched Miles march around the parking lot in his version of full military parade.

"I've been thinking about Pietro Greco taking over the Rossi Family," Trent said. "I don't think there is a Rossi Family anymore. I think it more likely that Greco changed sides."

Christopher nodded in agreement.

"He's smarter than Rossi was and tougher. He wouldn't be as easy to take out."

"He could have set Rossi up for the hit on the Barons of Lucifer," Trent pointed out. "Coupled with our computer game that emptied the bank accounts of the three partners, anyone on the inside could figure out that Rossi wouldn't be around much longer. If Greco's as smart as you say he is, I'd bet he changed sides."

Kiettisuk Jetjirawat's day started off well.

He slept later than usual. The stress of the past few days was beginning to catch up with him. But now that he had successfully eliminated his three partners and was the surviving, therefore inheriting, member of the tontine, he thought himself entitled to some relaxation.

He thought he would take the Ruthai out for a few days at sea. Maybe he would look over the latest crop of fresh young girls he had just brought into the country. There might be one or two who would be pleasant company.

Then Pietro Greco arrived.

Rossi's former underboss now had freedom to come and go as he pleased at Kiettisuk's headquarters building in Little Saigon. The guards met him with friendly greetings, never thinking to challenge his movements.

This morning he arrived carrying a large valise. It attracted no attention. There had been so many attorneys in and out, all carrying similar containers. All filled with documents beyond the understanding of the Thai guards.

There were no guards outside Kiettisuk Jetjirawat's penthouse suite. With Rossi, the Mad Dutchman, and Abdul out of the way, it wasn't thought necessary.

"Sawatedee-khap, Pietro," Kiettisuk greeted Greco.

"Good morning, Kiettisuk," Pietro replied in English rather than the Thai greeting.

"Might I offer you a cup of jasmine tea?"

"Yes, thank you, Kiettisuk."

"It has been a very eventful few days," Kiettisuk Jetjirawat said as he poured tea. "I am grateful for your support, Pietro. Now I intend to seek relief from the stress we have all endured. I'm thinking of taking the

Ruthai to sea for a few days. Perhaps you would like to accompany me? I've recently brought in a group of new girls. We're entitled to indulge ourselves after our success."

"Unfortunately the Ruthai won't be available for a few days, Kiettisuk," Pietro replied.

"Oh? And why not?"

"Captain Place has taken it to dry dock," Pietro explained, "for some needed work."

"I see," Kiettisuk said, speaking slowly. "Where is he having this work done? Why wasn't I told of this? Who authorized it?"

"He took it to a shipyard owned by a man who knows how to be discreet," Pietro said. "You weren't told because we wanted to surprise you. And as to who authorized it, Captain Place and I did."

Pietro opened the large valise as he spoke.

Kiettisuk felt his eye twitching. The superstitious Thai believed that if his right eye twitched, it was a sign that something bad was about to happen. If his left eye twitched, something pleasant was approaching.

His right eye was twitching.

Pietro Greco drove away in the dark SUV. The valise secured under the dashboard on the passenger side held, in addition to his Heckler & Koch submachine gun, a large sum of money. Around $750,000, he approximated. He had forced Kiettisuk Jetjirawat to open his safe before he killed him.

Kiettisuk also saw the wisdom in signing a bill of sale for the Ruthai. Captain Place now owned the vessel free and clear. And legally.

Pietro knew the gang leaders all kept a healthy supply of contingency cash on hand. Rossi's safe had yielded only $500,000. Fortunately he knew where to find the key to the late don's safe deposit box. He emptied it of $1 million.

With over $2 million in his late bosses' money, tax free, plus funds he had set aside himself, he was well fixed to move into retirement. Of course, he would pay Captain Place $100,000 for passage to wherever the former underboss wanted to go.

The captain was also the new owner of the yacht, which was even now having its name changed. He wasn't sure what Place had decided to call the yacht. He was sure that with $100,000 in cash, accompanied by ownership of an $8 million yacht, the captain would be happy.

Pietro had begun preparing a new identity for himself some time ago. Within a week he would have a new Social Security number, passport, driver's license. A new name.

He liked the name he had chosen for the next chapter in his life. It was far removed from his previous life.

It didn't take long for Christopher and Trent to learn the fate of Kiettisuk Jetjirawat. The big cop's phone rang as they were leaving the gun shop. Kiettisuk's chef had called 9-1-1when he discovered his former boss' body.

Trent dropped Miles at his condo. He skipped into the building happily clutching his new "toy." Trent promised to visit soon to teach him to clean and care for the shotgun.

The usual security guards at Spitting Cobra headquarters were not in sight. The armed men melted away when they realized their leader had been assassinated.

Christopher was in Kiettisuk's apartment. He had questioned the chef. The man was hysterical. He was working in the kitchen. He didn't even know someone had entered the apartment. He had heard no voices. No sound of any kind.

Kiettisuk had ordered a late breakfast. The chef discovered the body when he came in to inquire whether his boss wanted lunch.

This time Christopher pointed out the open and emptied safe to Trent.

"Whoever did this was as familiar with Kiettisuk's headquarters as the person who carried out the hit on Rossi," he said.

"I'm telling you, Christopher," Trent responded, "It's the same man. Pietro Greco changed sides."

"Yeah, I think you're right," the cop said. "And now he's changed sides again."

"Now he's working strictly for himself."

"You know he has a good chance of making a clean getaway," Christopher said. "I don't know where to begin looking for him. He has a house just down the road from the Rossi compound. We've gone through it. There's nothing there. He lived alone. He left not even a ticket stub to a movie theater."

"We might never find Greco," Trent said. "But we accomplished what we set out to accomplish. The fiduciaria no longer exists. The Rossi Family, Spitting Cobra, the Barons of Lucifer and the Scourge are either completely collapsed or so weakened it will be decades before they will be a danger again."

"And Rossi's alliance had already weakened the other major gangs in this part of the country," Christopher added. "We might have a chance to get a little control over organized crime in this city."

Police Chief Charles Marvin was not naïve. He understood crime would always be with them. It was part of the human experience.

At least for one day he was feeling victorious. He was at first skeptical of Operation Den of Snakes when Captain Albright and Sergeant Booth proposed it. It was complicated, risky, and unpredictable. And it worked.

Now he had a phone call to make. He hated to ruin her weekend but he feared that once news of all that had occurred became public she would run.

He nodded to the two uniformed officers standing in his doorway. As they left the room, he dialed her number.

"Amanda," he said when she answered, "please come down to my office."

Deputy Chief Amanda Justice was frozen with fear. Don Rossi hadn't answered her calls all week. She knew it was over for her. She couldn't let them put her in jail. She wouldn't survive it.

She considered briefly the service weapon holstered on her hip. But no, she couldn't do that. She didn't have the courage for it. For now all she could do was get out of this building. She would figure out an escape plan later.

She learned she didn't have that option either when she opened her office door. The two uniformed officers were respectful.

"May we accompany you to Chief Marvin's office, Deputy Chief Justice?" one of them asked, politely as he removed her weapon from its holster.

Amanda suddenly felt weak. She walked on shaky legs toward the chief's office, an officer on either side of her.

Technology, specifically the Internet, made it easier for Jimmy Shadow to be kept informed. Information had already been received via burst transmissions regarding the death of Jonathan Rossi and the collapse of Rossi's fiduciaria. Jimmy had also learned of the destruction of the entire Rossi Family, the Barons of Lucifer, and the Scourge. Now came word that Spitting Cobra was also neutralized.

These events, happening one on top of the other, convinced Jimmy the decision to ignore Rossi's last request for help was the correct one. Jimmy would not have wanted to be caught up in the chaos resulting from Rossi's over reach.

Now Steve Burgess was the object of Jimmy's attention. Sources had responded quickly. Burgess was still in town. He was still a danger.

Jimmy Shadow was a greater danger.

Burgess didn't know that Jimmy was watching him.

On the terrace of the Nob Hill condo, Trent sipped Rebel Yell bourbon on the rocks; Darcey enjoyed a Napa Valley Chardonnay.

Darcey had thawed some pulled pork saved from an earlier, more extravagant dinner. With a little onion, shredded cabbage, cheese, and pinto beans, the pork made excellent tacos.

Friday, August 19th

Trent's hands shook so violently he was unable to hold the coffee mug. It had been almost a week since the last symptom. Then came the tremors.

Not since their first visit with the doctors had Darcey seen this look on his face. Fear in his eyes. A desperate fear. He looked pathetic. It wasn't a good look for him. It wasn't what she was accustomed to seeing in him. It wasn't an emotion with which he was familiar.

She called Doctor Slim's office. The nurse said to bring him right in. The doctor would see him immediately.

She had to help him get dressed.

Doctor Slim and Doctor Raymond both made themselves available as soon as the couple arrived. They examined Trent thoroughly. They asked questions about the nature and timing of other symptoms.

"Since all the other symptoms have been of short duration," Doctor Raymond said, "I think we can safely conclude that this will not last long."

"What would you think about propranolol to ease the tremors?" Doctor Slim asked her.

"Yes, a Beta blocker would ease the symptom," Doctor Raymond replied. "I think we should give you a shot rather than pills. I don't think there will be a need to prescribe a daily dosage since it's likely this symptom won't last past today. If I'm wrong, we can always prescribe a longer treatment.

The doctors again reported to Darcey and Trent on the continuing work to find a cure. Again the doctors said they were optimistic.

As they started out the door, Trent stopped and turned back.

"With this shot you just gave me, is it ok to have a cocktail this evening?"

"Trent!" Darcey protested.

Doctor Raymond laughed.

"It's ok," she said. "Alcohol might make you a little drowsy but as long as you don't overdo it, a cocktail this evening should be fine."

"If your hands are still shaking you're not getting a cocktail, Trent," Darcey announced. "I'll do a lot of things for you but I won't hold a sippy cup so you can have a drink."

Steve Burgess had no problem holding a drink. He was in his favorite sleazy bar drinking heavily. And talking too much.

He let the bartender know that Sunday would be a big day. He bragged that he would be on Nob Hill on Sunday morning. He sneeringly said something about the "...high and mighty..." falling.

When he staggered out the door in mid-afternoon, the bartender stepped into the office. He turned on the lap top computer and sent a burst transmission.

Jimmy Shadow had a date. Jimmy knew Burgess' plan.

When the booze began to wear off, Burgess didn't remember talking to the bartender.

Captain Place had the helm, steering Dancer out of San Francisco Bay and into the open waters of the Pacific.

"You selected a good name, Captain," the man standing beside him said.

"Yes, it's a vessel that dances over the sea," Captain Place replied, an air of contentment about him.

The man standing beside the captain was once known as Pietro Greco. He had another name now. A new identity. He was looking forward to starting life over again. Life in a new place.

He breathed in the air of the open sea. It felt good in his lungs. Fresh. Clean. Free.

"In which direction should I plot our course?" the captain inquired.

The man thought for a moment. He looked south, toward Mexico. Escaping to Mexico seemed such a cliché. He looked north.

"North, I think, Captain."

"Any place in particular?"

"Just north for now," the man replied. "I'll know our destination when I see it."

Trent's hands were still a bit shaky when cocktail hour arrived. He didn't think he wanted Darcey to watch him try to hold a mixed drink. It would upset her if his trembling hand sloshed some of the liquid over the edge of the glass.

He made it quick. A shot of tequila.

A light dinner of bacon and eggs.

Saturday, August 20th

Guy waited until the lights in the condo went off. It was late. The street was quiet.

Then he waited another hour. He figured the wifey would be asleep. He was looking forward to waking Miles. His face contorted into a nasty countenance as he thought of the fun he might have with the small, effeminate man.

But he was here on business. He had to keep that in mind. He would have a little fun. And he would kill the man, who he remembered as being defenseless. Then he would strip the house of money and anything valuable that he could sell.

This would be a pleasant night's work.

It wasn't difficult picking the lock to the condo's entry door. He stepped inside and stood still, letting his eyes adjust to the dark.

Gradually the layout of the home presented itself to him. He saw the hallway to the right that no doubt led to the bedrooms. That was where he would find wifey. That's where he would go first.

He laid the FN Herstal personal defense weapon on the kitchen counter. It was a powerful weapon. He wouldn't need it to handle the wifey.

He had taken two steps toward the hallway when the beam of light focused on his chest. Guy knew what that meant. He stopped still.

"Put your hands on your head and get on your knees," Miles ordered.

Guy's mouth went dry. He obeyed. Quickly.

When Guy was kneeling, hands on his head, the lights in the room were switched on. Guy was stunned to see the small man he had called wifey standing in front of him. Miles was dressed in a long, pink tee shirt that came almost to his knees and pink fluffy slippers. His usual sleeping garments. His face shone with the overnight creams and oils he had applied. His usual bedtime ritual.

212

But it was the vicious shotgun pointed directly at him that got Guy's attention. The would-be burglar looked over at the weapon he had laid on the counter. Could he reach it before Miles could fire?

Miles saw the movements of Guy's eyes as he looked toward the weapon.

"Please, go for it," Miles said, confidently. "I know you think I look ridiculous...that I'm a defenseless faggot. But I promise you I will blow you in half before you can touch that weapon. So by all means, go for it."

Guy didn't move.

"You were very brave when you had Darcey and me bound, unable to protect ourselves or each other, weren't you? You were nothing but tough when my unarmed husband confronted you."

Guy began to whimper.

"Scott was armed only with his love for me and you, you piece of filth, you killed him."

"I didn't do it. One of the others shot him."

"You coward," Miles voice raised a decibel level. "You know exactly what happened. You ordered your man to kill me. And my husband, the only man who ever treated me decently in my life, my husband threw himself in front of the bullet. He did it to save...what was it you called me? Oh, yes...his wifey. You most definitely killed Scott. And I should kill you."

"Please don't kill me," Guy begged. "I'm sorry about your...your husband."

He felt his bladder voiding itself involuntarily.

Miles saw the darkening stain spreading across the front of the man's pants.

"You're peeing your pants!" Miles exclaimed, as he walked into the kitchen.

The kneeling man started blubbering as he felt the urine running down his leg.

"You fool!" Miles shouted. "Back up. Get off the rug!"

It was awkward backing up on his knees but Guy was too frightened to disobey. He crawled backwards.

"You peed on my rug! My very expensive rug. Do you know how hard it is to get the smell of urine out of a rug? I should kill you for that alone."

Guy hardly felt the blow on the back of his head before the blackness overwhelmed him. He fell forward. Face down in his own urine.

Trent's phone rang. It was almost midnight. It didn't matter. He was suffering from another symptom of his disease. Insomnia. He had been unable to sleep for the past two nights. He was in the living room doing one of his favorite things when he couldn't sleep. Watching an old black and white western movie.

Glancing at the ringing phone, he saw it was Christopher.

"Can you meet me at Miles' condo?" Christopher asked. "Someone broke in."

"Is Miles all right?" Trent asked, anxiously.

Christopher chuckled.

"I'd say Miles is as good as he's ever been."

Trent woke Darcey. He knew she would want to go with him.

Christopher and Nancy were already at the Capra Way condo when Trent and Darcey arrived. Uniformed officers had cuffed Guy and taken him away along with his personal defense weapon, which had been placed in an evidence bag.

Christopher had told them Miles would come to the precinct the next morning to give them his statement.

"And don't let him change his pants!" Miles had shouted after them.

Now the five friends were alone in Miles' home.

"Why didn't you shoot him, Miles?" Christopher asked. "He broke into your home armed with one of the deadliest weapons on the market. You could have blown him away and probably received a commendation from the mayor."

"I was tempted," Miles answered honestly. He was posed dramatically in a chair, his legs crossed, the feathery tendrils of his slippers waving with each movement of his foot. He was caressing the shotgun that lay across his pink clad lap. "But I don't want to kill anyone. Not really. I just want to make sure no one can ever harm me or the people I care about again."

"So what did you hit him with?" Darcey wanted to know.

"Remember that cast iron skillet you and Trent gave us? Scott loved steaks cooked in that pan. And it's very heavy."

"You knocked him out with a frying pan?" Trent asked.

"It's a fine pan, Trent," Miles said. "And as Mr. Hickok said, shotgun shells cost money."

214

Miles followed his friends to the door as they left. He watched them walking down the hall to the elevator.

"I'll be back to work Monday morning, Darcey," he said. "I'm ready now. It's what Scott would want."

Sunday, August 21st

Jimmy Shadow had a plan. A good plan. Timing was everything. He wasn't worried. Jimmy was up against Steve Burgess. Burgess wasn't much of a threat.

Trent had been able to fall asleep when they returned from Miles' condo shortly after midnight. Darcey let him sleep until eight o'clock before she woke him.

Preston Johnson had invited them over for Champagne this morning. It was an unusual invitation. In the years he and Darcey had been friends, he had either taken her out for meals or he had come across the hall to her condo.

But for whatever reason Preston wanted them to enjoy refreshments on his terrace on this Sunday morning. It was important, he told her. He was her friend. If it was important to him, it was important to her. They would be there, she told him.

Trent awakened feeling rested. As had become his habit, he lay in bed for a few minutes taking inventory of his body.

Hands steady.

Eyesight and hearing normal.

No aches or pains.

No fever or sweats.

A symptom free day!

Burgess awoke hungover. There was nothing out of the ordinary about that. He was usually either drunk or hungover. He reached for the gin bottle and took a big swallow. That made him feel better.

By 9:30 he was near the building on Nob Hill, the revolver he had taken from the body of the dead biker was in his belt, hidden by the

216

light jacket he wore. He waited patiently for the concierge to leave his desk in the lobby.

As soon as the lobby was empty, he moved as quickly as he could to the elevator. He went only to the 14th floor. From there he used his key for the secure floors to enter the emergency stairs and climb up to the 15th floor. He arrived there winded but, he thought, unseen. He stopped in the stairwell to catch his breath.

Looking through the small pane of reinforced glass in the stairwell door, he was surprised to see Trent and Darcey come out of their condo. He watched as they stepped across the hall and rang the doorbell. An old man opened the door, welcoming them in.

This was a complication, Burgess thought. But not much of one. The man who had opened the door looked ancient. Burgess thought he could be easily handled.

He didn't know Jimmy Shadow had already spotted him.

Preston Johnson was dressed as elegantly as ever. He was wearing a tan blazer, dark brown slacks, and a light blue shirt with a blue and red striped ascot around his neck. The ever present cane was in his hand as he hugged Darcey and shook hands with Trent, welcoming them into his home.

"I'm expecting another guest," Preston said. "I think I'll just leave the door open. It'll save the effort of walking back and forth."

"It's no trouble," Darcey said. "I'll take care of the door."

"No, dear, just leave it open," the old man repeated. "I have a treat for the two of you that mustn't be disturbed."

He motioned them to his kitchen island where sat a bottle of Champagne. Both the bottle and its covering foil were dark.

"Trent, I would like you to have the honor of pouring this bottle for us."

Trent's eyes grew wide.

"Is this what I think it is?" he asked.

"If you think it's a Shipwrecked 1907 Heidseick, then yes, it's what you think it is," Preston face showed his pleasure at Trent's reaction.

"Preston, this bottle is much too valuable to open," Trent objected.

"It's wine, Trent. It was made to be drunk. And this bottle has waited far too long to be enjoyed."

As the younger man began to open the wine, Preston explained Trent's astonishment to Darcey.

"During World War I, a cargo of this wine was en route to Tsar Nicholas of Russia when the ship was sunk by a German U-Boat. It lay at the bottom of the sea until 1997. While most of the shipment was destroyed, there were several bottles left. The temperature of the water and the level of pressure were perfect for maintaining the high quality of the wine."

"And I believe a bottle of this goes for close to $300,000," Trent added. Preston merely smiled, his Champagne flute in his hand. Two others sat on the table. Trent poured all three.

Preston merely smiled. He held his flute up to them. The three friends gently touched glasses.

"To the two of you," he toasted. "I owe you much. I wish a long and happy life for you."

They sipped, rather than drank, the precious wine.

"It's amazing," Darcey said. "This is a surreal experience. Thank you for sharing it with us, Preston."

"Yes, thank you," Trent said. "But I'm puzzled. You said you owe us something. I don't understand."

Preston looked into his flute, swirled the liquid around gently, and sipped again.

"There are things you don't know, Trent. Things I regret very much. But I think all will be made clear soon."

"Well, isn't this just a picture?" came the snarling voice from the doorway. Burgess held the small revolver on the group gathered in Preston's home. He had eased down the hall after Trent and Darcey entered the old man's condo. He had been standing by the door, listening.

"Ah, I see my other guest has arrived," Preston said. "Come in, Mr. Burgess. I've been expecting you."

Trent was startled for the second time within ten minutes.

"Burgess?" he said. "What are you doing here? How do you know this low life, Preston?"

"I'm here to finish what I started in New Orleans, Marshall," the ex-cop said. "This time I'm going to do it right. I was the one who put that bug in your clothes, Mr. Big Shot. You have me to thank for your illness."

Trent said nothing. Preston Johnson stared at the flute in his hand. He sipped the wine again.

"But you're still alive and I'm tired of waiting. I decided to come over here today and shoot you and your woman both. Won't bother me to shoot an old man as well," Burgess said, stepping closer to where the group was gathered.

Preston drained the last of the wine in his glass.

"You have such little class, Burgess," the old man said. "You are the biggest mistake I ever made."

"The biggest mistake you ever made? What are you talking about?" Burgess blustered.

There was a near silent click as Preston pressed a button on the gold handle of his cane. He slid the twenty-three inch carbon steel blade from the black hardwood shaft, using it to slap the revolver from Burgess' hand.

"We'll just be rid of that silly looking little gun," Preston said. He pressed the sharp tip of the blade half an inch below Burgess' sternum.

Burgess looked at his revolver on the floor. He looked down at the blade pressing into his flesh.

"What...I don't understand," Burgess stammered.

"Your mistake was in not telling me you wanted the bug to kill Trent Marshall," Preston said. "Trent Marshall is a friend of mine. Now you shall pay."

"Wait...don't do this..." Burgess pleaded.

"At least, Burgess, you will go to your grave with the knowledge that you're the only person who ever saw the face of Jimmy Shadow."

"Jimmy Shadow? You're Jimmy Shadow?"

Preston didn't answer the question. He gave a slight lunge forward, pressing the blade. The thin, strong steel slid smoothly, painfully through Burgess' body. Then Preston stumbled, almost falling.

Burgess stood stupidly for a few seconds looking down. He could see the gold handle of the cane protruding from his body. He didn't have enough life left to consider the sharp point that had come out his back.

The dead body of the ex-cop crumpled to the floor.

Trent caught Preston before he fell. He helped him into a chair.

"Now you see what I owe you, Trent. I owe you your life."

Trent and Darcey looked at each other.

"I don't have much time left. There was a particularly strong poison in my flute. Please let me explain quickly."

With his last breaths he told them the story of Jimmy Shadow. Ending with the contact from Rossi on behalf of Burgess.

Darcey was repelled.

"Preston, you're a murderer! How could you do these things?"

"Yes, you're quite right. Though no doubt there have been some victims who were innocent, I have always told myself I was doing the world a service by ridding it of evil people," he gasped. "But yes, I murdered. And at the end of my life I almost killed one of the finest men I've ever known."

The old man was weakening quickly. He tried to retrieve something from his pocket but his arms were growing heavy.

"Trent, please," he said, "the vial in my pocket."

Trent reached into the side pocket of the tan coat, finding a vial of powder.

"Give that to your doctor," Preston said. "I got it from the source who provided the bug that bit you. Tell your doctor to use this powder to make an antiserum which should arrest the disease now in your blood. Tell her to make a vaccine with it also and give that to you as well. You must have both!"

Trent nodded.

"Let us help you now, Preston," Trent said.

"No. No. It's much too late," Preston said. "Hopefully your doctor will only need a small amount of the powder to save you. Perhaps they can use the remainder to develop a cure for related illnesses. I know it's not much but it might provide some small good to atone for all the bad I've done."

Darcey was filled with conflicting emotion. This man she had come to think of as a father figure was not only an assassin but had come close to killing her husband.

Preston reached a hand out to each of them. They let him touch them.

"I'm so very sorry," he said, his breathing becoming ragged. "I hope someday you can find it in your hearts to forgive a wicked old man."

Saturday, September 26th

Trent and Darcey met Christopher, Nancy, and Miles for dinner at Jardiniere, one of San Francisco's finest restaurants. It was Scott's favorite.

Miles was doing well. He still called Darcey in the middle of the night occasionally. But those late night calls were becoming less frequent.

He had settled into his new role as Chief Operating Officer of DJA Designs. He and Darcey were working on plans to open a second office in New Orleans. Miles had just returned from his first visit to the Crescent City, exhausted but exhilarated by the ambience of the Vieux Carre'. He told his friends he had been embraced by the old city.

A few days after Preston Johnson, aka Jimmy Shadow, and ex-cop Steve Burgess died, Darcey was contacted by Johnson's attorney. He informed her that she was the sole beneficiary of Johnson's estate. It was a large inheritance in cash and investments. The only real estate was the condo across the hall from Trent and Darcey.

Darcey continued to struggle with conflicting emotions as they pertained to Preston Johnson. It was difficult to reconcile the friend and father figure with the assassin who had murdered scores of people. The man who was very nearly responsible for killing Trent.

She decided she could not keep the money. She donated the entire sum to the Salvation Army. She put the condo on the market with the intention of donating the proceeds of the sale as well. Unfortunately the value would be lessened due to the disclosure of the two violent deaths that had occurred on the property as required by law.

Doctor Raymond used some of the powder Preston supplied to make the antiserum and vaccine, which she administered to Trent as Preston Johnson had directed. She was studying the remainder in the hope that the powder's properties could be duplicated for use in the treatment of similar diseases.

They didn't yet know if the antiserum and vaccine was working. Though the symptoms weren't quite as severe, Trent still had days when he was confused. Disoriented. He had a few severe headaches. The symptoms didn't last long. Darcey did the best she could to comfort him and ease his pain.

Christopher turned over all the information Scott had provided about Rossi's money laundering operation to FinCEN, the Financial Crimes Enforcement Network. Those files were leading to arrests and seizure of funds in several countries.

There was talk about promotions for Christopher and Lieutenant Mitchum. Nancy's chief had also let it be known that she could expect her career to flourish thanks to her work with Christopher's team. Her chief liked it when his officers held their own with the SFPD in breaking up crime rings. He was especially pleased when his people proved equal to the federal cops.

When they got home after dinner, Trent opened a bottle of Merlot. He took the bottle and two glasses to the terrace where Darcey stood looking out over the city, a secretive, satisfied smile on her face.

"Can I pour you a glass of wine?" he asked.

"No, thanks."

"You didn't have wine or a cocktail at dinner either," Trent noted. "Are you feeling ok?"

"Never felt better. Alcohol just doesn't sound appealing right now."

Trent came to stand beside her, sipping the Merlot from his glass.

"Oh…by the way, we're pregnant," Darcey said.

Trent took another sip of the Merlot. He put his arm around Darcey. Together they watched the fog rolling in over the city.

www.ingramcontent.com/pod-product-compliance
Lightning Source LLC
Chambersburg PA
CBHW051647260626
47170CB00004B/1375